O, BISCUIT!

LYNNE HINTON

ISBN: 978-1-966343-85-1 (hard cover)
      978-1-966343-86-8 (soft cover)

Edited by: Rikki Jarrett and Erika Nein

Published by WARREN Publishing
Charlotte, NC
www.warrenpublishing.net
Printed in the United States

For Martha Shore:
Of all the voices in my head, yours is the funniest.

PROLOGUE

Willis Lemmons's face and shirt were covered in blood. He reached just above his right eyebrow to feel a gash, wide enough for his finger to slip inside and long enough for the blood to pool in the corner beside his temple. His eye was swollen shut, and he could sense a knot forming just above the nape of his neck. He thought he was going to be sick, so he didn't move. He just stayed where he was and tried to order his thoughts. He didn't remember exactly where he was or what happened to cause the injury. He tried to recall the hours before, but everything felt weighted and blurred.

He didn't think he was at the creek bank near Blankenship Bridge, where he had a small tent and bedroll, his books, and a few items of clothing. It didn't appear that he was behind the dumpster at the Piggly Wiggly, where he often waited for the manager to throw out the outdated bread and crushed cans of beans, and where he always found long dry pieces of cardboard and sometimes entire birthday cakes. Willis didn't see the familiar outlines of the storefronts around the town square or the rear entrances of the places with canopies where he sometimes slept when it rained. He wasn't near the church. He thought he heard the sound of water and wondered if he was farther up the bank, near the spot where the trout spawn, where the fishing was good.

Maybe what he heard was a fountain, like the one in the center of the courtyard in town, where children tossed in coins, making wishes for toys and miracles, and where, when he was really desperate, he reached in and pulled out quarters and dimes for a burger or a new magazine, sometimes a beer. He thought it might be the fountain in the circle driveway of the nursing home where he visited his mama at night, standing by her window while she slept, playing on the harmonica the songs she used to sing to him when he was a boy.

But Willis didn't really think he was in Owensboro or at the nursing home. There was no flashing light at the intersections, no neon sign blinking Open at the Saddleback Bar, no banner in front of the Baptist Church declaring Jesus Saves, the floodlight hidden in the grass. No Staff Only parking sign posted at the door of Evergreens. No county courthouse or sheriff's station, no two-cell jail he'd stayed in before— nothing marking the places he had wandered all his life. No, this didn't look like anywhere that he knew perfectly, but he still heard the sound of water and suddenly remembered the fountain in his brother's driveway, the small one with a dolphin in mid-leap, a single stream of water spilling from its lips.

Willis had always liked that fountain and used to sneak over at night to watch the lights shimmer against the smooth sides of the dolphin and the other spouts spraying water in varying heights, colored by the small lights strategically placed inside. He and his brother talked from time to time back then; Marvin even let Willis stay in the camper he kept on the south side of the property. But that was before the fire and the blackouts and the sheriff's visit that led to Willis's arrest and Marvin's legal actions that kept Willis one hundred yards from the house built on the lake, north of town. Willis couldn't remember the last time he had been in the vicinity of Marvin's house, the last time he had seen the dolphin up close.

He glanced up and noticed the porch and the curved eaves, the long brick walkway ending at the front door, the cement planters—empty since it wasn't yet spring and the bulbs were not yet blooming—and the tall windows covered with dark, heavy curtains. While he registered everything he saw, Willis tried to remember what led him to his brother's house, and what caused the gash on his temple, the bump on his head, and the slow way he felt. He inhaled deeply and pulled himself up, bearing all his weight upon the bench that wrapped around the fountain. He managed to turn around and sit down, exhausted from the slightest of movements. He could see from his sitting position that the front door was open, and he thought it odd that his brother hadn't closed it, since Marvin was fastidious about keeping outdoors out and indoors in, demanding his guests remove their shoes before entering and say their goodbyes before opening the door and turning around to stand in the entryway—a Southern manner of making a final farewell.

Marvin was deathly allergic to almost everything, but especially bee stings, keeping an EpiPen in his pocket at all times. Since he was a boy, he would redden and blister from mosquito bites and horseflies, poison ivy, and ragweed. Their mother layered him in long-sleeve shirts and scarves and socks anytime he was in the yard, the manner of dress he still chose when he went outside—something he rarely did.

Willis used to tease his younger brother about his pale complexion and fear of insects since the older of the two preferred outside to in, but he stopped it when Marvin almost died from the sting of a wasp that had built its nest unobserved by members of the Lemmons household or any of its staff. Marvin was about ten when it happened. Willis had found his brother—his face swelling, eyes rolling back in his head—and was able to deliver the shot into his leg and save his life.

Once Willis saw the grave consequences of his brother's encounter with the outdoors, he began protecting Marvin as best and as often as he could, standing guard at the front door of their parents' house when Marvin exited and entered, checking every corner and hiding place, knocking down nests, and even asking for an EpiPen to keep for himself in case Marvin misplaced his own.

Willis had assumed he would stay beside and protect his brother for the rest of their lives, so close they were as young boys. But Marvin left home at sixteen and never looked back, attending college early and then graduate school, leaving Willis to fend for himself and survive their father's heavy hand the best way he could. Willis stayed a few years before his mother's accident, then decided to join the army; years later, he came home.

Willis stood up from the fountain bench and walked to the door.

"Marv," he called out as he neared the entryway. "Marv, you mean to leave the door open?" He glanced around inside but did not hear a response from his brother or anything else from the doorway. He took a breath and made a small move inside the foyer, unable to recall the last time he had actually stepped foot in his brother's house.

"Marvin? You home?" Willis reached up to his forehead and felt the gash again, hoping the blood was dry and would not drip onto the floor, knowing his brother would not be pleased if he had to clean the white marble because of a mess Willis had made. He looked down at his feet and knew he was already breaking rules by not taking off his shoes. He considered his options: Take off the pair of old sneakers or back away and head to his tent.

It was the moment he lifted his eyes away from his feet that he saw the leg of a man just inside the sitting room to the left of the front door where he was standing. The leg was in khaki pants, bent, and there were no other parts of the body to identify who it was from where Willis stood. Trying not to track the floors with his dirty shoes, Willis peered around the corner from the hallway, and that was when he could see that the leg belonged to Marvin, who was face down, lying in his own pool of blood, still spreading into a larger spill, it seemed, beneath the leather sofa and out onto the Persian rug Marvin bought on a long-ago trip to Spain.

Willis forgot about protocol in Marvin's house and hurried to his brother's side, turned him over, and was instantly struck at how beautiful his brother really was, how peaceful he looked, no longer worried about what might sting or poison him.

Willis sat beside his brother, cradling the top of Marvin's body in his arms. He didn't think to call 911 because he knew death when he saw it. He knew the absence of life and breath, and he knew it was too late for doctors or paramedics to bring him back. Gently, he reached up to the sofa and placed a pillow beneath his brother's head and stood up. He noticed the knife and, without thinking, picked it up. It was not one he recognized; then again, there wasn't much in Marvin's house that he did recognize. He hadn't seen his brother for years, and he was pretty sure Marvin had remodeled the mansion a couple of times since first building it.

As he glanced around, Willis suddenly began to understand the gravity of the situation—the appearance of such a thing as the estranged brother, standing next to the dead body of Marvin Lemmons. He thought of sitting in the county jail, of the list of offenses he had on record with the police, the way people in town treated him, the way his own family treated him, and he knew the best thing for him to do was to get out of the house as quickly as he could. He leaned down once more and pulled Marvin into himself, a means of a final goodbye, then gently placed his dead body back on the floor. He reached into his brother's pocket, taking the only true reminder of what he remembered most about him. Willis stuck the EpiPen in the front pocket of his jacket, the knife in a side pocket, and hurried out the door.

CHAPTER ONE

Buford is my morning coffee—strong and dark, with a lingering sweetness like the vanilla latte cream left as a sample by Dreamland Dairy in last week's delivery. And I suppose that makes me his biscuit: plump, pale, and thick with layers, a slight edge.

We meet every morning, straight up at five a.m., to sit at the window table just by the door where we watch sleepy downtown Owensboro come to life. Buford runs the barbershop, BJ Barbers, situated right next to the bakery on Main Street. We opened our businesses six years apart, Buford first, having come into a little money from the sale of the family farm, followed by year after year of him encouraging me to open my own place. It was badgering really—first when Daniels's Shoe Shop closed after Maurice Daniel got Alzheimer's and Mrs. Daniel closed his place, then at Nickel's Five and Dime when Walmart opened at the edge of town. He finally convinced me to take out a loan and purchase Millie's Diner, a constant in this town for as long as I can remember that was eventually closed when Millie's son was arrested for bank fraud. Once the loan was approved and a few updates were made, we've been here, side by side, for over twenty-five years.

Buford and I became friends when we were eight-year-olds, standing at the bus stop alone. The older kids, including my brother Draymond, had moved onto the junior high bus, leaving us with the handful of other elementary school children. Cathedral, my sister, was still in preschool. She rode in a van from the church that picked her up from home.

I knew Buford, of course, prior to that age; classes at Owensboro Elementary School were small. I sat behind him in first and second grades—our last names starting with the letter *P*—along with Leanna Peters, whose family moved to the mountains in second grade after her dad died in a tractor accident.

The school bus stop was at the top of Longfellow Street and was the last stop before the bus turned around and headed back into town. It was the first and only integrated bus stop in Owensboro, serving the children from Second Town—the scrabble farmland beyond the main streets where Black people could buy property and build homes and operate a few businesses—and Dixie Crossing Trailer Park, where I lived with my mama and two siblings.

I inherited Grandma Lawton's bad eyesight and, being shy, never told anyone what I could and couldn't see. I memorized the eye chart on the day of our vision tests in first and second grades, and my memories of my early years remain murky and soft, the thoughts of faces and words as something from faraway.

It was Buford who gave me my first pair of glasses. To this day, I don't know how he knew I was cheating on the eye tests or where he got the black-framed glasses that slid down my nose when I held my first chapter book in my lap, sitting on the fat limb of the white oak tree behind the Owensboro Library where I spent most of my afternoons. I only know that, after Buford slipped me that grown-up pair of eyeglasses, I felt as if I had woken up from an eight-year-long sleepwalk. For the first time, my life had focus. I wore glasses for most of my life until I finally had a surgery a few years ago that gave me twenty-twenty vision.

"This is the last jar."

I feel him behind me before he tells me we're almost out of molasses. He is warm and broad, a deep breath, and I feel myself lean into his light.

"Maybe Georgia has a box in her basement. I'll ask her later." I make a mental note to ask my only employee what she has stored at home, knowing she always has extra jars of jams, jellies, and syrups.

Buford leaves the jar on the steel table in the kitchen and heads into the dining room. I hear the space heater come on, the chairs taken off the tables and pushed into place.

"Ferge's early," he says as he walks back into the kitchen.

I pour him a cup of coffee, add half a packet of sugar, stir it, and hand it to him. He must have seen the sheriff driving on Main Street.

"There's a tray of cinnamon-raisin in the warmer, and the butters have seven minutes."

"I'll wait," he replies, taking a sip from his favorite mug.

"Right," I answer. "Molasses."

Buford smiles.

"So, I'm thinking about adding another station," he tells me, and I stop scraping the sides of the mixer bowl and peer up at him.

"You thinking about bringing in a partner?" I ask, knowing Buford has been opposed to having another barber in his shop for as long as I've worked next door, recalling the struggle he had the first five years with Percy Strahan, who unfortunately came with the place when he bought it. Percy was the previous owner's brother-in-law, and he never could cut hair or give a decent shave. Buford finally paid him to go.

He shrugs. "Lucille's youngest is going to school in Wilmington, figured he'd need a place to start." He takes a seat at the stool in front of the table. He's wearing his tan smock and brown pants. Everything is neat: the creases in his pants pressed; the smock, crisp and starched.

"Leon?" I ask, trying to mask the surprise in my voice.

He narrows his eyes at me and then glances away. "I know," he says softly. "I just thought maybe he could use ..." His voice trails off.

"A break?" I finish the sentence and go back to scraping the dough with my long wooden spoon.

"You're right," he says, and I don't add anything more. He knows that I know he has given his nephew more money than he's made in a year. He knows that I know he has a soft spot for his older sister's boy, the one who suffered the most in the divorce, the one that reminds him of himself. He knows I know that he gave him a car when he turned sixteen, which he wrecked six months later; paid Leon's tuition for community college when he said he wanted to be a fireman; gave his sister bail money more times than I can count … He knows that I know it all.

"It's your money, Buford. And he's your kin. And you always say, 'you do what you got to do.'" I pause. "Besides, it's not up to me to tell you what's best."

"Funny, but that's never stopped you before." He smiles, and I roll my eyes at him.

The buzzer on the stove goes off and he gets up, finds the pot holders, and pulls out the steaming butter biscuits. I wipe the flour off the tabletop and lay out a towel so he can put the tray down.

"Best biscuits in Owensboro," he says.

"Only biscuits you eat in Owensboro," I reply, grabbing a table knife from the drawer and gently slipping it between the biscuits and the sides of the muffin pan, lifting them up slightly so they won't stick.

"That's just what you think," he replies while I slide two biscuits onto small plates. He takes the dishes, along with the butter and molasses, and heads into the dining room while I grab my cup, fill the thermos, and follow him to a table.

"How come nobody makes molasses anymore?" I ask as I spread butter on the biscuits. I wait for him to twist the ring off the molasses jar, pop the top with a spoon, and pour the thick syrup onto our breakfast.

"Helen Johnston's daughter still does, down by the pond at her mama's home place. They get cane from over near Franklinton, and she and her boys spend a couple of weeks every summer boiling it." He finishes dousing both biscuits and then slides his finger across the top of the jar and licks it. He winks at me as he does this.

"I thought she moved to South Carolina," I respond, taking that first delicious bite of hot biscuit and homemade molasses. I close my eyes while I chew.

"She did. But I guess she doesn't want to let the tradition go, so she comes back here every July and makes a batch."

"How do you know this?" I ask as he takes a bite. He closes his eyes too—neither of us ever tiring of the delight in our mornings.

"Cutting hair," he replies after he's finished his bite and wiped his lips.

"Right," I say, pouring coffee into my cup, remembering how Buford knows about everything that goes on in Owensboro since apparently the men in the barbershop gossip as much as the women down at Thelma's hair salon.

We sit in silence as we eat, the thinnest light of the morning sun just starting to fade the black sky. I notice the robins are out and the courtyard is vibrant with new grass. There's no one moving on the streets, and we turn toward each other in surprise when we hear the whirring of the police siren somewhere near the station.

I'm about to say something about crime getting started early or how Ferguson must have gotten a call from his mother from the next town over when we hear the knock on the back door of the bakery.

Buford gets up, and I watch him as he moves past the kitchen. I can see all the way down the hall to the door and when he opens it, I recognize right away who's standing there.

"Lord, have mercy," I say as I stand up, knocking over the jar of molasses with my arm.

"Lorna Gayle, get a towel!" Buford calls out, the body slumped into him.

I run into the kitchen, thinking somebody has finally gone and killed Willis Lemmons.

CHAPTER TWO

"I've got some dish towels," I tell Buford as I rush from the kitchen to the door.

He's pulled Willis inside the hallway, has him propped against the wall while he assesses the injuries. Willis is, it turns out, not dead, but he has a significant wound on the front of his head, a knot on the back, and appears disoriented. I'd say he also looks disheveled, but I've come to accept this is how Willis Lemmons looks most days. He is always a bit of a mess, but this is different. Something has happened, and I can't tell if he fell and hit his head or if someone assaulted him, since it's certainly not out of the question that he's been victimized. There are no locked doors where Willis lives.

He's been staying on the streets of Owensboro for as long as I've owned and operated the O, Biscuit Bakery. He told me he gets squirrely inside a house, can't breathe in closed-in spaces, and prefers being outdoors, in nature, alone and away from the prying eyes of law enforcement or roommates or the judgmental citizens of our fair town. He never comes into the shop but instead waits outside at the back door, where he showed up today and where I always slip him a bag of biscuits and a tall cup of coffee. Buford says it's PTSD, that something happened when Willis was in the service, coming from Afghanistan before we pulled out. But nobody has ever gotten Willis to explain what changed for him over there.

Truth is, Willis was always slightly different from everyone else. He's a few years ahead of us, but I still remember how he walked the halls alone at school, head down, hair in his eyes, trying not to see or be seen. Everybody knew that after Marvin left, their daddy doubled down on abusing his wife, finally beating their mama so bad one time that it put her in Evergreens. Willis, already held back a couple of years in school, traumatized by his home life, and apparently something from war, is still trying to find his way to this day. He's never chosen to live inside since he returned from the war, and he is triggered by backfires and raised voices.

Buford has always known more than anybody about Willis and his military service, his injuries, and the consequences of war. Of course, Buford also served. He signed up after graduation, became a medic, and, as he likes to tell it, traveled the world. He has his own demons from his time on the battlefield; and, similar to Willis, he chooses not to elaborate on why he never goes to the fireworks display held every July Fourth down at Whitman's Lake or why his hands shake when it thunders in the spring when the storms are frequent and long.

I've asked him about what happened on more than one occasion, but Buford just shakes his head and tells me some things ain't meant to be talked. I fire back and tell him most things need to be talked and usually the things we refuse to share are the things that need the most attention. But more than forty years after Buford's honorable discharge, he's still a closed book. It's just his way, and I guess that's part of the reason I hesitate getting married. Closed books don't usually make the best partners.

"He's got a concussion." Buford is shining a tiny light in Willis's eyes, and I wonder for a second how long he's been holding a thin flashlight in his pocket and why he keeps one there.

"And he needs three or four stitches." He leans into the injured man.

I hand him a clean dish towel, and he gently presses it against Willis's wound.

"Call 911," Buford tells me, and I stand up and feel around in my apron for my phone.

"No," Willis suddenly speaks.

Buford and I glance first at each other and then at Willis.

"No hospital. No doctor."

Well, this is surprising. The questions start to mount.

"Willis, this gash is pretty deep. You need to have it looked at," Buford says.

"Then look," he says and lifts his head.

I catch Buford's eye, my face a question mark. *Should I call?*

Buford shakes his head.

"I can use superglue," he tells Willis and, I guess, me.

I'm just trying to sort through the shock of having him show up at the back door before dawn and trying to understand what in the Sam Hill is going on.

Willis nods, and I think this may have happened before. It just seems like this is something that's familiar to the two men, but for the life of me I have never heard Buford talk about gluing together skin or taking care of Willis's medical needs.

But it is Buford, and he is discreet, and he does give Willis money and free haircuts and shaves and lets him take a shower at his house. We both take care of Willis; me with the gift of free biscuits a few times each week, coffee, leftovers from my dinners, desserts from new recipes I might be trying; I even slip him a bit of sherry from a bottle I keep in the storage room for my fancy uptown desserts when I see him with the shakes. But, clearly, Buford does more than me.

"Can you go to the shop and bring me the black bag in the closet? It has medical supplies, you know, a first aid kit." Buford reaches into his pocket and pulls out his keys.

I'm about to argue for an ambulance, but then Buford looks at me again, telling me with his eyes, gentle and tender, to do as Willis asked, to keep this just between us. I sigh and take the keys and carefully step over Willis, open the rear door, and walk outside. I hear Buford ask a question, but I can't make out all the words. It's now a private conversation between the two men, the two veterans, and I can tell it's not meant for me because of the soft way Buford is speaking, how his voice is low and measured, like how he talks on the computer to his grandson who just turned three. It is talk intended just between them, and I do not stand and listen.

I open up the barbershop and switch on the lights and then turn them off since I don't want to call attention to the fact someone is in his place, even though I know it's unlikely anyone is walking the town square. Still, Willis clearly desires privacy, and I think it's best if no one knows we're in our shops.

The darkness settles, and there's just enough morning to help me see how to get to his closet. I turn my cell phone's flashlight on and open the closet door. Everything is neat and in its place, including the black bag I am there to retrieve, situated on the third shelf, right at eye level.

Buford is the neatest person I know. I'm sure being in the military caused some of that, but Buford was picky even before then. His locker in school was the cleanest one in the hall. And he always dressed in pressed shirts and pants, his sneakers never scuffed or dirty. He had folders for every subject and didn't stand for clutter. I saw his bedroom just once when I went home with him to study for the biology exam in ninth grade. I think I embarrassed him when I asked if I could go home and get my camera and take a picture since I had never seen such a clean room.

I stand at the barbershop closet, knowing Buford needs his bag but also recognizing that the two men may need a little more time without me in earshot. And since I'm thinking about that time I saw his bedroom for the first time, I'm suddenly remembering how it felt to walk from the bus stop with him at fifteen, how nervous we suddenly both became, and how his father drove up while we were sitting on his bed going over test questions about the anatomy of a frog we had dissected earlier in the week. Buford became visibly shaken by the surprise arrival and had me hide in his closet until he figured out what his father was doing home from his shift job at the plastics manufacturing plant. I must have sat in the closet where he and his brother kept all their clothes for an hour as Buford talked with his father. After a while, his father yelled something, and I heard a scuffle of some kind, but I didn't come out of the bedroom. I just waited like I was told, knowing better than most the benefits of a good hiding place.

Everything was neat in there, too, and I didn't know if his brother was just as picky or if Buford just ordered everything for them both. I assumed it was Buford's touch on things, that he was the main one in charge of the boys' closet. Finally, after I had counted all the shirts and pants, and moved aside the shoes that poked me when I sat down, the door slid open and he leaned in, smiling, and said something like, "Coast is clear," or "He's gone." I'm not sure I remember exactly, just that he had a red mark on his cheek, and when I asked if everything was okay, he replied, "As good as it gets."

I shake aside the memories, figuring the two men have had enough time alone, grab the bag, and close the closet door. When I glance out the front window of the shop, I am surprised to see somebody peeking in, their face cupped by their hands, and I freeze. It can't be later than six a.m. The sky's not yet shed the night's full darkness, and I have no idea who would be trying to see inside Buford's shop. I hold the medical bag to my chest and wait. In a few seconds, the person takes a step back from the window and walks away. I stay unmoving for a minute, and then head to the rear door. I open it carefully and peek out. When I don't see anyone, I step out quickly—making sure the door locks behind me—and hurry to the stoop of my place. Buford opens the door before I knock.

"Somebody's out front," I tell him as I step once more over Willis as he sits propped against the wall. I can't see through the blinds on my front window, so I can't tell if the person I just witnessed trying to see in Buford's shop is peering into my store, but I know they can tell I'm there. The kitchen lights can be seen from the front.

I turn to the men. "Willis, is someone following you?"

He glances away and shakes his head.

"Willis, who did this to you?" I ask.

He doesn't answer, and I head to the front door, deciding I got every right to know who is prowling around our shops this early in the morning. Buford stops me with a light touch on the arm. He puts his finger to his lips, and we wait silently as someone tries to open the door. He doesn't answer, and I start to head to the front door, and I quietly and quickly pull the rear door shut behind me. I check the knob to make sure it's locked and then turn the dead bolt because all I can think is that whoever hit Willis is coming to finish the job.

The shadow at the front window leaves, and Buford and I glance first at each other and then at Willis.

CHAPTER THREE

Buford exhales and kneels in front of Willis.

"Okay, this is going to sting," Buford says as he takes supplies out of his bag. He has gauze and scissors, a bottle of alcohol and a vial of medicine, and a tube that looks like the small bottle of glue I keep in my toolbox. He dabs some alcohol on a piece of gauze and gently places it on Willis's forehead. Buford holds the gauze on the wound for a few seconds. Willis doesn't react at all.

I like to watch Buford work. I've seen him bandage a few scrapes and bruises of children who have come into the store after falling on the sidewalk or in the alley. He's cared for a number of my own emergencies, including a bad burn on my arm when I grazed a pan of raisin biscuits and a few cuts from the knives I use to slice sausage and pieces of ham. He is slow and meticulous, and it's clear he knows what he's doing. I just find what he does enjoyable to watch, like an artist at work or seeing compassion take form.

He wrapped Georgia's wrist every day for weeks when the cast came off after she broke it slipping on the ice one winter. He's taken out stitches from Ferguson's knee after he had a fall playing softball. He's administered ice packs and heating pads, and used every size of adhesive bandage in the box, but I've never seen him glue up a gash using the same product I use to repair broken coffee mugs. I observe as he squeezes a few drops on the bottom of the cut, gently pulls the thin skin together, and presses it carefully between his fingers.

He's wearing gloves like he always does when he's providing first aid—plastic gloves that he keeps in a drawer at his stations and in this first aid kit. Still holding the wound, he asks me to gently pat it once more with alcohol while he uses his other hand to find tiny butterfly bandages. He places four of them in a row on the cut, then leans back against the wall, pulls off the gloves, and slides down.

"How much longer before Georgia gets here?" he asks.

I pull out my phone. It reads ten minutes after six. "Half an hour?" I say, the answer a kind of a question since I'm not sure when my second baker will arrive. "She's taking her granddaughter to school this morning."

When she's not babysitting, Georgia usually gets to the store around six, has a cup of coffee with us at the front table, and then finishes the baking.

Buford nods. He knows the granddaughter, Flora. In fact, I'm pretty sure he's bandaged her up a few times too.

"Good, that gives us some time to make a couple of decisions."

Willis glances up at Buford and shakes his head.

"We need her help," Buford tells him.

Willis drops his face. "I should just go to Ferguson," he says, and I think he means to make a report about who assaulted him.

I'm about to agree, phone in hand, ready to make the call, when Buford interrupts.

"I don't think that's best." He pauses while Willis and I watch him. "Let's just find a place for you to rest awhile and see what unfolds."

"Why can't we call Ferguson?" I don't understand why Willis wouldn't want the sheriff to know about the assault.

Buford gives Willis a look.

"Marvin's dead," Willis replies after a few seconds of silence. "Stabbed."

"What?" I ask, my body reflexively pulling away from Willis as if this bit of news is a snake that bites. "How do you know this?"

I eye the door, thinking there might actually be a man with a butcher knife outside. I rack my brain for what I could use as a weapon—a rolling pin, maybe a skillet? My knives are known more for buttering than defense.

Willis turns to Buford for support or, I don't know, an answer maybe.

"He was there," Buford finally replies. "He doesn't remember what happened."

"You were there?" I say, not following, noticing how my voice has suddenly grown all pointy and judgmental. "Where is 'there'?"

"Marvin's house," Willis answers softly.

"But you aren't allowed to go there," I say, stating the obvious.

Both Buford and I know about the restraining order Marvin took out on his brother. The two of us, in fact, went with Willis to court to hear the ruling because he hadn't wanted to go alone. We both closed up early that day and walked over to the courthouse to hear what the judge had to say.

Marvin wasn't there, just his attorney, who explained that the younger brother could no longer allow Willis on his property. Marvin claimed that Willis was destructive and careless, causing damage to the trailer where Marvin let him live and the cleared lot behind the house.

"Frankly, Judge," the lawyer from Charlotte had said, "Mr. Lemmons is afraid of his brother. He just doesn't trust that Willis is safe to be around."

"That's not true," Willis had whispered, shaking his head from side to side. "That's just not true." But he didn't have a lawyer sitting at his table, just the town barber and a baker, both of whom enabled his drinking and were the only ones there to stand up for him in the place of missing family and legal representation.

The judge had quieted Willis, wouldn't hear his side of the story—a side that explained he had not done the damage to the open field, and that the fire in the trailer was not started because of falling asleep while smoking like his brother said, but because of somebody else messing around there, or maybe poor wiring—poor wiring that he had mentioned to Marvin on previous occasions. Willis insisted he never smoked inside, hadn't smoked at all in a couple of years, but he was not to be heard. He was ordered to pay a five-hundred-dollar fine, an amount he'd never raise, and to stay a hundred yards away from Marvin's property and Marvin himself.

"I don't know why I was there," Willis says. "I woke up next to the fountain, and I don't remember anything."

"Did you get in a fight? Did he hit you?"

There is no answer.

"Willis, did somebody kill Marvin and then assault you? Should we be worried they're following you?" I glance around from side to side like somehow the murderer snuck in when I wasn't paying attention and is now close by.

"He doesn't remember anything, which is why I think we should let him take some time, see if he can recall the events of last evening before he turns himself in." Buford is eyeing me, hard, like he's trying to convince me not to call the authorities and also not to agree with Willis that he should talk to the sheriff.

I do not respond.

Buford knows how to trim hair, how to hold the layers in between his fingers and snip the ends. He knows which straight razor to use and how to sharpen it so that it gives a close and smooth shave. He knows how to place the hot towel across the face so that the nose and the mouth are never covered and how to blow dry and style, cover bald spots, and comb over hair so that it doesn't call attention to the thin places. He knows how to keep an impeccable station, how to mop without leaving streaks, how to sterilize his barber tools, greet new customers and keep them for life, how to coax little boys into the chair for their first cut, and how to listen to what his clients are hoping for and then prepare them for the best that can be done with the too-curly or sparse hair they have.

He's just shown that he can take care of deep gashes and bandage wounds. He can fix the engine of any make and model of truck or car, clean and dissemble and reassemble a firearm, cut up a chicken, cook an entire dinner with vegetables, bake homemade bread and dessert, and grow the best garden of anybody in Owensboro. Buford knows more than most. And because Buford is Black, grew up in the South and still lives there, Buford has a particular knowledge as to what the police will do with a homeless man like Willis, the judgments made based on the way a man looks, what they will see when they notice the wounds on his head and find out he was present at and then fled from a murder scene.

Buford knows the sheriff, has cut his hair for years, and even though they grew up together, attended school and played ball on the same teams, calls him a friend even, Buford also understands that people see and make conclusions based on skin color and employment status, current address, and prior records. And as much as Buford trusts Sheriff Ferguson Gentry, as much as he knows the man to be good and honest and fair, he also knows how it will go for Willis if he shows up at the sheriff's office, injured, unclear about his whereabouts for the last twenty-four hours, saying he had been at a place he was ordered to stay away from, and had seen his brother stabbed to death on the floor.

Buford knows Willis needs a lawyer and a little time to try and recall what exactly happened between him and his brother. Buford knows this as good as he knows what is likely on the horizon for the man everyone calls the town drunk.

"Let's just give him some time," he says again, hoping he sounds convincing enough to keep us both off the phone.

I don't think it's best to keep the law out of this situation, but I also have my own history with the sheriff. I understand the decision.

"Do what you got to do," I say, just as we hear dueling sirens moving in our direction.

CHAPTER FOUR

The sheriff's car and the deputy's truck race past the bakery. We hear them turn down Main Street, heading in the direction of the lake. The three of us take a collective breath when we realize they are not stopping for Willis. Apparently, they are not on the lookout for a fugitive and those who are protecting him.

"Somebody must've found Marvin," Buford says, packing up his first aid kit. "That means we don't have a lot of time, Willis." He closes the bag. "I think we need to find you a good place to get yourself together, somewhere out of the way."

Willis shuts his eyes and shakes his head. "I don't know where to go except my place at the river. I can stay there."

Buford bites his upper lip, likely thinking about the situation and the best way to move forward.

"I think they'll look for you there. I'm going to take you to my house, let you get a shower, something to eat, maybe lie down a bit. I'm coming back to work, but we'll figure out what needs to happen when I get home this afternoon." He turns to me like maybe I've got something to add.

I just shake my head. "Who do you think found Marvin? Who called the law?"

Neither of them answers.

"Okay, I can agree that bringing in the sheriff isn't the best thing right now, that Willis needs some time."

Buford nods. He knows why I'd come to that agreement.

"But I know *somebody* needs to sort through exactly what happened between the two of you, *somebody* needs to make sure there's not some murderer walking the streets of Owensboro." I pace for a minute. "Buford's right, though. Maybe after a few hours of rest, you'll remember what happened. Maybe a shower and a nap will help jar your memory."

Willis glances down.

I turn to Buford. "You know we may hear about this."

"We got some time," Buford answers. "Ferge can wait."

"Okay," I reply, knowing it's a risk for all of us to hide Willis. The sheriff could accuse us of standing in the way of justice. But if that's the price we pay for keeping Willis safe, so be it.

"Maybe I'll hear some talk in the shop later," Buford says.

I imagine he'll hear something; it's just not guaranteed to be useful since he mostly hears bad jokes and stories of how things used to be before there was electricity and indoor plumbing. Still, Buford learns a lot.

He stands up and offers his hand to Willis. Willis takes it, and though he's a little wobbly, he's able to get to his feet and remain standing. They head to the door.

"Here, wait," I say and move into the kitchen. I bag up two biscuits from the warmer. Force of habit, feeding people—thinking a biscuit can cure all manner of trouble.

Willis glances over at me as Buford takes the bag. "Thank you, Miss Lorna. You're always good to me."

I give him a long look, remembering the boy at school, the one bullied, the one always alone, and then I reach out and hug him. It's awkward, and he stiffens at my embrace.

I step back, realizing I crossed a line. Willis has never liked to be touched.

"I'll take your bag to the shop," I tell Buford, knowing they need to get going since it's now light outside and customers will be at my front door soon.

I check my phone. It's six thirty. I open up at seven. I expect Georgia to come busting through the door any second, and I still need to clean up the molasses that spilled on the floor. I have a lot to do to get the morning going. And I'd like to have some time to try and see what I can find out about what happened at Marvin's.

I unlock the door and carefully poke my head out to check the parking lot. There are still only three vehicles: the store van, my old truck, and Buford's Cadillac. I stand aside as the two men walk past me. Buford gets Willis buckled in the passenger seat of his car, then walks around to the driver's side. He smiles at me and nods as he gets in.

I hold up my hand in a wave and then head back inside.

I clean up the spill in the dining room, then take the biscuits out of the now-cooled pans and place them in the heated serving dish. I start another pot of coffee for the kitchen and retrieve the batter I mixed first thing this morning from the proofing shelf. I start spooning it into the small muffin pans I had already greased and floured. It's the hot biscuit dough, made with a little chili powder and diced jalapeños. I don't make them every morning, but I usually try to have some at least once or twice in the week. There are a few construction workers who come in, asking for *pan caliente*, hot bread. When they first asked, I thought they meant biscuits from the oven, acting like I knew what they were saying since I pride myself on having taken two years of Spanish in high school. I pulled out the pan of cheese biscuits, and they didn't seem to understand. Later, I learned they meant something to eat with a little heat, not bread freshly baked.

One of the men brought me the jalapeños from his garden to show me what he wanted, so now I make up a few "hot" biscuits to have on hand. It's mostly the construction workers who came up from South Florida who want them, but sometimes one of my regulars will ask for something different, and I give them the Caliente Special. But that's usually only once. Then they don't ask again.

"Damnation, that granddaughter of mine is going to steal my last breath."

Georgia. I smile as the door slams behind her.

"Was that Buford I just saw pulling out? And who was that he was carrying with him? Was that Willis Lemmons? And why is the mop out? You done and spilled the inventory?"

She's already frazzled as she enters the kitchen, and we haven't even shared a proper greeting. But then again, Flora is a handful.

I don't answer about the mop or Buford.

"I got the cinnamon-raisins done, butters in the warming tray, and I'm making a few hot biscuits since I think the crew is still patching up holes on the west side."

"*Pffft.*" Georgia always makes noises when she doesn't like what someone is saying. "They'll be patching up them holes for as long as I'm patting down dough. They need to just go on and repave the whole street."

I feel heartened that I was able to change the subject and not answer her about Buford and Willis. I don't see the reason for bringing Georgia into the know when there's actually nothing yet to know.

"You get Flora off to school all right?" I ask as I scoop batter into the tin.

"That child is on my last nerve," she tells me as she puts her lunch in the fridge and grabs her apron. "She's wanting to wrestle on the boys' team." And then she gives it a "Hmm-mmm-mmm," for good measure. "You ever heard of such a thing? Girl ain't no bigger than a minute, just got into middle school, and now she's wanting to roll around a gym floor with boys twice her size. I don't know what kind of craziness her daddy puts in her head."

Georgia heads into the front room and turns on the commercial coffee maker, the lights, and the hot water baths for the biscuit trays, and sets out plates and tongs and all the things we need when the customers come in. She returns to the kitchen and puts on oven mitts and then picks up the warmers and takes them to the main dining room, placing them on the display line. She covers them, but not before snatching herself a biscuit and placing it on a napkin.

She likes butter and grape jelly, has the same breakfast every morning. Georgia will taste the others, but she never eats a new kind of biscuit. Even with a flair for the supernatural, a bent toward favoring the paranormal, she is mostly very traditional when it comes to some things. She likes her biscuits plain, her talk direct, and she's still mad that they removed home economics from the junior high curriculum. She tells me at least once a week how she thinks girls need to learn to cook and sew at school. She will have a hard time with her granddaughter on the junior high wrestling team, a real hard time.

"Where's Buford going?" Clearly, she hasn't let go of what she saw in the parking lot. I could not distract her for long.

"Home, I think." I start rattling pots and pans, acting like I'm going to start cooking the eggs and bacon.

"He taking Willis somewhere?" She's eyeing me now 'cause she reads me like a book.

"Mmm," is all I give her. I hurry into the walk-in freezer to get away.

I hear her move to the front door and yank open the blinds, put out the open sign. I know she'll sweep the front sidewalk next and then wipe down the two small tables we keep out front in good weather to give us more visibility for passersby.

Georgia's daughter, Mae, had that idea. She apparently saw some French movie and thought the appearance of a café gives the bakery a little more shine on Main Street. Mae's always got ideas about new ways to do things. She helped me order the tables and chairs for the bakery and still brings artwork she thinks will show nice on the walls. She does have a good eye for decorating, I do have to give her that. Some of her marketing strategies have worked too—Biscuit Bucks brought in a lot more business—but Mae does occasionally have some far-out notions, like the time she wanted to let people bring in their pets, claimed it was all the latest rage.

I know that happens in eating places in the big cities, but I had to put my foot down on that idea. I promise, if I had said yes to pets and emotional support animals being allowed in my shop here in Owensboro, a farmer would've walked right in the front door with a pig or a barn owl, just trying to be funny. I told Mae there are some boundaries that have to be maintained in a place like our town.

Georgia is standing at the kitchen door when I come out of the freezer. She's jangling something in her front pocket. She pulls out a fist and throws dice on the counter. This is relatively new. When I first met her, Georgia read tea leaves, claiming they gave a more accurate weather prediction than the one from the six o'clock news. And for a few years, she spent hours counting birds because she was sure that seeing five crows was a sign that somebody was sick, and that six of them together meant somebody was dead. She would spot three picking the grass together and suddenly just stop what she was doing to count.

She stares at the dice as if they're telling her something she needs to know, and then she picks them up and returns them to her apron. "Whose blood is on the wall in the hallway, and why is there a medical bag in the dining room?"

I'm so startled, I drop the tub of grease.

CHAPTER FIVE

I have never lied to Georgia. And even though I learned what to say and not say to protect me and my siblings, how to keep the bill collectors satisfied, what to tell the social workers and school counselors so as not to have them make a home visit, I am not a good liar. I fidget and start to turn red just below my collarbones and then feel it spread to my forehead. As long as I have known her, I could never not be truthful to Georgia. She just knows me too good.

I clear my throat and set the tub on the counter. "It's Buford's," I say, turning my back to her so I don't have to look into those inquisitive eyes. It's not that I'm intending to misrepresent the facts of this morning; I just don't know enough of it to answer a lot of questions. And Georgia always has a lot of questions. As hard as it is to say what I know, I hardly think it wise to bring someone else into this conundrum.

"The blood or the bag?" she asks.

Here we go.

"Hmm?" I act real busy again.

"The blood or the bag?" she asks again.

"The bag. Now, can you start on the next batch?" I'm moving plates out of the sink, getting spoons lined up, going to the refrigerator for eggs. "Did you unlock the door?"

She glances behind her toward the front of the shop. "Not yet," she responds, and we both turn to the clock on the wall by the dishwasher: 6:50. We still got ten minutes to talk, and I don't have any more ideas of how to keep her from the line of questioning she seems determined to stay with. I am trying to honor Buford's wishes that we not share the news about Willis, but it is hard not to tell Georgia.

She stares me down like the truth might suddenly march across my face in big bold letters, even though I don't actually know any truth and my forehead is presently weighted down with bangs wet with perspiration.

I raise my eyebrows and smile. I turn on the charm and feign ignorance. I do the dance and Georgia knows it, but after a few minutes, I hear her sigh. She has decided to let it go.

"Uh-huh," she says and heads out of the kitchen, but not before she places Buford's medical bag on the table in front of me. "Maybe you should take it to his place. Maybe he might need it again."

I exhale, recognizing a reprieve when I get one. I walk over, pick up the first aid kit, grab the key to Buford's place, and quickly move in that direction. I don't mention to Georgia that I'm stepping out, doing what she said. I open the rear door to my place, then to his, return the bag to the third shelf in the hall closet, lock his door, and get back inside the shop and await her next question.

I know I'll have to tell her everything soon enough, and I know Owensboro is too small for a secret like Marvin Lemmons being killed to stay hidden for long. In fact, I'm a little surprised somebody isn't standing at the door to run into the shop and break the news.

I hear the jingle of the bells from the front once I've found my way into the kitchen and figure the biggest story since Willard Scott from the *Today Show* came to town to film Betty Pettyjohn's one hundredth birthday party is now just about to break.

"Ya'll open?" is the familiar sound from the first customer of the day.

"Right on time, Judge Farley," Georgia says.

I decide not to go out into the dining room, opting to stay away and just hear what our municipal court justice might relay to Georgia.

"You want one or two this morning?"

"Give me two," he responds. "It's going to be a busy day at the courthouse."

"Yeah, crime on the rise this week?" Georgia replies, a typical day's banter with Judge Farley, a wee bit of tease in her voice. I hear her bag up the butter biscuits, knowing she never forgets to add little packets of apricot jelly—his favorite—napkins, and a plastic knife.

"Give me a large coffee too," he tells her. "Ferguson called me before I had a chance to make a pot at home."

"Oh?"

And I lean in their direction. Maybe I'll get the official report about what's happened so far. Maybe the judge can clear everything up. Maybe he'll tell us that they caught the killer, and I can call Buford and tell him Willis is in the clear.

"You want milk or cream today?" Georgia isn't going to pry like I wish she would, like she just did with me. She could at least ask a follow-up question about the sheriff.

"You got any of that half-and-half?"

I wonder why he isn't talking about the murder, and then I think about our supplies and realize I haven't put out the cream and sugar or the thermos of milk we keep at a counter for customers to doctor their hot drinks like they like.

I walk over to the refrigerator and find the carton of half-and-half. Georgia comes in and studies me like I'm some sort of science project. She shakes her head, jangles the dice in her pocket, and takes the carton.

"Here you go," I hear her tell the judge. There's a pause in their conversation while I assume he pours the cream into his cup of coffee.

"Thank you, Georgia," he says. "You look real nice today." Then he must whisper something to her because she makes that "*Pffft*" noise again.

"See you, Lorna," he yells out, and it startles me.

"Morning, Judge," I call back as the front door opens and closes. Someone else comes in, and I wait again to hear the story being told, but all I hear is a kind of light chatter, like I hear when I'm standing a few feet away from the sports radio talk show Buford sometimes keeps on in his shop.

I decide instead of trying to eavesdrop on dining room conversations or worry about Willis and Buford or make any judgments about Marvin or even try and get questions answered, I will do the thing that has always calmed my anxious spirit: I will lose myself in biscuits.

I lift off the plastic wrap from a bowl of dough and take a whiff. It's dough I made a couple of days ago without adding the cream and baking soda, since putting in the soda and wet ingredients early and then setting the dough aside causes the biscuits to lose some of the rise, leaving them heavy and dense. I need to use it today, or it'll have to be tossed since I never leave dough refrigerated for more than forty-eight hours, knowing it just starts to get gross after that.

I grab the buttermilk and the sharp cheddar cheese I shredded when I made the dough and set the ingredients on the steel table in the center of the kitchen. Georgia is talking to somebody, Robbie Miller, I think, from the florist shop across the town square, or maybe it's somebody else from the courthouse, I can't say for sure. Even though I'm as curious as a cat to see who knows what, I close my eyes and stay focused on my baking. I find my rolling pin and cut off a long piece of parchment paper, then sprinkle flour on it. I inhale and mix the buttermilk, the baking soda, and the cheese into the batter and stir it all together, and then I exhale.

Sometimes I don't roll out the dough and cut it for these kinds of biscuits. Sometimes I just use my spring-loaded quarter cup scoop and drop them onto the pan. When I do them that way, they have that kind of Red Lobster-look to them, a rustic biscuit appearance that some folks seem to think makes them more authentic. But this morning, with everything going on, everything I know and don't know, I need to roll.

I drop the dough on the paper, get my pin, slide a handful of flour up and down the rolling part, and start my favorite part of making biscuits. Everything becomes silent. I don't listen to who's talking out front. I don't try to make out what somebody might want or need from the kitchen. I try to forget about Willis and Marvin, about Buford taking him home.

I don't feel any urge to walk into the dining room and into the townsfolk's speculations right now; I just push and pull the rolling pin toward and away from me, lean in and draw back, my feet firmly planted on the floor, my belly grazing the table. Forward and back, side to side until the great clump of dough is flat and rectangular. It's soothing, rhythmic, and as always, it becomes my meditation.

Forward and back. Side to side. I have to stop myself or I end up rolling it too thin, having to clump it together again and starting over. Sometimes I do that on purpose, just to keep feeling this feeling, this rocking of my whole body, the breath of morning that helps me find space in my brain for gentle thoughts, room in my heart for more of what's missing. Today, however, I try to roll it just thick enough.

It was my grandmother who taught me how to make biscuits. She'd come stay with us once in a while when Mama fell off the wagon or took up with some man who promised her the moon and then just drove her down to the beach until he tired of her.

Her drinking and leaving used to upend me and Draymond; Cathedral being so young, she didn't seem to notice. But when Grandma Lawton started coming and sitting with us, we didn't mind Mama's absence one bit. Grandma Lawton, as blind as she was, would make the biggest cat-head biscuits we ever had. She would clean up the trailer, sew patches on the holes in our jeans, dig up the ground around the front steps and plant pansies if the weather was right, even play ball with us. We liked having her there so much that sometimes we tried to talk Mama into going out of town or added liquor to her iced tea just so we could call Grandma Lawton and tell her to come.

I grab the cutter and drop it into the dough, carving out biscuits, taking them one at a time and putting them on the tray I had already covered in parchment. I put them three to a row like Grandma Lawton taught me, sprinkle a little flour on top, and roll the excess together with my fingers. Then I flatten it out with the pin so I can cut two more, finally leaving one long thin piece of dough.

"And that there's the snake biscuit," she would say, and me and my siblings would fight over who got that one—sometimes having to wait till it baked and then slice it up because Cathedral would start to cry and me and Draymond would turn to fists.

"You get the head, Lorna Gayle," she'd inform us, "and Draymond gets the rattle tail." Cathedral would be just fine with a round biscuit as long as Grandma Lawton blew on it and cooled it down with butter, calling it some favored critter like a beetle biscuit.

I take the thin piece and curl it around the top row, smiling as I remember how much I think about those early days when I'm cooking dinner or baking biscuits.

"Sheriff's on the phone," is what immediately pulls me out of my happy place and back to the unsettling things at hand. "Says he needs to talk to you." Georgia has just popped her head around the corner.

I feel my heart rate start to pick up, and I put down the rolling pin and slide my hands up and down my apron.

"I'll get it in here," I say, grabbing a towel and walking over to the phone on the wall. Trying to center in on my morning meditation, I take in a deep breath and pick up the receiver.

CHAPTER SIX

"This is Lorna," I say into the mouthpiece. I try to sound warm and cheerful, not at all as if I know Marvin has been murdered and Willis was hit on the head and is now hiding out at Buford's, not at all as if I have reason to sound guilty.

"Lorna, it's Ferguson."

"Morning, Ferguson. What can I do for you?" *Warm and cheerful,* I tell myself. *It's just a normal day at the bakery. Willis wasn't here, and I don't know anything about anything.*

"I'm going need you to leave the store," he says, his voice all professional, the words all choppy and swift. Ferguson talks like this when he's doing his police business.

"Uh, okay, for what?" And my mind starts swirling like dough in the mixer. *He's found Willis. He's arrested Buford. I'm going to be charged for harboring a fugitive. I wonder how much a lawyer costs and whether they let you have biscuits in prison.*

It's almost impressive how wide and far-reaching my imagination can go when I think trouble's just made a phone call to my number.

"We need something to eat out here."

"What?" As far-reaching as my mind went, I did not consider delivering biscuits as the purpose of this call.

"There's about six officials out here, counting the ones from the station and the ones from the county, and none of us have had any breakfast. It appears we're going to be here a while. I would send Darrell to come get them, but I got him wrapping tape around the house, so can you bring us some biscuits?"

"You want biscuits?" The warmth and cheer have melted into a little bit of being dumb.

"You got biscuits, I presume."

"Yes, of course," I reply, trying to sound like this is just another order on just another ordinary day. "You want me to come to you and bring biscuits?"

There is a long breath blown into the phone. It sounds like Cathedral when I used to ask her where she was going on a school night. After Grandma Lawton died and Mama finally got to go somewhere farther than Wrightsville Beach with a new boyfriend, I took over raising my younger sister. Draymond helped a little, but by the time he turned sixteen, he was mostly staying with friends and working at the tire shop.

"Six people," Ferguson repeated. "Could be a variety, some egg-and-sausage, maybe one of them boxes of coffee?"

"Now?" I swear I am not trying to be difficult.

"Yes, Lorna. Now. Or whenever you get some biscuits wrapped up and the coffee made."

"Okay."

"You want to know where we are?" And now Ferguson sounds all gossipy, the way I've seen him act at Buford's when he's got a secret and wants somebody to ask him about it.

"Marvin Lemmons's?" I said it before I thought it through. And just like that, I see Buford's face, all eyeballs and surprise, shaking his head like I know he'd do if he heard that I had just let on to the fact that I knew Marvin was dead.

There's a pause in the conversation, and I think I have really done it now. I know I cannot be trusted with illegal activities like hiding Willis. Buford was right to get him out of the shop, or I'd have probably dialed the state police trying to ring up the milkman for a new order.

"Yeah ... how'd you know that? Did Mavis already come in to get biscuits?"

Mavis, thank God! She was in! That was who I heard in the dining room while I was rolling out the cheesy dough. It wasn't Robbie Miller from the florist, it was Mavis and everybody knows that Mavis loves to gossip. "Yep, she came in a few minutes ago. You want me to see if she's still here?"

There's a moment of silence, and I wonder if he's still considering other ways I might have known his whereabouts.

"Nah, that's all right. She needs to get to the station anyway, wait on the reports we've ordered. Coroner might need directions since he's coming from Winston-Salem. I had to call everybody in early."

"Mmm-hmm," I say, listening closely.

"She tell you what happened?"

"Who? Mavis?"

"Yes, Lorna. Mavis, my assistant, the one who was at the biscuit shop a few minutes ago, who may in fact still be there, and who knew where me and Darrell had to go this morning, who knew because I told her that Marvin Lemmons is dead."

"Oh."

"Lorna Gayle, are you all right? You don't sound good. Should I call Eugene at the diner for some food?"

"Oh, no, no, no, Sheriff. I'll get you some biscuits, and I'll bring them out there to you. It's all just a little much, isn't it?"

"Yeah, yeah, it's just terrible is what it is."

"Terrible," I repeat.

"All right then, see you in about an hour?" I hear other voices besides Ferguson's. I hear him slide the phone away from his mouth and answer a question about whether or not they need to put down plastic on the floor in the entryway.

"Of course, put down plastic or use the newspaper from the boot of my car. Just don't mess with anything around the body. And for

Christ's sake, Darrell, do not go tracking mud into the victim's house. Wear them paper booties I'm always giving you."

I just wait, figuring he'll get to me in a minute.

"Now, what were you saying?" he asks me.

"Nothing, just that I'll pack up what I have and see you in about an hour."

"All right, all right," he replies.

"You need anything else from town?" I ask.

He pauses. "You got any of that brown butcher paper, you know the kind that comes on a long roll?"

I figure he thinks that might be better on the floors than newspapers, but I don't have any of that, just rolls of plastic, and not the kind for walking on.

"Nah," I answer. "You want me to stop by the station and see if you got some there?"

He seems to be thinking.

"No, I don't know if Mavis could find it, and I can't recall where it might be. Haven't used it since ..." His voice trails off, but I'm listening real close because I think he might mention another town murder, and I can't say why or how, but it feels somewhat exciting. I don't know what has happened to me, but suddenly I'm as nosy as Georgia.

"Nah, it's all right, just bring us the food. I suspect we're going to be out here for a long time."

"Okay, Sheriff," I say, sounding all professional, like I'm working alongside him and Darrell and not just catering a murder scene. "If you think of anything else you need, just ring me back and I'll bring it over with me."

"Thank you, Lorna. We'll see you when you get here."

"Uh-huh," I say and hang up the phone. I'm facing the wall, processing what just happened.

"Marvin Lemmons is dead," Georgia says, standing at the door to the kitchen, staring in my direction. "Mavis just broke the news, which is more than I can say about you."

I feel her eyes burning a hole through my neck.

"You want to tell me whose blood that is now?"

I don't turn around, don't answer Georgia. I just try not to let on that I am so relieved that Mavis can't keep a secret, I almost want to give the sheriff's secretary breakfast for free.

CHAPTER SEVEN

"How many more?" Georgia is helping me bag up biscuits to take to Ferguson.

"I made four sausage-and-egg," I tell her. "Maybe I should just do a couple of egg-and-cheese." I've never catered a crime scene, so I don't know how hungry law enforcement officers are when they're checking for fingerprints and getting statements from witnesses.

I do know a little about homicides and first responders because me and Buford make it a habit of watching all the *Law & Order* reruns on Channel 13. It's kind of like eating breakfast together in the mornings; we have dinner once a week and watch murder mysteries. It's always Wednesday nights, and we order pizza from Eugene's. We also get together other nights and over the weekends, too, but we don't generally watch television shows then, just the nightly news and *Jeopardy*.

I check the clock and notice that it's been about twenty minutes since the sheriff called, almost an hour since Buford and Willis have been gone. He usually opens the barbershop at eight, and I wonder if he's going to make it in time to do so this morning and whether or not he has any early appointments today.

"He said there were six of them, maybe more by now, but I don't guess we're expected to feed journalists and neighbors," I say. I think about who else in Owensboro knows about Marvin and wonder if Frank Kelly from the weekly *Tribune* got a call, if he sent his brother RJ to take photographs of the house, the body.

"You suspect they'll send someone from Raleigh to solve the crime? How does a small town like Owensboro manage a murder? Are we sure Ferguson even knows what he's doing?" I'm not sure why I think Georgia will know the answers to these questions, but Buford's not here, so I might as well ask her.

"Ferguson ain't no Matlock, that's true, but I think he knows his way around dead people."

"What makes you think that? How many dead folks do you actually think he's handled? And to be clear, Matlock was a lawyer," I correct her.

"What?" She's wrapping up a cheesy biscuit in aluminum foil.

"Matlock, Andy Griffith. Well, and now Kathy Bates. Anyway, he was a lawyer in that show. You're thinking of when he was the sheriff in Mayberry."

"Am I?" She stops what she's doing to consider what I'm saying. "Well, it don't matter, he figured stuff out even if he wasn't the sheriff. Matlock has skills; the both of them."

"Right," I answer, deciding to make a couple of egg-and-cheese to take along with me.

"You think it was a crime of passion?"

"A crime of what?" I ask.

"Passion. Like maybe Marvin had a secret love affair and the husband found out and killed him. Or maybe it was one of those beekeeper employees, and they got mad at him and jumped out of a bush somewhere and whacked him."

I think about the employees from Marvin's warehouses, how they wear white jumpsuits and how we always say they look like beekeepers. "It's possible," I say.

"Or maybe it's a serial killer," she adds, peeking around like she thinks one of them might be in the dining room. "One of them crazy kind who cut up the body and put parts in the freezer." She glances behind me. "Do you think we should check the freezer?"

I give her a look. "Wait, you think a serial killer killed Marvin and then put his body parts in our freezer?"

"Well, not Marvin's parts, since I guess he was all put together when they found him." She pauses. "Did they find all his parts?"

"I can't say, Georgia. But they did know it was Marvin, so there must have been enough of him to identify his body."

She nods like she's really considering parts of Marvin. "Well, maybe he's not in there, but there could be somebody else's parts."

"In our freezer?"

She purses her lips together and keeps nodding very slowly.

I don't even know how to respond, so I head into the kitchen, shaking my head. As I leave, I hear the bells jingle on the front door.

"Hey, Miss Georgia, how y'all doing? My oh my, but you sure look busy with all them bags and foil. You making a to-go order?"

I roll my eyes. Donna Jennings has just walked into my shop. It's not even an hour after we opened, and she has already gotten here. I doubt she knows about Marvin; then again, maybe that's why she's here early, hoping for a bit of the latest town gossip.

"Donna."

I hear the edge in Georgia's voice. She does not approve of what Donna is doing.

"It is such a beautiful day today, isn't it? Seems like our weatherman got it right this week. Spring is coming early this year."

"It's not early, Donna. Spring is exactly on time."

"Is it now?"

I can see our customer touching the sides of her hair, dressed to the nines, lipstick perfectly applied, heels and matching purse, probably a new pantsuit with a silk blouse—fixed up in some fancy color like watermelon or lavender.

"You know, I would love a few of the cinnamon biscuits to take to a house showing I got this morning. And I'll have a cup of hot coffee, a large, and Mama, what would you like today?"

I hear a chair being slid across the floor and mumbling from the front.

"Mama, don't pull out all those napkins," Donna is yelling.

Donna Jennings runs a real estate agency and brings her mama to the bakery when she's got a house to show or an appointment with a seller. She leaves her here like we run a day care for old people. It irritates Georgia, but I don't mind.

Ms. Abigail gave piano lessons when I was little, a free offering to all the children living in the trailer park. She was always kind to me and my brother and sister, and her dementia is just in the early stages. She's not much trouble. I just feel bad for her when Donna leaves her here through her nap time and she falls asleep sitting up. Sometimes she keeps her eyes open when she's hard asleep, and there's been more than one occasion when some other customer thinks she's dead. But you get used to it.

"Donna, we got a lot going on this morning, so we can't watch Ms. Abigail all day."

"Oh, it's not all day, Miss Georgia. It's just a couple of hours is all." There's a pause. "What you got going on?" she asks.

I hear Georgia's "*Pffft*" and hope she's not getting ready to tell Donna about Marvin or, worse, tell Donna off.

"Mama, I told you to quit with the napkins. How does egg-and-bacon sound for a biscuit today?"

I can't hear how Ms. Abigail answers, but I go ahead and add another egg to the skillet, pull out a couple slices of bacon, and throw them on the small grill next to the burners on the stove. I flip the egg already cooking.

"So, Miss Georgia, sorry about that, what is making you so busy today? It's certainly not a lot of traffic in the dining room. Does it have something to do with all that police activity this morning?"

There isn't anyone else in the front, and I'm sure Donna thinks this is part of the reason that dropping off her mother to stay for hours isn't a problem. I'm sure she thinks it's just like a college kid sitting in a coffee house all day. But even though Ms. Abigail isn't a lot of trouble, she's definitely not a college student.

I listen to see if Georgia's going to tell her about Marvin.

"It's just a busy day," she replies.

I guess she's going to keep the information to herself, but it's certainly not because she's suddenly become a pillar of discretion. She just doesn't like Donna.

"Busy?" Donna's hoping to hear the skinny.

"Your mama want coffee?" Georgia is not biting.

"Mama, you want coffee?"

I don't hear Ms. Abigail respond.

"Just give her a glass of milk. Coffee can sometimes give her a tummy ache, doesn't it, Mama?"

It gives her more than a tummy ache, I think, remembering the mess we had in the bathroom last week after she drank two cups of coffee in the afternoon. That was Friday, when we close at one o'clock and Donna left Ms. Abigail until three. I think the bathroom accident was as much as her being mad she got left as it was drinking coffee.

Georgia rings up the sale, and I hear Donna over at the table where I'm guessing Ms. Abigail is sitting. She's talking to her, but I can't make out what she's telling her, probably something like how she won't be gone long and just to stay where she is.

Poor Ms. Abigail, I think, but I imagine it's hard on Donna, too, trying to take care of her mother and work full-time.

Still, Georgia is right; I'm going to have to say something to her at some point. I can't be expected to watch out for her, especially when her dementia gets worse. It's like trying to keep your eye on a toddler. And Ms. Abigail is fast. I've seen her outwalk Donna.

I put the egg-and-cheese biscuit on a plate and walk it over to the older woman sitting at the table near the window. Donna, it appears, has already left the building.

Georgia has brought her the glass of milk, and she just shakes her head when I walk around her to get to the only customer in the dining room.

"Here you go, Ms. Abigail," I say, placing the biscuit on the table in front of her, knowing I need to leave to get to the crime scene.

"Marvin Lemmons was an a-hole," is what she says, and just like what happened with the tub of grease earlier in the morning, I almost drop the plate.

CHAPTER EIGHT

"What did you say?" I ask Ms. Abigail, so shocked to hear her outburst. There had been no discussion of Marvin Lemmons in the bakery this morning since she and Donna arrived. And from the sounds of Donna's end of the conversation, not asking Georgia any real estate questions—like wanting to know who Marvin's next of kin is and whether or not they might want to sell the house since Marvin is now deceased—it didn't appear that Donna knew.

"You're Margarete's daughter," is how she answers without saying anything else about the dead man.

"Yes, Ms. Abigail, but what did you just say about Marvin Lemmons?"

"But you're not Cathedral, not Cathy. She was the better piano player."

I see that the thread of her thoughts regarding the murdered man is now lost, somewhere in a knot with the other threads in her mind.

"She was," is all I can say. And it is true, after all. Cathedral was gifted in her music, though she didn't stay with it.

"Shame about Margarete," is what Ms. Abigail says next, and I wonder what she thinks actually happened to my mother.

"Yes, ma'am," is how I answer. "Enjoy your biscuit," I add, walking away. Georgia follows me into the kitchen.

"I do not understand for the life of Abraham why she thinks it's okay to bring her mother in here and leave her for hours on end." Georgia is still mad about this current situation.

"It's hard to be a caregiver," I say, edging past her.

"Abby needs to be at Evergreens," is how she responds, and I know that's probably where she'll end up eventually. It's the nursing home on County Road Number 11, the same place where Willis's mama is. It's not terrible, but then again, it's not where anybody I know wants to live.

"Donna is doing the best she can."

"By leaving her at a bakery all day?"

She has a point.

"You know that woman has enough money to pay somebody to stay with her mama when she's running all over town buying and selling every house from here to South Carolina." Georgia reties her apron strings since they've come undone. A strand of hair has also fallen from the bun of her long gray hair on top of her head. She reaches in a pocket, jingles the pair of dice while she's got her fingers in there, and pulls out a bobby pin. She slides back the fallen lock and pins it to the side of her head.

From the door, I glance over at Ms. Abigail, who is picking apart the biscuit, taking out the egg and placing it to the side of her plate, then the bacon. She tears off a tiny piece of biscuit and takes a bite, and then she makes a line with her breakfast along the windowsill—egg, then bacon, the biscuit, like she's setting a tiny glass menagerie of animals on a shelf.

"You know I am speaking the Lord's truth," Georgia says.

"Just keep an eye on her," is what I tell her as I take off my apron and get ready to take the delivery to Ferguson. "And don't let her eat what's she playing with. Those windows ain't been cleaned since I opened up here."

"Probably longer than that," Georgia replies.

I bag up all the biscuits, along with two boxes of hot coffee that drained all our makers, and I grab a handful of paper cups, napkins, creamers, packets of sugar, some of those little wooden stirrers we got for buying coffee from that online distributor, and a few bottles of water from the fridge. I put everything in a box from the freezer and then put the box on the cart I intend to wheel out to the parking lot and load into the van.

We don't typically make deliveries, or at least we don't advertise that we do, but I often use the van to take breakfast to hospital employees, or over to the school for a breakfast, to the Baptist Church for their women's missionary society meeting, or sometimes to Donna's open houses. But driving around Owensboro with a box of biscuits is not why I got into this business.

"You got a meeting?"

Buford's pulled into his parking space, rolled down the window, and is speaking from the car.

"Where have you been?" I ask, thinking I sound worried and wondering if he is picking up on it.

"Just trying to get Willis settled. Why, is something wrong? You seem upset."

I guess he picked up on it.

"Ferguson called."

Now he looks worried.

"He just wants biscuits," he continues, "but I don't feel good about all this."

"He at Marvin's place?"

"Uh-huh, and Mavis broke the news to Georgia, so I guess it'll be all over town before you get in and start a shave."

"Mavis does love to talk about her work. Maybe that's a good thing."

"Maybe," I reply, thinking he's right. If Mavis keeps talking, maybe we'll hear if they're trying to find Willis. Maybe I could go by the station pretending I'm on a mission for Ferguson, searching for that brown butcher paper.

"You'll just have to keep Mavis coming in for breakfast."

"Now that's an idea. Maybe I could give her some extra Biscuit Bucks. How's Willis?" I ask, without any more thought on giving away my coupons, the cart now wedged between me and the Cadillac. "He know anything more? He gonna talk to Ferguson?"

Buford shakes his head. "All he knows is that he woke up with a gash on his face, a bump on his head, and found his brother stabbed dead in his living room. What he knows is just enough to make him suspect number one."

"Ferguson would certainly think that," I say. "You reckon Willis will talk to you?"

Buford shrugs. "Hard to say." He turns away, and I'm staring at his profile. He has perfectly chiseled cheeks, sideburns that would seem just a little too long on anybody else but shape his chestnut-brown face just right. "He'll talk to somebody in time," is how he answers, and I wonder what the two of them came up with while they were gone.

"Well, Georgia's in there. She found the medical supplies and apparently Willis got some blood on the wall near the door."

He turns back to face me.

"She also saw the two of you driving out of the parking lot."

"What did you tell her?" He wants to know.

"Nothing," I answer. "She thinks Marvin was killed by a serial killer who cuts up the body parts and hides them in a freezer at a bakery."

He raises his eyebrows. "That sounds about right for her, but how did you manage not telling her anything?" He also knows Georgia is like an old dog with a bone. It might be buried a hundred times, but it's going to get dug up just as much.

"Buford, I'd love to talk, but I got to go," I say, knowing I need to get the biscuits out to the lake before Ferguson calls again.

"You take all the hot ones?" he asks, eyeing the box on the cart.

I smile, reach into the box, and pull out a sausage-and-egg from the bag. "I made a few extras," I tell him as I reach through the window and hand it to him.

He takes it from me, touching my hand as he does. "Hey," he says, and I stare him right in the eye like I know he's asking me to do since he's still touching my hand, holding it really. "It's going to be okay," he says, and I can't help but think of the last time I heard him say that and how it turned out he was so wrong.

CHAPTER NINE

I haven't been out to Whitman's Lake since last summer. July Fourth, if I remember right. Georgia, Buford, and I went together to sell biscuits at the community holiday festivities. We stayed until after lunch, hot dogs grilled up by members of the Kiwanis Club and catfish biscuits—the biscuits made by us, the fish caught by the local Boy Scouts, the proceeds going to the scouts. We were there just long enough to sell out of the inventory and watch a softball game between the first responders and the county hospital staff. Buford wanted to leave before it got dark since he didn't want to be at the lake once the fireworks started.

Georgia stayed and got a ride back into town with her daughter and Flora. She likes to watch the fireworks display, claims she likes the sky all loud and flashy and likes to watch everyone singing the anthem when the fireworks are over. It gets her every year, she says, to watch Mayor Rowan trying to remain upright with his hand across his chest without falling over.

Buddy Ro drinks a lot. Him getting elected as mayor of Owensboro the first time was kind of a town joke. Nobody else was running, and a few people just put Buddy Ro as a write-in without thinking too much about it. Next thing the town council knew, they were swearing in Ralph "Buddy" Rowan, the manager of the mattress store in the strip mall west of Owensboro, as the new mayor.

That was at least fifteen years ago. Now, we've just come to accept his leadership, if that's what you want to call it. Mostly, we just like to watch him show up drunk and try to finish a speech. Several of the men actually wager bets on how long he can stand up in front of a crowd before he starts singing a bar song or reciting Psalm 23 instead of the Pledge of Allegiance. He does give our little town a reason to come to the city council meetings, granting us the appearance of civic pride to other cities around us, which we all sort of respect.

Whitman's Lake is owned by the county, and for the longest time, there was no building anywhere near the water. It was just dirt roads and boat ramps all the way around the big body of water fed by Belew's River. I'm not sure what happened to the zoning laws and development restrictions that were in place for years. I just know that some time ago, we all heard that Marvin Lemmons gave a big donation to members of the council and to Buddy, who was just starting his reign as mayor, and before anybody knew it, Marvin was the chair of the zoning commission and was building a mansion on the north side of the lake.

It turns out that the city council meeting when Marvin was elected, unlike all the others, was not public, so nobody knew what was happening until Mr. J.H. Julian, the president of the Owensboro Bank, told the men at the barbershop that Marvin was moving out to Whitman's. Everybody acted like they thought that things seemed to progress too fast and without much oversight, but nobody made a stink. So after that announcement, it wasn't long before a few others started building out there near Marvin, and nothing really changed in Owensboro.

As I recall the development at the county lake, I begin to wonder if Marvin managed his business with the same sort of sketchy practices; that maybe some business deal went sour, sent some customer over the edge, or maybe when he built his house all those years ago, he made somebody in town mad enough to kill him, and they've been waiting all this time for revenge. But that doesn't seem likely.

There's still public access, and folks take their boats out there, fish from the banks, and swim in a roped-off beach area. Now there's just a road that goes up to the mansions that has a gate stopping anybody from driving around that way. Lakeview Estates, they call it, and I guess, like Buddy Ro becoming the mayor of Owensboro, we all just got used to it. I doubt a murder came from that.

I glance out the windows as I pass by the farms and wide strips of meadows. Daffodils are blooming a little early this year. Apple trees, the hardwoods, dogwoods are all budding. We didn't have much of a winter in North Carolina, so I expect the summer to be hot and the bugs to be awful.

Georgia always says that if the winter doesn't give us ten days in a row of frost, mosquitoes and gnats lay all the eggs they want around puddles and creeks, on the banks of the lake, and once spring shows up, insect life abounds. She says it has to be ten—not nine, not eight—ten. And just as she does when she sees the crows gathering, Georgia counts.

I have never questioned her science since she's always been right as far as I know. A short and mild winter has always meant more heat in June and an increase in the sales of calamine lotion during the late spring and summer at the drug store. I know this because before I started the bakery, I worked the counter at Mr. Denton's pharmacy. We always stocked up on the aloe and the calamine when spring came around. You just learn things like that when you're trying to match the needs of a town dealing with bites and rashes and bugs.

Mr. Denton was a kindly old pharmacist but a less than stellar businessman. However, he did always mind the trends and made sure to order what folks wanted. He died from a heart attack after his wife left him for the school principal. He had the foresight to order extra doses of penicillin and boxes of condoms around prom night and graduation, but not enough to recognize Mrs. Denton's extra hours of volunteering at the school library and the way she got all blushed and clumsy when the principal came to the store to buy school supplies.

I always thought she was having an affair with the girls' basketball coach, Annie Ledman, since the coach seemed to always be at the store hanging around the pharmacist's wife. I learned later she was just passing notes between the principal and Mrs. Denton in exchange for extra equipment for the team—ice packs, heating pads, Gatorade, that sort of thing. She was Principal Allen's wingman, I suppose, and after Mr. Denton died, I could tell Coach Ledman was really sorry for aiding and abetting the infidelity. She'd come around the store acting all downbeat and remorseful, left flowers on the dead man's grave, and ended up moving to a community college in the mountains, teaching math—apparently giving up coaching and the high school drama altogether.

I drive out past the town limits, notice the cemetery and give a nod to all the dead ones from town, my mama included, and then head out the county road that leads to Lakeview Estates, where Marvin built his house. I watch as the sky brightens with the morning sun. It's going to be hot today, and I hope that means business will be good at the bakery. Sometimes you just never know, but it does seem that we sell more biscuits and Pepsi in spring. Last year, I tried to market iced coffees after Mae made the suggestion, but that didn't really go anywhere in Owensboro.

People balked at the idea of cooling down a cup of coffee with cubes of ice and charging more than a regular, claiming that if they wanted their coffee cold, they'd just pour a cup and leave it on the counter instead of paying extra for me or Georgia to make what was meant to be hot, now all of a sudden cold.

"Just give me a Pepsi," they'd say, shaking their heads and mumbling when the offer of iced coffee was made. Like Mr. Denton figured out about the need for aloe cream and calamine lotion in April, we learned that what might be popular in your large town bakeries does not guarantee success in Owensboro. You can follow the trends, but just make sure they have something to do with where you actually live.

I turn off the main road onto the lake road, and I can see the blue water from where I'm driving. There are white caps since the morning wind is a bit high, and a few boats are anchored around the private docks near the houses. I guess the word is now out, and folks are trying to see what they can see by land and by lake. Some of the people in the boats have fishing lines in the water, but some of the boats just have people sitting in the front, shading their eyes, and watching.

I make the turn for the Estates and get to the gate where Maynard White is working as the guard. I roll down my window as he steps out of the shack.

"Lorna," he says as a way to greet me.

"Hey, Maynard."

"You making deliveries now?" He tries to peer around me into the van.

"Ferguson made a call, asked me to bring something for the boys working up there."

"Marvin's dead," he tells me. Apparently, Owensboro doesn't honor any HIPAA laws or privacy concerns, so that even the security guards will gossip.

"I heard," I say, wondering if he knows anything more.

"Well, I can guarantee you there weren't no break-in," he adds, and I make a note of his observation.

"Yeah, how's that?" I might as well learn as much as I can. I sit up tall in my seat.

"James Dean worked the night shift here at the gate shack. Says nobody came in or went out after dark that doesn't live here or wasn't with Mr. Friddle's family. He lived a few doors down from the entrance here, died at the hospital yesterday." Maynard seems real proud of himself for knowing this tidbit, puffs up like a party balloon.

"But that still leaves a bunch of people who do live here as suspects, right?" I say. "And then maybe somebody said they were with the dead man's family but weren't really."

I see a little air seep out, and for some reason, I keep going. "And there's always the lake. Maybe somebody came in by boat. Or maybe it was somebody who came in during the day and waited until night, like a repairman or delivery person like me. Maybe they came out after James Dean left and before the new shift started, that being you, I guess."

Deflated now, he stares at me like I've got three heads. He scratches his chin and glances out over the van like he's pondering.

"Maybe you should check the video feed of everybody who's been in and out for the last week." I suddenly feel like I'm channeling Matlock, and I tell myself to make a note to tell Georgia.

He shakes his head, and I wait for his answer.

"Can't do that."

"Yeah, why not?" I ask, thinking it must be some security measure.

"Camera's out."

"How about a daily log?"

"Don't keep no log," he replies, and I watch him fill up again with air. "But I got a good memory, and I remember who came through here yesterday." He hitches up his pants by the belt loops. "Preacher came and stayed till the family got here, I think, in Mrs. Friddle's guesthouse, trying to be a blessing, I'm sure. Harper Rainey from the funeral home, of course. And I did see one person walking out, running really, when I first got here. He was down at the other end of the fence. Not sure exactly who it was and not sure how he got in, just saw him go out the lake access gate. May have just been a morning jogger, but I'm going to try and find out who it was."

I try to keep my mouth from flying open. And before either of us says anything else, before I can ask about security cameras and footage from houses near the entrance, we both turn to see a car pulling in behind me to go through the gate.

"You take care, Lorna. I'll see you on the way out." He pats the side of my van, waves at the person in the car, and then he opens up the gate.

CHAPTER TEN

Darrell is the first one I notice when I get to the crime scene. He's got the yellow tape wrapped around a light pole in the front, looped around the head of the dolphin in the fountain, and he's unrolling the spool to take it down the driveway to the mailbox. He lets me pull in before he wraps it around the tall black base of the box. He has a cigarette hanging out of his mouth. I roll down my window again as I pull up beside him.

"Hey, Darrell," I say, putting my foot on the brake.

"Hey, Lorna … Hell of a mess up there," he tells me, as he glances over his shoulder. "You might want to stay outside."

I'm thinking I hadn't considered anything but staying outside Marvin's house. I never had a plan of going into a dead man's residence where the police were gathering evidence. I realize I hadn't given it a lot of thought, but I just figured I'd leave the boxes of food outside in some tent I assumed they'd have up. A sheriff's tent or crime-scene ground-zero site, like they always have on the television show. But then I think, maybe going inside would be fun.

I turn to Darrell, and he's taking a long pull of his Marlboro Red while he leans on the mailbox.

"You closing up the driveway?" I ask, wondering how I can pull out if there's tape stretched across the exit.

"Nah, just blocking off the front yard to keep folks from gathering up there." He holds the roll of tape in one hand as he flicks the ashes from the end of the cigarette with the other. "You bring breakfast?" He peers around me to try and see into the van, just like Maynard.

"Yeah. You want a biscuit? I got sausage-and-egg, cheesy biscuits ..."
I try to recall what else is in the box.

"You got coffee?" He puts the large roll of tape under his arm,
drops the butt of his cigarette, and then crushes it out with his shoe.

"I do," I tell him, wondering if he's going to pick up the butt he just
dropped, but it's clear he doesn't plan to do it, at least not while I'm
parked here with coffee in the front seat.

I put the engine in park, and reach over to the passenger seat, find a
cup, and open the spout on the box of coffee to pour him some. "You
take anything in it?"

He shakes his head. "Just black," he tells me.

I hand him the coffee and, since I was apparently smart enough to
gather some intel from Maynard, decide to see what he knows. Darrell
has been a deputy for about a year, and he's not known for any gifts in law
enforcement. Buford says he got the job because Ferguson lost a bet with
Darrell's father and had to hire him as the payoff. Darrell mostly likes to fish.

"Ya'll know what happened?" I ask, trying to sound interested but
not too curious as to appear as if I have any agenda.

Darrell takes the coffee, enjoys a sip, and shakes his head. He stares
out at the lake, gets a kind of lonesome gleam in his eyes. "Knife
wound," he answers and then turns to me like he realizes he wasn't
supposed to tell me anything. "You know Marvin?" I guess that's his
way of changing the subject.

I ponder Marvin Lemmons, consider the question. Like everybody
else in Owensboro, I knew him, and I didn't think much of him. I've
always had more of a relationship with Willis than him. Marvin was
older than me by just a year. He was smart, top of the class every year.
But he was not generous with all that he knew. He seemed to enjoy it
when others struggled over something he picked up easily. He always
acted as if he looked down on everyone else, as if he was somehow better
than the rest of us. I watched as he pretended he didn't know Willis,
avoiding him in the halls, sitting at a different table in the lunchroom.

And then, because of his severe allergies, he was always excused from gym class, sitting in the stands, wrapped up in sweaters, staring down at the rest of us while we played dodgeball or ran laps. I'd catch him leering at the popular girls, but he never spoke to any of them, and he never noticed me. Since he left high school early to go to college before the rest of his class, he didn't go to prom or march in graduation. He and Willis had those things in common, but Willis seemed lost, whereas Marvin just seemed annoyed.

He owned a few warehouses over in Second Town where they said he kept large pieces of equipment. He did something with building computer rooms, got the parts, installed everything so that the rooms were secure and perfectly clean. I know a few people who work over there sometimes come into the bakery wearing those head-to-toe white jumpsuits, hairnets, paper booties. Georgia named them "the beekeepers," and none of them seem to be from around here. But I don't even know what it is they actually do out there. Truth be told, I didn't know Marvin really. I just know what happened with Willis. And I know Marvin lived up here on the lake. I know he was successful, never married even though it's been said he became a sort of ladies' man when he got rich.

I don't know how the other folks in Owensboro thought of Marvin, but I never cared for him. Too uppity for my blood, and I never approved of how he treated Willis. I didn't like him before, but I really didn't like him after the court case and the restraining order he put on his brother. I know I had trouble with my siblings, but I'd never say they couldn't come to the house or walk into my business. And when our mama died, Draymond and I divided things up evenly. We didn't fight about her insurance or the trailer, even though her estate was real different from Old Man Lemmons, I'm sure. But everybody in town knew Marvin didn't give Willis a penny. He found some way to keep all that family's inheritance to himself and make sure his mama stayed at Evergreens. When Mr. Lemmons died from a heart attack, never having served a day in jail for almost killing his wife, that was about the time Willis set up a tent at the creek and about the time Marvin came home to Owensboro for good.

Buford trims Marvin's hair when he can't get to his stylist in Atlanta. He says Marvin's nice enough, tips well, doesn't really talk too much to anyone, is polite but doesn't like to wait. If there's not an open chair, he'll just leave. But Buford's with me on this opinion: We both think he did his brother wrong. And considering this, I wonder if somebody else in town thinks the same thing, enough to want to do something to make Marvin pay—something like stabbing him to death.

I turn to the deputy standing outside my van and wonder if anybody in the sheriff's office is checking these things out: angry business partners or customers, disgruntled fishermen who lost access to their favorite fishing hole, silent supporters of Willis. I give Darrell a hard look, trying to imagine what he thinks happened. He's a good twenty-five years younger than me. He's the baby brother of Thomas Swindoll, and Thomas was at least ten years behind me in school. I look at him. He's so young and innocent, and I wonder if what Buford said is true—that he got the job because the sheriff lost a bet. I wonder if he's got any ideas about the murder or even if he's happy in his work, especially on days like today when his job has to do with something so grisly. But then I see him staring at the lake again like he's spotted an old lover, and I think he's not long for the deputy work.

"I guess I knew Marvin about as much as anybody else in town," I finally answer, not sure he has even been waiting on one.

"He sure has a good view from here," he replies, that longing now not just in the sad way he's staring out but also in his tone of voice.

"He does," I respond and then think we're talking about him like he's still going to enjoy his view.

Darrell sighs, takes out the pack of cigarettes from his front pocket, pulls out a fresh one, and then searches around for something to do with his cup of coffee while he lights the cigarette. I reach my hand out through the open window, and he hands it to me. Once his cigarette is lit, I give him back the cup.

"You been fishing this week?" It's clear to me that I'm not going to get too much news from Darrell so I ask him about what he really likes to talk about.

"Caught a walleye," he says as he nods and takes another drag. "A walleye," he repeats. "They say there ain't any of them 'round here, but I got pictures. I was planning to fish later today but ..." His voice trails off, and I realize his grief.

"Does the sheriff actually work on murder cases? Maybe this crime gets passed onto another agency, something like the state police?" I realize I don't have a clue about how these things get handled, but I keep going. "Maybe it'll be somebody else doing all the work and you'll still get to go," I say, trying to sound hopeful.

"Maybe," he answers, without much conviction or enthusiasm. "Ferguson really wants this one though," he adds.

And we both turn to look up the driveway, where the sheriff is standing near the house with his hands resting on his gun belt. He's just staring in our direction, and I know I need to get up there.

Darrell quickly puts out his cigarette, like he's suddenly in trouble, and takes the roll of tape out from under his arm. He hands me the cup of coffee like he can't have any more.

"Wait, why does Ferguson really want this one?" I ask, thinking about what he just said.

"Figures he already solved it," he answers. "Thinks he don't need no help from outside the department." He bends down, picks up the cigarette butts, and sticks them in his front pocket. "Calls this a 'local drama,' 'family dispute.'"

He steps away before I can ask what kind of evidence Ferguson has, why he thinks this way.

"Thank you, Lorna," he says and starts walking to the other end of the yard.

CHAPTER ELEVEN

"I swear that boy is going to be the death of me," the sheriff says as I step out of the van.

I turn to follow his gaze and see Darrell getting wrapped up in the yellow tape. He's trying to untangle himself, and even from where we are, we can see the tape is sticking to his hair and his clothes. Ferguson just closes his eyes and shakes his head.

"You want the food on the cart?" I ask him since I don't see any good coming from commenting on his deputy.

"Nah, just wait a second and I'll get somebody to come and take it inside." He yells to the people in the house. "James Earle, Lester—come out here a minute."

I open up the side door of the van when two men come over from the house. I slide up the boxes where they can get them.

"You know Lorna?" Ferguson asks the two men, and we all shake our heads. It's hard to see their faces since they're both wearing masks, but I'm pretty sure I don't know them.

"James Earle and Lester work for the county office. They're taking prints and photographs for me." They nod at me without speaking or holding out their hands, which are covered in gloves.

They're wearing the same kind of white suits the people working over at the warehouse wear, that white paper jumpsuit that ties in the back with strings. I wonder if it's because of COVID, or if it's some sort of security measure, or if Marvin has started decomposing.

"Lorna Gayle runs a bakery in town; has the best biscuits in Owensboro," Ferguson tells them.

"I'm still the only one with biscuits," I say, thinking of how many times Buford and I have had this conversation.

"Eugene has biscuits," Ferguson responds.

"Eugene has dinner rolls," I note. "He just calls them 'biscuits' so the locals will still eat his dinners."

"True, true," the sheriff replies. "Just take the boxes into the kitchen in there. Looks like there's coffee and napkins and everything, so try not to make a mess."

I step out of the way without having spoken to James Earle and Lester or having them speak to me. The two men take the boxes, stacking up what they can in each other's arms, and then walk away. I guess I'll not be going inside, after all. I'm a little disappointed.

"Not very talkative," I say to the sheriff.

"Yep, they're sort of serious in the workplace."

"You been with them before, then?" I ask, still unclear about how many murders the sheriff of Owensboro has actually worked.

"More times than I like to count," he answers, and this surprises me since I can't recall the last time I knew of a homicide in our fair town.

"We get a lot of overdoses," he says, as if he knows what I'm thinking. "And sometimes the death might just be due to natural causes, but if they aren't at the hospital or Evergreens, we have to make reports, gather evidence, you know, just to have it in case something ever comes up."

"Like a similar death," I say, nodding, as I suddenly remember one of the episodes of *Law & Order* where there was a home health nurse killing her patients and nobody noticed for a long time. When one of her victims—the mother of a detective—died and had not taken ill, the detective became suspicious. I feel myself wanting to gloat a bit about that particular episode because I solved the mystery a good fifteen minutes before Buford. He thought it was somebody in the neighborhood killing elderly people for their drugs.

"Anyway, thanks for bringing us something to eat," Ferguson is saying and reaching for his wallet.

"It's fine, Ferguson," I say, waving away his attempt to pay for the biscuits. "Consider it a sign of gratitude for your service to the good people of Owensboro."

He smiles, rests his hands on his gun belt again. "Did you know Marvin, Lorna?"

He's staring right at me like I might be a suspect, and before I know it, my neck starts to go red.

"I knew of him, really, more than knew him," I stammer a bit, and I start to feel like maybe I killed Marvin and forgot.

"Yeah, a lot of people say that about him." He smooths the sides of his head where his hair is sprayed down stiff. Nothing moves with his action.

I start to wonder how many people Ferguson has asked this morning if they knew Marvin Lemmons. I glance around but don't see any of the neighbors gathered on the street. Everybody seems to be staying away.

"Why you suppose that is?" I ask, finding my voice.

"He was a private man," Ferguson answers.

"What's in the warehouses?"

He turns to me again.

"I mean, what kind of work is it that he does?" I clarify.

"Installs the computer rooms in industries, builds the floors and the walls to keep them fireproof and wired right for servers and so forth, knows how to lay the tile and hang the siding so that the space is both secure and pristine. He does pretty well, I hear."

"Did," I correct him, and he seems confused. "I don't guess he does well anymore."

"No, you're right about that."

"So, is it murder then?" I figure since we're talking like this, I might as well stretch it out.

Ferguson smiles. "Now you're sounding like R.J. You writing a book?"

I grin, trying to act innocent and play along. "No, not at all, I'm just curious, like everybody, I imagine. Not every day we get something this big in Owensboro. I have to say I feel slightly uneasy thinking something like this could happen here." I pause. "You think we're safe?"

He slides a hand over the top of his head, smoothing down his hair. "I think you're just fine, Lorna Gayle. No need for panic. But you're right, there'll be a lot of questions and speculations about this one, I 'spect." He says this and then appears as if he's trying to get a piece of food from between his teeth using his tongue.

I glance away to give him a bit of privacy since it seems like this is a kind of personal hygiene activity. I have always been courteous and polite about such matters. It's just neighborly.

"Georgia watching the shop?" he asks, and I think that he must be finished with his dental work.

"Yep, she got in about the time you called," I tell him and close the door to the van.

"And Mavis already came in?"

"Uh-huh," and I hear myself swallow and wonder if he thinks it was a gulp, a guilty gulp.

"She talks more than an administrative professional in a law enforcement office should probably do so."

I shrug since I don't have a clue as to what would be a good response to that statement. I do not disagree with him, but I also know she provided the wind to the sails of the lie I made earlier on the phone.

"Okay, Sheriff, well, I guess that's all you need from me this morning. I hope you get some good leads, and this thing gets solved real quick."

A car is coming in the direction of the driveway where we're standing, and we both turn to see. It's a black SUV, fancy looking, all washed with tinted windows.

"Goshdang, it's the feds," is all Ferguson says, his brow suddenly all knotted up.

Somehow, I get the feeling Darrell was right about the sheriff. If they're here to help, Ferguson does not appear too eager to partner up.

CHAPTER TWELVE

The SUV has parked behind my van, and I don't see how I can make a quick and easy departure now that four people are all exiting the vehicle. I turn to Ferguson, and he's just shaking his head. He kind of moves his mouth sideways, takes in a breath through his nose, then blows out a sharp exhale. He's getting ready for something.

"Sheriff," says the man who was sitting on the passenger's side as he walks toward us.

I just stand where I am, holding my ground, I suppose. These are people who carry themselves tall, with authority and presence, and I try to match up.

Ferguson just nods. "You fellows are here a bit early." He has a small twitch in the corner of his right eye.

"It's a federal case, sir." The younger one, the driver, says this, and we all turn at once to the bearer of this news. Even the older one who got out of the vehicle first and made the initial greeting seems surprised to have heard something coming from the agent beside him. He doesn't appear that pleased, and the young one shrinks slightly. I almost feel sorry for him.

"I haven't heard any instruction from Raleigh," Ferguson replies. He lifts his hands that were hanging to his sides and rests them on his belt. He is someone not yet ready to move.

The older man, the one in charge I now understand, holds out his hand behind him, and a woman from the rear of the group places a paper in it. He then reaches it out to Ferguson, who takes the paper.

I can only see the top, which has Federal Bureau of Investigation on the letterhead, but I can't read what clearly is getting under Ferguson's skin.

"We'll need to evacuate the scene, especially anyone who is a nonessential party." The man is glancing around the front of the house like he's taking mental notes.

Ferguson clears his throat. "You want to explain to me why this has you boys so interested?" He hands the paper to the agent.

The woman in the rear moves out again, just enough to make herself seen. Ferguson doesn't acknowledge her though. I guess to him they're all the same, male and female—all "you boys" in this group.

"Let's just call it a need-to-know situation, and when you need to know, we'll make sure you're up to speed."

I can't help myself, my eyebrows have raised, and I have placed my right hand on my chest. That sounded straight out of a movie, and I can't say why, but I feel somewhat protective of Ferguson.

The sheriff clears his throat again, turns to glance away.

"Why don't we begin again?" The FBI agent appears to make an attempt at a smile, but it's forced and not at all genuine. "I'm Special Agent Paul Causey. This is Agent Williams, Brody, and McMillian." He nods at the three people with him, and at the sound of their name, they nod in return. "We are here to help you manage the situation of the deceased found in his home in Owensboro. We appreciate the professional way you have handled the unfortunate event up to this point, and we will continue to manage the scene with the same level of mastery it is clear you have provided."

Ferguson eyes all four agents and then returns his glance to the agent in charge, Causey. He doesn't reply.

The agent is about fifty, I'd say, white—pasty, really, like he stays inside most of the time—salt-and-pepper hair, trimmed nicely, standard black suit they're all wearing, even McMillian, the woman in the rear. He's medium build, slightly taller than the others, and has a serious face.

"Sheriff Ferguson Gentry," comes the response while I'm sizing up the agents, thinking they seem exactly what they are. I suddenly realize they're all staring at me like they're waiting for me to take their order or bring them the daily special.

"Oh, I'm just …" and I fumble with my words, understanding they're expecting an introduction. I start to feel a wee bit out of my element, so I just shrug and hold out my hand, which no one takes. "I'm Lorna Gayle Pitchford," I say, shaking my head. *Lord, I'm just wanting to get out of here, is what I am.* "I brought food for everybody," I add, dropping my hand.

"Biscuit Bakery on Main," Ferguson notes. "Ya'll should try it on your way out of town."

And this makes me laugh slightly.

"Well, if it's all right, let's step inside and you can catch me up on the proceedings of the Owensboro Sheriff's Office heretofore."

And now I laugh out loud. I haven't heard the word *heretofore*, well—considering it now—never.

The agents glare in my direction.

Ferguson nods a few too many times, I think, and he turns to me. "Thank you, Lorna. It was mighty nice of you to bring us breakfast." He turns and walks toward the front door, and the three men and one woman standing in front of me—the feds, "the boys"—turn to follow. Agent McMillian is putting on rubber gloves as she walks past.

I move toward my van to leave, thinking I'm going to have to drive on the lawn to get around the FBI vehicle, when I hear somebody ask from inside the house, "Are those body bags spread out on the floor? I thought there was just one victim?" I suddenly wish I had brought Ferguson the butcher paper he was needing.

"They from Raleigh?" Darrell has walked up from the street. He still has a short piece of yellow tape stuck to the side of his head, but I decide not to call attention to it.

"Uh-huh," I answer. "Not very friendly," I add.

"Never are," he replies. "All business, them people." He's peering at their SUV. "You reckon it's bulletproof?" he asks and steps closer, lightly kicking the front tire.

"You could try it out and see," I answer, showing what I mean with the lift of my chin at the gun on his belt. I smile.

He responds by sort of nodding with his whole body, flashes a quick grin at me, then glances around.

"Marvin's my first murder," he says quietly and shakes his head like he's not happy to be dealing with such circumstances as we presently find ourselves. "You see him?" he asks.

I shake my head. "I didn't go in."

He exhales long and slow. "His eyes were open," he tells me, his voice gone all small.

I try to think about the last time I saw Marvin. I think it was before Christmas. He had been to Buford's and gotten a trim and a shave, and he stopped in the shop to get a cup of coffee. He talked on his phone most of the time he stood there waiting for Georgia to pour it and ring him up. He was cagey as he talked, glancing from side to side like he thought somebody might be listening, holding his hand over his mouth so nobody could make out what he was saying.

He wasn't bad looking, kept himself in good shape since high school. He was tan, which I thought was different for Marvin, since I remembered him being only ghostly pale when he was young. And he wore a thick blue sweater, a scarf around his neck, dark slacks. He kept his hair cut short, military-like, had a nice natural wave to it, Buford said, but Marvin never wanted it long. He was tall, seemed quite comfortable in his skin, and when he saw me watching him from the kitchen, he just stared in my direction.

He stared the longest time, and then the look on his face changed, like he remembered something, like he remembered who I was, which I knew was impossible, and he smiled ever so slightly, but still, I could see it. Marvin smiled. And I thought, as I stared back, watching the sinister way he was recalling something from the past, that no one would ever know he and Willis were brothers, so different they were on the outside.

He stayed on the phone as he waited at the counter, and when he left, Georgia claimed he was rude, talking on the phone the whole time. In spite of the distracting phone conversation, the staring, and the menacing half grin, I just thought he was busy—otherly engaged, as Buford liked to say about the customers who never talked.

"It was like he died surprised," Darrell adds and kicks the tire of the SUV again.

"Sounds about right," I answer, thinking again of how contented he seemed when he stopped in for coffee a few months ago. "I doubt Marvin ever thought something like this was coming."

CHAPTER THIRTEEN

"Feds?" Buford is sweeping around the chair near the front window. He's already had at least one customer this morning.

I stopped by his place before heading over to the kitchen. I check the clock on the wall and see that it's about noon, which means I got to get next door and cut the ham and stir up some red-eye gravy for lunch. It's been advertised in the paper as the Bakery Biscuit Special today, and I know we'll get a handful of folks counting on it. Especially with something like the murder of Marvin Lemmons, people will want to talk.

"They tell Ferguson why they were there?" He keeps sweeping up the pieces of hair, white ones, so I know he's cut the hair of somebody old.

I shake my head. "Just that it was a federal case," I answer, recalling the young agent piping up with that bit of news.

"They take the body yet?" he asks, now emptying the dustpan into the garbage can under the sink.

"I don't know," I reply. "Two men from the county medical examiner's office were in the house, a couple of cars I didn't recognize. I don't know who else was inside, but I didn't see anybody from Harper's."

Harper is Rainey Harper from Score Harper's Funeral Home. Like his daddy and his daddy before him, Rainey usually handles all the white people in Owensboro. Buford's cousin, Jimmy Hargrove, takes care of Second Town.

Buford stops what he's doing and seems to be thinking. "I guess they take the body in a van from the coroner's office, not the funeral parlor."

"I suppose," I reply, suddenly wondering whether Marvin would actually get a funeral, not having any other close family who could make a decision in town other than Willis.

"J.H. said the lawyer in Charlotte's been notified. And Marvin apparently had a girlfriend in Florida, a flight attendant he took to the country club a few times, had her phone number in his wallet. He mentioned that nobody's seen Willis to tell him the news."

He pauses and glances over at me, and I nod, knowing our secret. "And the Baptist preacher was going over to Evergreens to tell Mrs. Lemmons," he finishes.

I think about Willis's mama and wonder what she knows, if she'll understand her youngest son is dead. After Old Man Lemmons threw her down the stairs, sending her into a coma, everybody said she'd fight her way back. They said she was strong and determined, that she'd endured worse, but after a year, then two, then ten, then … well, I don't even know any more. Nothing's changed. She just lays over there in a room at Evergreens, hooked up to a ventilator breathing for her, a catheter and feeding tube, just lost to some place where nobody can reach her.

There was a rumor a few years ago that Marvin was going to take her off the life support, that he had told that lawyer from Charlotte to draw up the paperwork and was planning to take care of it all, but I heard from Georgia that the Baptist preacher, who is really the only one who still visits her other than Willis at her window, talked him out of it, went to his house and told him that she was in God's hands and to let it alone.

I'm sure Marvin didn't soften at some word that his mama was being protected by the Good Lord, but much to the surprise of everybody in town, he listened to the preacher and left things alone. That was a very long time ago, and Willis never said nothing about it, but I know he sometimes goes over to the Baptist Church and cleans up the sidewalks after a windstorm, empties the trash every Monday, and not due to the fact he takes their charity. I think he knows the preacher talked to Marvin not because of any all-out devotion to the sanctity of life but mostly because of him. Willis may not go inside Evergreens, but he loves his mama more than anything. I don't think he'd stay around here if she was gone; in fact, I'm not sure he'd still be alive. I think the preacher understands that, and I'm grateful for what he did. Willis deserves a little kindness. Maybe that's also part of the reason I'm going along with Buford. I care about Willis, too, and even though I'm worried about what we're doing, I want to protect him. I want to find the real killer and keep Willis away from the sheriff.

Still, I hate what happened to Mrs. Lemmons, and I hate she lives like that. Sometimes if me and Buford talk about end-of-life stuff, I think about her and know that's no way to live. If she is still hanging on to keep her oldest boy alive, that's more of a sacrifice than I could make for anybody, even my child, if I had one.

Not long after she went into the nursing home, a year after being over at the county hospital, I had papers drawn up stating that I don't want to live like that and gave a copy to Buford. If I'm dead in the brain, then don't hook me up to anything. And if it's too late and the tubes are in, then Buford gets to decide when I've had enough time to try and make it back and when to shut everything off. I know it was hard to put that on him when we ain't really family, but I knew I couldn't burden Draymond, my only living relative, with that kind of choice. Buford understands me, and he's done the hard things before, so he agreed and promised to take care of me no matter how that care came packaged.

"You think it's good news for Willis?" I ask.

"What?"

"I don't think the feds would be involved if they thought it was a domestic case. And if it was as simple as a brother killing a brother, wouldn't they just leave it in the hands of local law enforcement?" Seems like I saw this on an episode of *Law & Order*, but I can't remember the specifics.

Buford is thinking.

"The FBI only gets involved if it happens on federal property or when local law enforcement agencies ask for help or when multiple jurisdictions become involved or when it's a mass shooting, right?" I remember doing a search after watching television that night.

I imagine Buford must remember that episode. "Could be," he says.

"Well, I can tell you for certain that this local law enforcement did not ask for their help. Ferguson was madder than a wet hen when they drove up. And in all the time I've been serving Ferguson biscuits, I have never heard him say a curse word. Although, I don't think goshdang really counts as cursing." I stop for a second.

"The murder wasn't on federal property, and it was only Marvin who was killed, no others, and not by gun violence."

Buford chews on his bottom lip. "Yeah, I think you're right. This is good for Willis. Marvin must have been involved with something the FBI knows about."

"Uh-huh," I reply.

"You sound like you know more than what we watch on TV," he says. "You been reading up on the law and not telling me?"

"I do a little more than just cut out recipes and bake biscuits," I answer. "I got some skills," I add with a grin.

"Always knew it to be so," he tells me.

"You know, I have to say," I tell him, "I'm a little suspicious when most nobody seems to understand what a man does for a living, like Marvin. Doesn't it feel a bit suspect, all them people donned from head to toe in white paper like they work at the chicken factory or with hazardous waste? Ferguson says it was computer installation work, but nobody ever talks about what they do over there, like they've taken a secret oath, and he never seems to hire anybody from town." I pause. "You notice that?"

Buford doesn't answer.

And as we ponder things, I think about the warehouse workers coming in for lunch, how I don't know any of them or their people. Georgia once thought they were immigrants working for less money, but they're mostly white and all speak real good English, at least that I've heard. They don't struggle with the language like the men from South Florida working on construction crews.

Buford checks his work around the chair. "You know, those warehouses are less than a mile from the entire population of Second Town, and he has only one local guy employed there—Leo Landry, who works at the security gate out front. He never goes inside, not allowed. Even the janitors are from somewhere else."

I make myself a note to see if I can talk to Leo and learn anything from him. I file away the thought and return to the conversation at hand. "Georgia thinks Marvin drove down to Texas and picked them up at the border."

"These aren't undocumented people," he replies. "They're just not from around here."

Before either of us can make further comment, the front door opens, and Buford and me recognize who it is and then turn to each other, sharing what I can only imagine is the exact same memory.

CHAPTER FOURTEEN

"Hello, fine folks," he says, like he's from the 1800s. "I'm trying to find the sheriff," the lawyer from Charlotte announces.

I realize I don't know the man's name. I've just always called him *the lawyer from Charlotte*. And I am about to say something smart to him like, "Yeah, well, does the sheriff in Mecklenburg County keep his office at the barber shop?" But I think better of myself, choosing to refrain from the sarcastic tone.

I'll be honest, I don't like this guy—this lawyer without a name—with his wavy brown hair slicked back, narrow hips, and tan cheekbones. I remember him well from the trial against Willis: the smug way he spoke to the judge, the way he refused to look at his client's brother to even acknowledge that he deserved to be heard in the court, the manner in which he smiled when the ruling went in his favor—how pleased he was with himself. I didn't like him then, and I don't like him now.

He's big money, more money than I'll ever know, more money than I'll ever want. It just shows in how he walks and holds himself; how he dresses, not a wrinkle or a smudge on his silk suit; how he judges everyone else. Reminds me of Marvin. If he had dollar signs on the inside of his eyelids, it wouldn't surprise me one bit.

He's so far out of my league, I don't even know where we might meet up except in a courtroom or maybe if he was ordering breakfast. It certainly wouldn't be for socializing or going to church or shopping at the Piggly Wiggly. He doesn't even seem to know how to talk to me and Buford. In fact, it's as if he can't decide between the two of us standing here who he should even address, and not because he's trying to be inclusive and broad sweeping with his attention; I'm sure it's because he's never really addressed anyone of color or any woman with not much more than instructions on how to detail his car or how many copies to make—or maybe if she were younger and richer and thinner and more beautiful than me, a few charming lines that gets her where he wants her, probably in the backseat of his sports car or in the penthouse of some hotel.

"He isn't here," Buford answers since the lawyer has now decided just to attend to him, choosing gender as the higher value.

"Has he been in this morning?" He just stands in the door, neither in nor out, just blocking the way for anybody else who might want to enter or exit.

"I haven't seen Sheriff Gentry today," Buford says, and I just watch as he fades away into this person giving a report to a member of the court. I've seen him do it before. He slides in and out of this compliant citizen role that I understand is a way of survival for Black men in the South.

"You try your client's house?" I decide to make myself heard. I decide I can participate in this conversation without being either catty or dumb. I know words. I've even talked to the FBI and figured out some things. I can answer a question, although I did just answer a question with a question, something Georgia says can be rather annoying on my part.

And then he does turn to me, like he's just seeing me here for the first time, like I just showed up, walked in the door, or appeared out of thin air. He pauses before making a reply, and I don't know if it's because he doesn't want to acknowledge me, doesn't want to answer the question, or doesn't understand the idea as presented.

"He's not there," he finally replies, and this causes me to wonder where Ferguson went, if the FBI really has taken over, forcing the local authorities away from the crime scene. Then he just stares at me for a moment longer than he should, and I suddenly don't want to be in this conversation any longer. "Do I know you?"

"I don't think so," I reply, and for whatever reason I feel myself redden.

"Yes, you're a friend of Willis Lemmons." He studies me, and I wonder why he didn't say that about Buford since we were both standing opposite of him with Willis at the trial.

"You might try the courthouse," Buford says.

He keeps staring at me and then turns again to Buford. "What?"

"Sheriff Gentry," Buford explains. "You might try the courthouse."

"Right," he answers. "Except that's where I was, and his secretary said he was heading down here to the barbershop to talk to some folks."

"Well, I haven't seen him this morning. If you want to wait, we can see together if he shows up, or I'm sure you can get his cell number from his office and just call."

"Yep, I probably can do that," he responds and then glances around Buford's shop like he thinks the sheriff is hiding somewhere.

I decide to go with the honey over vinegar communication style even though I like this man a whole lot less than Ferguson. "You want a biscuit?" I ask. "You must be hungry dealing with all you're dealing with at the moment."

He doesn't respond, just gives me a look.

"What time did you get into town this morning?"

A forced grin forms across his face like he knows I'm trying to get information.

I wait for a few moments, but clearly he's not answering.

"Well, biscuits are hot if you want one. Buford, I'll see you later," I say, thinking I won't get much from the lawyer, and start to move toward the rear door.

The phone rings, and Buford picks up. He walks over to the desk where he keeps his calendar and starts flipping through the pages. Somebody's wanting to make an appointment, which is rare for Buford. Most of the men just show up when it suits them.

"What about Willis?" The lawyer stops me before I make it past Buford standing at the desk. He glances up from the appointment book when he hears the question.

"I'm sorry," I say, turning around.

"Willis Lemmons," the lawyer says.

"Willis isn't here either," I answer, then look over at Buford. Then I turn again to the man from Charlotte. "What is your name?"

"Has Willis been here?" He doesn't seem to want to answer my question, but I figure I'll just Google him when I get home tonight. It shouldn't be that difficult to find out this man's identity.

Buford makes the appointment and ends the call. He walks around the desk to face the lawyer still standing in the door. "What's that?" He stands between me and the lawyer, and I know that's my way out.

"Willis Lemmons. I'm sure you've heard about Marvin ... so has his brother been here this morning?"

"Buford, you still want the lunch order?" I don't know why I think he needs my help, but I just reinserted myself into the conversation.

"Thank you, Lorna, I'll walk over to your shop in a few minutes and pick it up."

The lawyer turns around and glances at me, smiles. "You run the place next door?"

Buford is still watching me, seems like he's waiting for me to answer.

"O, Biscuit Bakery," I answer, nod at Buford since I'm done with this man and his questions, and start walking toward the door. "Still happy to fix you up with breakfast if you want."

"You and Willis are close."

And I stop.

"Is there something you want to ask me?" I feel on my tongue how sharp the words sound.

"I'm just trying to find the family member of my client. I'm sure I will need to discuss some estate issues, probate information. It would serve us well to find Willis, and I recall you standing with Mr. Lemmons when he was ordered to stay away from his brother's property and to pay some court costs, which if memory serves me, I don't think have been paid."

"I was there as well," Buford notes, stepping back in the conversation.

"What?"

I've turned around now to watch the two of them.

"Me, I was there, too, as a friend to Willis."

"Funny, I don't remember you." And he narrows his eyes at Buford.

"Well, that's understandable," Buford replies.

"What makes that understandable?" the man responds.

I'm watching the talk between the two like it's a tennis match.

"Just that you were very busy with stating the case of Marvin, I can see how you didn't pay close attention to who was sitting with Willis."

"Maybe," is all he says.

"I'm going to go." And I start again to head to the exit. "We have country ham biscuits today, if you want something to eat," I tell him. "Maybe you can give me your business card, and if I think of something important, I'll give you a call. Besides, I never know when I might need a lawyer."

He grins and pats his coat pockets, doesn't pull out a card. "Fresh out at the moment, but I know where to find you."

I shrug. "Suit yourself. We're open Monday through Saturday ... best biscuits in town."

He doesn't reply.

"See you, Lorna," Buford says.

"Later," I answer, and then I take my exit, trying to shake off the ick I just got doused with.

CHAPTER FIFTEEN

"I had to make another pot of coffee because I knew we needed extra for the red-eye." Georgia is pouring coffee into the skillet on the grill. There is no one at the counter, and Miss Abigail has her head on the table. I assume she's taking her morning nap, but there's a part of me that thinks I should check her breathing.

"Thanks, I can take it from here," I tell her as I see the woman in the dining room jump like she just fell in a hole in her dream, sit up, glance around, and then drop her head onto the table again. I place the keys in the bowl by the kitchen door and take the apron off the peg and put it on, tying the strings around my waist.

"So, what did you find out?" Georgia is standing at the grill, holding the spatula in her hand like she's going to swat a fly, which I hope is not what she's getting ready to do.

"He is really dead," I answer, walking to her. "And Ferge isn't saying much."

"Mmm-mmm-mmm …" she says and shakes her head. "Stabbed?"

"Looks that way." I decide to tell her more since I know the talk is already flying around town by this time. "He was killed at home. No witnesses at this point. No video footage at the front gate." I remember Maynard's reports and the lack of any help or evidence that is likely to be forthcoming from the guard shack at the Lakeview Estates.

"We got any suspects?" she asks, like she's now on the case.

I think about what I know, which isn't much. Maybe a shady business deal gone bad? Maybe somebody trying to protect Willis? Maybe somebody mad about a rich person taking away the town's lake? Maybe that creepy lawyer?

I turn to her before answering, and I watch her gaze move over to the magnetic strip above the center table where we hang the knives. Maybe she's imagining these instruments of our good cooking suddenly turning to weapons. Maybe she just needs a paring knife to cut up the strips of ham. I decide not to ask. "No suspects that they've named."

She narrows her eyes at me. "They keep the windows closed?"

"What?" I take the spatula from her hand and start stirring in the drippings.

"The windows at his house, did they keep them closed?"

I shake my head like I'm not understanding.

"To keep his soul from flying out," she tells me. A rule of death I do not know.

I ponder the question.

"Well, even if they kept the windows locked up, the door stood open for the entire time I was there," I reply. "I didn't notice a soul escaping though." I pour a tiny bit of molasses into the skillet, remembering that I need to ask her for another jar.

Some people put honey or a pinch of brown sugar in the red-eye gravy, but I prefer a teaspoon of molasses to give it sweetness.

"Don't mock me," Georgia replies, and we both turn to the front door when we hear the bells jingle, signaling us that someone has come in.

"I wouldn't mock you for the world," I respond, a smile settling in place.

"You should watch yourself. Maybe go home and take a shower." She waits before greeting the customer.

"You think Marvin's soul somehow flew out and landed on me? You think a shower can get his soul off my skin?"

She gives me the evil eye.

"Ms. Thelma," she says and leaves the kitchen.

I hear the polite talk between Georgia and the owner of the Curl Up and Dye hair salon just up the street. Thelma always comes in for a biscuit on Country Ham Day. She likes the cinnamon raisin ones too, but she's partial to the ham.

"I need some gravy," Georgia calls to me, and I turn down the heat on the grill and keep stirring.

"Got it," I yell to her, finish stirring, and then spoon some gravy into a Styrofoam cup and take it out front.

"Good afternoon, Thelma," I say, and she smiles in my direction.

"Lorna, so good to see you." She takes the cup as Georgia bags up the biscuits she's ordered. "You hear about the murder?" she asks, her eyes all big as she glances around like somebody might be listening.

I nod.

"It's set me on edge. I'm going to start locking my door from now on."

"Probably a good idea," I respond.

Thelma shakes her head. "Anyway, I'm just here to take Miss Abigail in for a wash and trim." She's handing Georgia a twenty-dollar bill. "Donna said she'd pick her up from my place."

"Well, let's hope you didn't make any evening plans," Georgia says, and I cut her a look. I'd prefer if Georgia didn't speak out of turn about our customers.

Thelma puts the change Georgia hands her into her wallet. "You do not have to tell me anything I don't already know. I hear she also leaves her at the Catholic Church in Thomasville when they have bingo on Friday afternoons." She leans into the counter to whisper. "You know Miss Abigail does not like to be in the Catholic Church, says it makes her wobbly, all them statues of Jesus everywhere." Then she glances around again and crosses herself quickly.

"We don't think you've actually been to church unless you get a little wobbly," Georgia notes.

Thelma appears confused.

"Pentecostal," I say.

Thelma nods and smiles, then raises her hand to her neck and fiddles with her necklace.

I glance over at Miss Abigail now waking up. She wipes her chin and takes a gander around like she's seeing everything in the shop for the first time.

"Speaking of," Thelma glances around now too. "I got asked to do Mrs. Lemmons's hair later today."

Now for the life of me I cannot make the transition from statues of Jesus in the Catholic Church to fixing a comatose woman's hair. I'll need to wait on Thelma to fill in the blanks.

"Can you believe it?" she asks. "She woke up."

"Martha Lemmons?" I ask.

"The very one," she answers. "One of the girls who works there said she's been praying some prayers to the saints while she sits next to her bed, which I don't actually think Mrs. Lemmons would approve since she's a bit like Miss Abigail when it comes to that brand of religion. And, besides, everybody knows she's close with Reverend Goodlaw from the Baptist church." She takes the bag of biscuits Georgia is holding out. "Only appreciates his praying.

"But anyway, she was praying to Mary or Jesus the Christ, or Saint Jude, hard to say really since nobody actually knows for sure, and then Martha's eyes just started flickering, and she stared right at the girl praying and asked about Marvin."

"Marvin?" Georgia is the one asking. "She knows? And is Saint Jude the one who runs that children's hospital in Memphis?"

Thelma nods to the first question and then shakes her head and waves away the second.

"Reverend Goodlaw was there this morning to break the news. 'Course nobody thought she would hear him, but apparently the news about her dead son just flat woke her up. He told her about his passing, said a good Baptist prayer like she likes, stayed a little while and left, and that's when the girl that works there went in the room to pray to somebody and she woke up."

Georgia and I look at each other.

"And now she wants her hair fixed?" Georgia asks, which is not really the first question that came to my mind.

Thelma seems confused. "Oh, I think it's mostly because she hasn't had her hair cut in a long time. Gladys Nobles, the head nurse, called me. She thinks there's going to be a lot of company calling on the woman—thinks it would be best if they had her presentable." She glances over at Miss Abigail, who is now writing something on the window. "This being a miracle and all."

"A miracle in Owensboro," Georgia responds.

"Yes, appears so. I guess what they say is true." Thelma leans forward. We both wait for it. "When God shuts a door, He always opens a window." She puts her right hand over her heart and Georgia follows suit, and I think they're going to do the Pledge of Allegiance.

"To let out the spirit," I say and elbow Georgia, who elbows me back, harder.

"Well then, ladies, thank you for my lunch." She turns to walk away and stops at the table where Miss Abigail is sitting. "Come on, Miss Abigail. We're going to take you to the beauty parlor to get your hair done."

Miss Abigail glances up at Thelma, who is standing over her, and then she turns to me and Georgia. "Somebody should tell Willis about his mama." And she stands up and the two of them walk out together.

CHAPTER SIXTEEN

"You think it was the prayers said to some saint, or the news about Marvin?" I cooked up a few more slices of ham since what we had is gone and there are two more hours before we shut down. I spoon them into the dish on the serving line.

"Well, if it was a prayer to anybody else up in heaven other than Jesus, then you know my thoughts about all that kind of magic praying." Georgia is wiping down the table where Miss Abigail had been sitting. She pulls out her chair and lets out a sigh. I guess there's going to be sweeping involved in the cleanup.

"We don't need no help getting to God," I say, knowing her stance on intercessory prayer but also knowing her leanings toward the mystic and how not everything she believes goes together.

"None," she says emphatically and heads to the broom closet. I want to ask her about her set of dice and how she incorporates future-reading from numbers in her religion, but I don't really have the energy for that conversation.

I hear her mumble something about Donna and needing a saint to show her how to take care of her mother, but it's clear she's just ranting to herself. This is not really two-way talk.

I watch through the front windows and see a few people walking the streets. Nothing too strange about the day, it seems, well, except the murder and now the miracle. Nobody is running about or standing on the street corner shouting the rapture has come, just the usual traffic of bank people and a few women from the law offices taking a walk on their lunch break. It's a warm spring day, and I can see the tiny pink blossoms on the cherry trees around the town square, the yellow coat of pollen on the tops of cars, the new bulbs we plant every fall on the town's anniversary—adding to the winding rows of daffodils and tulips, the red and yellow now marking the sidewalks. It is a nice time of year in Owensboro.

Buford loves the autumn, with the brisk westerly wind, the butternut squash in bloom, pumpkins and sweet potatoes for his soup and pies, the sound of the high school marching band on the field near his house, college football. Georgia favors summer, eating watermelon on her front porch, going to the lake with her granddaughter, fish fries at the fire station, and tent revivals. But I like spring.

I'm not crazy about the allergies every year, but I like the feel of wearing a sweater in the morning, the leftover chill from a cold night, the angle of the sun, the surprise of color, like the daffodils and the tiny purple blooms on the catmint Buford planted as a surprise one year in my window box. I like the thought of something that seemed so dead and lost come to life, buds on an old dogwood, the greening of barren fields, the kindness of evening breezes, the light rain, strawberry picking. April and May are like waking up after a bad marriage is finally over or leaving the hospital with a cart of balloons and cards—the surgery and stay all done—or being able to stand at a grave without crying. In spite of sneezing and the required nose spraying, spring has always given my soul a lift.

The bells jingle on the door, and I glance away from the flowers on the square to see who is coming in.

"Miss Lorna, how you doing this morning?"

"I'm just admiring the flowers, Preacher."

Reverend Goodlaw comes in from time to time to have a biscuit, chat, probably hoping I'll start attending his church. I'm sure he considers his visits to the town businesses as part of his pastoral care to community members, but he also has a soft spot for the country ham. I usually get a free blessing when he stops in, and he gets a punch on his Biscuit Bucks card.

"They are quite lovely this year," he says, turning around to see what I see. He spins around and walks to the counter.

"You still have some ham left?" he asks, eyeing the serving dish.

"Just heated up some slices," I answer, reaching over to pick up a piece of foil. I scoop a biscuit from the tray, set it on the foil on the counter, slice it open and slide in a big chunk of country ham, then I take a large spoon and add some gravy, put the top of the biscuit in it, and wrap it up. "I'm assuming you're wanting this to go." The Baptist preacher never eats in the bakery. I think he likes to unwrap it and enjoy it while he walks.

"Yes, yes," he answers, pulling out his wallet and holding out his coupon card.

I punch a hole in one of the circles. He only needs four more and he gets a free biscuit and a new card.

He takes it back and then pulls out a ten-dollar bill.

"I guess you know about Marvin," he says after he takes his change and adds some to the tip jar near the register.

"I have heard about him, yes," I answer, wanting to ask about Mrs. Lemmons and if he knew about the change brought on by prayer, but I decide to let him bolster up the conversation. I decide to hear what he knows.

"It's a tragedy," he responds. "But there was good news to come of it," he adds, and I figure he must have gotten called about Martha.

"You mean his mama?" I ask.

He nods. "I was there, visiting Mr. Greeson on the memory unit when they came and got me."

"And she was awake?"

"Bright eyed and sitting up," he tells me. "The closest I've been to a miracle since that car wreck on Route 90."

I think back to the incident to which he is referring. It was about fifteen years ago, if I remember right. A car sped out of control and rolled over an embankment. Charlie White and his son were driving back from a high school basketball game out of town. They were both trapped in the front seat, car upside down, and Laney Draper drove past right after it happened and stopped to help. When he saw that the car was about to set fire, he told everybody that he couldn't see how to get them out, that they were trapped, so he dropped to his knees and prayed and then felt himself become strong. He walked to the car and was suddenly able to pull both Charlie and Donnie out of the wrecked vehicle and drag them to safety. Pastor Goodlaw was next on the scene, and he preached about what he witnessed for months, saying he felt the Spirit as soon as he got out of his car; claimed Laney was touched by God and still in His presence, that he had been gifted by divinity to be able to reach inside the car and pull them both out even though they were buckled in, and saying that neither of them could budge beneath the crushed roof.

Laney never talked much about it, not like the pastor, said he just heard a voice telling him what to do, and he followed it. And he felt strong and mighty and was able to pull them both free. Charlie and Donnie both said they saw two people that night, two people pulling them out of the car, even though Laney was the only one there until the preacher drove up to the scene.

Everybody knew it was something special, and it was said that Charlie quit drinking and paid up all his outstanding loans, joined the church, and became a deacon. Donnie graduated and went to Bible school in Charlotte; pastors a little church in Mecklenburg County now.

I guess the preacher is right; there hasn't been something this big and exciting in all this time.

"So she knows about Marvin?" I ask.

He nods. "She was real sad about that, cried a little, but then asked for something to eat."

"Makes sense, I guess, since she probably hadn't had a bite of anything in years." I consider wrapping up a few biscuits and taking them over to Evergreens when we close. Willis used to say that Mrs. Lemmons always liked a plain biscuit. "Funny though that she didn't ask anything about what happened."

He shrugs.

"What do you suppose caused God to wake her up?" I ask.

"Maybe God knew her other son was going to need her," he answers, squinting his eyes like he was thinking real hard about the answer. "Or maybe what they said about her is true."

I wait.

"She's a strong woman and was not going to go down easy."

"All these years in a coma is certainly not easy," I answer.

"True, true," he responds. "And I suppose the rest of what I know is true too."

I lean in to hear this truth.

"The comings and goings of God are never ours to fully understand."

And suddenly there is a crash coming from the broom closet and then we hear, "Jesus, Mary, and Joseph, there's a rat drowned in the mop bucket!" And Georgia is standing in the dining room with her hair fallen out of her bun. She's holding a dead rat by its tail. She glances up at Pastor Goodlaw. "Oh, I'm sorry, Preacher, didn't know you were here." She looks down at the rat and then again up at the clergyman, and immediately drops the drowned rodent.

"Georgia, why did you do that?" I ask, walking around the counter to where she is standing.

"Preacher got himself some Holy Ghost and I don't want to be holding no rat if he's going to start bringing more dead things to life."

And I turn to Pastor Goodlaw, who starts to open his mouth and then closes it.

There's an awkward pause in the bakery. The three of us just holding silence like Quakers waiting on the Light.

"You all have a blessed day," is what he says, and he just backs his way to the door. "And Lorna, when you see Willis, please tell him to come by the church. I'd like to offer my condolences." He gives Georgia and the dead rat one last glance and leaves.

CHAPTER SEVENTEEN

"He wants to see me?"

Willis is sitting at Buford's kitchen table. I brought the rest of the ham with me, and Buford is stewing some tomatoes he had in the freezer and opened up a jar of green beans, canned from last year's garden. I'm fixing the table since we're planning to eat dinner together.

"That's what he said," I answer him, knowing he's got lots of questions about Mrs. Lemmons. "Condolences for Marvin, maybe a prayer for your mama?"

I stopped by Evergreens on my way over to Buford's. Mrs. Lemmons was sitting up talking to R.J. from the paper when I got there. I just said my hellos and dropped off a couple of biscuits. I didn't get a chance to tell her anything about her other son, but she seemed just like her old self. Thelma had already gotten there and had done a good job fixing her hair, and one of the nurses had put a touch of makeup on her. She was wearing a new pair of pajamas that somebody must have given her. She was thin, frail, but she appeared a whole lot better than when she was in her coma.

There was a line of folks wanting to see her, talk to her, and I noticed as soon as I pulled up that Darrell was parked outside in the circle driveway. I don't know if the FBI ordered the surveillance or if Sheriff Gentry is still running his own investigation, I just know the deputy was sitting there, waved at me when he saw me walk up. I asked him what he was doing there, and he just said he was keeping an eye on things, that the sheriff told him to come, and that he was glad to get away from Marvin's. When I asked him if the FBI took over the case, he just shrugged like he didn't know or didn't want to say.

I was going to ask him more, but then my cell phone rang, and I took a call from the school about an order. By the time I finished, Darrell had taken his own call and just waved at me and rolled up his window.

I decided he was probably just keeping an eye on the facility for Ferguson, making sure Evergreens wasn't bombarded with news media and such. I didn't think his presence meant anything suspicious.

But Buford isn't so sure. He's convinced they're waiting for Willis.

"And she was awake?" He rests his head on his hand, his elbow on the table.

"She was talking about the things she remembered after she went down the stairs."

"She remembers things?" He raises up.

I put down the paper napkin in front of him, place a fork and spoon on top.

I shrug, making two more places for dinner. "I didn't really get to hear much," I tell him. "She didn't know me at first, so I told her who I was, and she remembered Draymond. I think he fixed her car some."

"We always went to him when she needed new tires," Willis replies.

"Do you want iced tea?" Buford calls from the kitchen.

I turn to Willis, who nods. "Two teas," I respond and hear Buford pulling out a tray of ice.

"I got to go to her," Willis says, and I glance over at Buford through the opening into the kitchen. He's standing at the sink, where I can see him putting the ice in the glasses, and he just shakes his head.

"I know," I answer, sitting in the chair across from Willis, remembering Darrell sitting in his car at Evergreens. "But let's just wait a little while, till the company slows down."

He turns away.

"Does she know about Marvin?" he asks.

"She does," I answer. "She remembers the preacher telling her before he prayed."

"You think that's what woke her up?" Asking the same question I had earlier.

I raise my hands like I'm not sure how to respond. "Maybe. It's hard to know about these things."

"It has to be though," he replies. "She's been lying up there so long. And suddenly she just wakes up on the very day they find her son murdered?" He puts his head in his hands and winces slightly when he bumps the wound just above his right eye. "It just has to be."

I glance over again to Buford, who is not watching us.

"Well, no matter what it is that shook her awake, it's a miracle, and now you have family who cares about you. This is a good thing." I try to remember what the preacher said, how he named it a miracle, how he claimed we can't understand the mysteries of God. I wonder if I should say something like that, but I doubt there's any words that will ease the confusion in Willis's mind.

Buford told me before we closed up shop that he had come home in the afternoon and Willis was sitting under a tree out back, said he couldn't stay inside, said he couldn't remember anything from being over at Marvin's and that maybe he should just catch a train and head west or maybe south. Buford talked him out of it, and I guess it worked since he's still here. Buford didn't tell him about his mama because we both decided he might leave for sure if he learned that news. We talked about it and decided we'd tell him at dinner and then stay with him, keep him from trying to go to Evergreens.

But then Buford had gone ahead and told him before I got there, said he was acting so low, it was clear he needed some good news. But Willis isn't taking the news real well. He's happy, of course, that his mama is awake, but now he's acting all bothered and worried. It's like he thinks she'll blame him for Marvin's death. That she woke up for reasons other than just grief, like maybe she was told something in the realm of unconsciousness about what happened between the brothers, something he doesn't remember, and now it's troubling him mightily.

"Willis, your mama knows you wouldn't hurt your brother. She knows you love him."

Willis looks down at his plate. "What do you think Preacher Goodlaw wants to see me about?" he asks. "He could have just passed along his sentiments."

"I don't know. Maybe he just wants to make sure you're okay."

"Maybe he wants to give you a Bible or a pamphlet about miracles," Buford chimes in from the kitchen, clearly having listened to our conversation.

"That's true," I say, but that doesn't really seem right. He could have given Willis a Bible and religious literature long before today. It does seem curious that he asked me to give Willis a message, like he knew I'd know where he is.

Buford walks into the dining room, carrying a bowl of green beans, the steam rising. "It could just be a way to put eyes on you," he adds. "To make sure you're alive." He puts the beans on a hot pad on the table. "Or he might be checking in with Ferguson, telling him what he finds out."

"I don't think the pastor would be doing favors for the law," I reply. "I think he just wants me to know he cares about you, Willis—that he understands this is hard for you." I head into the kitchen and find another bowl for the tomatoes.

"You're probably right," Buford says, following me into the kitchen. "I think maybe I'm a bit paranoid at this point." He smiles at me, brushes against me as we pass each other in the doorway. I'm taking the tomatoes to the table, and he's coming in for the drinks.

"You talk to Junior?" I ask as we both take our seats at the table.

"I called and left a couple of messages. Secretary said he was in court all day." Buford passes the platter of ham to Willis, who takes it and puts one slice on his plate.

Junior is Buford's oldest son. He's a lawyer in Raleigh, and we both thought having his counsel would be most important right now.

"He'll call tonight, I'm sure," he adds.

We pass around the bowls of vegetables, the plate of biscuits, the butter and a knife. When all our plates are filled, Buford bows his head.

I glance over at Willis, and we both follow suit. Buford reaches beneath the table, and I take his hand.

"For these blessings of food and friendship, we give you thanks, Dear Lord. We thank you for Mrs. Lemmons's miraculous recovery."

I glance up at Willis, but his eyes are closed tight, and he seems to be listening closely to the prayer.

"And we pray for insight and wisdom as we try to find the answers to our many questions. In the name of Jesus, we pray, Amen."

"Amen," Willis whispers, and when I turn to him, I see the tear rolling down his face.

CHAPTER EIGHTEEN

"He seemed better by the time he went to bed," Buford says, wrapping up the leftover strawberries from dessert. He served them atop thick slices of vanilla cake that had soaked in the fruit syrup overnight. He even made his own whipped cream. Next to biscuits, Buford's strawberry shortcake is my favorite thing to eat. He makes it like my grandmother used to make—extra sweet, extra creamy.

I reach over and take out one strawberry from the bowl he's holding and slide the plastic wrap back on top. Buford smiles, holds it out in case I want another, and when I shake my head, he puts it in the refrigerator.

"He ate everything on his dinner plate and even took seconds."

It's clear we both think it was a good sign that Willis had an appetite.

I finish up washing the dishes and then reach into a drawer for a drying towel. I take out a blue one from a set I bought him last Christmas. I dry a few things and put them away. I'm just as at home in his house as I am in my own, and he manages his way around my space and belongings with the same ease he has here.

I put up the glasses and think about how we almost married once, how not so many years ago we decided that I would move into his place since it was the bigger of our two houses, talking about how silly it was to maintain separate households since we stayed together most of the time anyway, agreed that since we acted like an old wedded couple, it would just be easier to make it official. It was a good and wise choice we thought, but then his daughter called from Germany and said she wanted to move back home after serving in the army, return to North

Carolina and start a new life, still not quite sure what she was going to do after her discharge. So we set our plans aside and Odelia stayed about three years, even took up cutting hair, claimed she would take Percy's station. It was all good and fine, but then she said she missed the military and signed up again for active duty. That was at least a decade ago, and she's been all over the world since then. She probably has twenty or more years with the government, makes good money, and is happy, married to a French woman she met on an assignment in Western Europe.

When she left, Buford brought up getting married again, but I think I got cold feet about suddenly having grown stepchildren, and I just didn't answer. Afterward, I figure Buford may have decided his package deal with all his family was more than he should ask of me, but the truth is we just didn't talk about it again. I don't really know why, but our arrangement worked before, and it still does. I don't think we miss out on very much in life, except waking up together. Sometimes I feel like I miss out on that, but then I see him at five in the morning coming in the rear door at the bakery. We have our coffee together, watch out the window, start in on a conversation we had the previous night, and it's like we haven't forfeited a thing.

Georgia is the only one who brings up our lack of vows and official designation for our relationship with any real frequency, claims we need to get married for the sake of our future, says that a wedding would do us all good. I think maybe me and Buford have gotten too settled in our ways and, besides, with my jaded history of family affairs, it just seems for the best not to make anything legal and binding.

Mama never married any of her children's fathers, and Draymond never took vows. Grandma was widowed by the time she started staying over, and most of my cousins are divorced. So I clearly don't have any solid knowledge about how family works. I just feel unprepared for marriage. Well there's that, and I suppose if I aim to get real truthful,

I'm a little nervous that if me and Buford do get married, I'm liable to mess up what we have, the good we keep between us.

I feel anxious that I got some curse laid upon my head by Mama, a curse that if a person gets too close to me, moves into my life completely and sees who I really am, he'll fly away like some snowbird late for warm weather. I just don't want to take the chance that getting married would actually lead us to moving apart.

"You want another cup of decaf?" he asks, opening up the top of the coffee maker, pulling out the used filter.

I open the cabinet door and step aside so he can pitch it into the trash can under the sink. "Nah," I answer. "I'll be up all night if I do."

"But it's decaf." He pulls out the carafe, holds it out with a grin like some happy waiter, and turns on the water. He'll just pour it out in the sink if I say no. He's getting ready for the morning.

"Still makes you pee," I reply, and I see his smile widen. He nods because we both have trouble sleeping. Sometimes it's because of having to get up and go to the bathroom every couple of hours, and sometimes it's just the way of things. Old memories, battle fatigue, a net of worries cast around the mind, the way I used to wake up to find trouble standing near my bed, having followed Mama home from wherever she had been out drinking; it could be any number of possibilities keeping us up.

Thinking now about my nighttime ways makes me wonder if maybe there's even more I got going on than a Pitchford curse that's keeping me single. Maybe another reason not to get married is that I don't want to pull Buford into the late-night wrestling matches I have become accustomed to enduring alone. Maybe just like he's saving me from stepchildren, maybe I think it's a kindness of sorts, him not having to get his sleep disrupted any more than it already is. And maybe we don't go ahead and tie the knot because we're both real clear of what we got tagging along with us into marriage.

"He was willing to sleep in a bed?" I ask, stacking the plates in the cabinet. I wasn't sure Willis would stay in the house after dinner, but after he said goodnight, he walked down the hall to the guest bedroom and closed the door behind him.

"I opened the window earlier. He said as long as he could hear the night birds, see the moon, he would be okay."

He takes down the canister of coffee, scoops a few spoonfuls into the paper filter, and closes the top of the coffee maker.

"This must be so hard for him," I say quietly, glancing in the direction of where Willis has gone to bed. I can't deny it, there is a softness within me for him, always has been.

"He's trying like you wouldn't believe to remember what happened, what he was doing at Marvin's, how he hit his head." Buford sighs, leans against the counter across from where I'm standing. He holds out his arms, and I go to him, place my head on his chest, and close my eyes.

I am safest here.

"How long do you think we have before they come for him?" I ask, my lips right at his ear. It's a question I have wondered about all day but haven't said it out loud to myself or Georgia or Buford.

From where I'm resting, I feel Buford shaking his head. He doesn't really know what kind of time we have, and I think we're both starting to realize that if Willis hasn't reclaimed any memories from the previous night yet, it's highly likely he isn't going to have some breakthrough days later. I think both of us believe the same thing—if you're going to remember something, it would happen sooner rather than later. I also think we've not yet lent our voices to this presupposition.

"I wonder why Junior hasn't called." I raise up from my position and look into Buford's eyes. He glances up, and I think he's seeing the clock in the den. I check the one on the coffee maker and realize it's after ten o'clock.

He stiffens and drops his arms from around me. "Wait a minute," he says and walks out of the kitchen. When he returns, he's holding his phone in his hand. "He did call," he explains. "I had it on silent mode, forgot to change it after work." He shakes his head and blows out a breath. "Dumb of me."

"Just a lot on your mind, Buford."

Buford taps the voicemail button, and I can hear Junior's voice letting his father know that he could be reached in the morning if they didn't connect tonight.

"I'll have to call him first thing tomorrow," he says, probably assuming it's too late to call him now. He is staring at the device in his hand, and I wonder why he doesn't think this is something that needs to happen tonight.

"And there's another call missed," he notes, glancing up at me. "There's no message, but Sheriff Gentry phoned about an hour ago."

We both turn to the window to see the lights of a car driving past, but neither of us says a thing.

CHAPTER NINETEEN

I got home after eleven p.m. I didn't leave until the car slowing past Buford's finally left for good.

We both stared out the window, staying behind the curtains, as the black sedan crept past, then went up to the corner, did a U-turn, and drove past again.

It wasn't the sheriff's car and not Darrell; it wasn't the FBI SUV. In fact, it wasn't anybody's vehicle we recognized, but they didn't stop or pull into the driveway. They just drove on past. I waited a little while before leaving, and I didn't see it anywhere parked down the street.

After I pulled under my carport, I told Buford that I hadn't been followed or seen the suspicious sedan anywhere near my place. I only live five minutes from him. Since I didn't see the car on any of the streets around or between us, we both decided whoever it was had left the scene completely. Still, I waited a good ten minutes before jumping out and running into the house. I admit I was nervous. Marvin's murderer is out there somewhere.

"Coast is clear," I say when we speak again to tell him I am safe in my home and everything seems fine.

Buford wanted to follow me home, but I told him I would keep him on the phone while I drove and check everything while he waited on the line. I told him I was worried that Willis might take the opportunity to leave if he heard both of us driving away. He was reluctant to listen, but in the end, he agreed he could get to me very quickly if something was amiss.

"You go in all the rooms?" he asks, and I start walking from the kitchen to the dining room to the den to the bedrooms.

I open up every door, every closet, even get to my knees and look under the beds. I walk around furniture, check behind the washer and dryer, thinking I need to vacuum back there, and finish in the bathroom next to my bedroom. I wait before my final signal, opening the curtain and checking in the shower. I've always told him that I'm afraid that's where the criminal will hide. Since Buford remembers this, he makes me check there before he'll hang up.

"All clear," I say again and take a deep breath. I'm not sure who I think might be hiding in my house, who was driving past in the dark sedan and why they might be stalking me, but my mouth is dry and my hands shake slightly. I take a long gander at myself in the bathroom mirror. I am clearly a bit on edge. I can see it in the way my brow is furrowed and the line of sweat just above my upper lip. I haven't been practicing my deep breaths and mindfulness meditations.

All this day with its secrets and murders and miracles, strange cars driving up and down the road, Willis getting hit on the head, all of it has me knotted up on the inside—the way I spent most of my childhood and adolescence, the way I thought life just was for everybody until I realized this isn't a natural mood or typical emotional landscape for others. I didn't really have a clear sense of the anxiety and how it ran things for me until late in my teens, when Mrs. Denton—the pharmacist's wife, the one who had the affair with the high school principal—asked me once after I graduated, "Lorna Gayle, why are you such a nervous soul?"

I remember feeling flabbergasted that she would say such a thing, even going as far as to recommend a pill that she knew her husband gave out to a few of the people in town—some teenagers from school, the Nervous Nellies, we always called them,—and suggested I see Dr. Henry, the town's only physician, to get a prescription.

"What do you mean?" I asked when she made the comment again for the second or third time. "Why do you say my spirit is nervous?"

"Because you flit. From the cash register to the phone behind the counter, to the broom closet to the front door. Lorna Gayle, you can't stay still. You're like a bird in the attic—you flit, girl, flit. I get tired just being here next to you. If you won't take a pill, then try meditation or deep breathing or something."

I turned to see what Mr. Denton had to say about it, about me, but he quickly glanced away, started counting pills, and refused to comment. He stayed away from gossip and reflective conversation; thinking about it now, maybe that's why Mrs. Denton went outside the marriage for companionship.

It's true, after all, what they say about people: We do love to ruminate about the comings and goings of others. There is some level of satisfaction noting the oddities of somebody who isn't kin. Without a partner's willingness to either discuss deeply personal affairs or share details about somebody else's maladies or troubles, it can be downright lonesome in a relationship, or so I imagine. Like I noted previously in my recollections, I don't actually know what stirs up the dust of discontent in a marriage, and I certainly don't know what happened to Mr. and Mrs. Denton. I only know that when she said what she did about me and my nervousness, I knew it stung too much for it not to be true.

I was a Nervous Nelly, too, and even though I didn't really want to get a prescription to stop me from "flitting," I did want some of what I saw in other people, in other young women. I wanted to learn how not to be so anxious all the time, to be comfortable in my own skin, to be still?

So I tried meditation, borrowed books from the library, and I started working to pay attention to how I breathed. It seemed for a while like it helped. Then I took to baking and found biscuits actually gave me the best state of mind. I didn't need to sit crisscross applesauce or light some calming candle. I just needed to roll out the dough, cut and spin the mold, place them on a baking pan, and watch them take form. I liked the mindfulness training and the deep breathing, but it was the biscuits that finally gave me relief.

Some folks even noticed once I started baking, said I appeared happy, asked if I had fallen in love. Mrs. Denton would sometimes come up beside me at the counter and take a big whiff like she thought I might have started drinking since she hadn't seen any outgoing prescriptions written on my behalf.

The intentional deep breathing did seem to make a difference, and the biscuit making had a way of calming me down, so I did both. I had a regular practice of meditation along with my baking, but then, I don't know, I just got lazy and quit. I guess I eventually grew out of the nervousness. After Cathedral left and Mama died, after I didn't have to take tests in school or deal with the mean girls, I think I just naturally calmed down. Plus, I knew if anyone in Owensboro found out that I was doing the meditation, they might call me a hippy or worse, so I just stopped—and right until now, I hadn't even remembered about how the practice helped.

I stand in front of the mirror, close my eyes, place my hand over my chest, and take in a deep breath. I steady myself, bend my knees slightly, and take in another deep breath like the meditation teacher on YouTube says.

In through my nostrils, count to five, hold the breath, count five more seconds, and exhale.

I feel the practice slowing my pulse, the deeper breaths giving me more oxygen, and I start to relax, start to feel myself ease. When I open my eyes, I see the furrow gone from my brow, and my hands are not shaking.

I turn on the faucet and cup my hands to gather enough water to splash on my face. I lean down and enjoy the coolness. I raise up, take in another deep breath, and reach for the towel hanging on the small hook next to the mirror. I am feeling almost sleepy, thinking I may actually have a good long night of rest when I suddenly hear the screen door at the front of the house creak open. I immediately forget to exhale.

CHAPTER TWENTY

"I think they're gone," I say, whispering into the phone. I am breathless. No meditation or even making biscuits will soothe me now. I couldn't draw a deep inhale if there was a money prize for doing so.

"I'm coming over."

I can hear him jangling his keys, opening the door.

"No, don't come, Buford. I'm fine. Don't leave Willis. Just stay on the phone with me while I go to the door."

"Why are you going to the door?" he asks, clearly not happy with my instructions to him.

"Because I think they left something." I knew whoever had been there had opened the screen door, did not knock or try to open the wooden door, and then retreated; just seems like there is something on my front porch.

"Where are you right now?"

"I am standing at the front window. I saw them drive away. They're gone," I say to reassure him. The porch light is on, and I can see no one is there.

"Okay, I am right here. If anyone is there, just yell, and I'll be there in five minutes."

I let the curtain fall shut. I don't respond. I'm thinking about how much damage can happen in five minutes. Questions race across my mind. *How long does it take to get off a shot? How far can I run in five minutes? Can I get to the bedroom and lock the door, holding off the bandit long enough?*

Then the answers start to swirl. *Takes about one full second to fire a gun. I may get to the mailbox in five minutes if I don't fall down the front steps. I don't think I'd make it down the hall, and why am I calling whoever might be standing on my porch a bandit?*

"Lorna, what are you doing?"

I shake away the questions and the answers. "Nothing, I'm still just standing here." I move to the door. I reach out, unlock the dead bolt that Buford put on the door years ago, claiming what I had was flimsy and unreliable.

I grasp the knob and take in a breath. Easily, slowly, I turn it.

"Lorna."

His voice startles me even though we are in a conversation.

"Don't scare me!" I tell him.

"Sorry."

I turn the knob until I can pull the door ever so slightly open.

I peek onto the porch. Just my head, and just the front of it sticking out from inside. The streetlight is shining, and the moon is full. The front light illuminates the empty space before me. No one is around. After glancing around the yard, the street—one way and then the other—I look down and see a large manila envelope.

I lean down and pick it up, without examining it closely.

"There's something here," I say, then hurry to get fully inside.

I pull the screen door completely shut and lock it, then close the door and turn the knob and the dead bolt, locking them both. I turn around and lean against the door, holding the package against my chest.

"Is it safe?" he asks. "Is it a package that could have something dangerous in it? Do we need to call Ferguson? Should you have brought it into the house?"

Too many questions, I think, and it's already in the house so that one is a second or two late. But after hearing him, I do throw it out in front of me.

"It's an envelope," I say, studying it from what I hope is a safe distance. "Probably not a bomb." I pause, remembering events broadcast on the news some years ago about suspicious mail arriving at courthouses and the offices of political leaders in Washington.

"Could it be anthrax? Should I put it in a plastic bag?"

Buford doesn't answer right away. "I doubt it's anthrax," he finally replies, like he's given it good thought. "And I'm not sure a plastic bag would help anyway."

I stretch out my leg as far as I can and kick at the envelope like that might help me know what's been left at my door. And as soon as I do that, I suddenly remember Frank Kelly, from over at the paper, telling me and Georgia that somebody had sent J.H. Julian, the bank president, a water moccasin in a box, a live one.

Frank had seen it himself when he heard the call on the scanner, drove over to the bank to watch Jimmy Neal take the snake out of the box and put it in a bucket, saying he planned to set it free out past the railroad crossing at the creek. There was a big discussion at the bank, and later at the barbershop, about the advantages of setting a moccasin loose and the stronger possibility of the real plans being made for the old cottonmouth, primarily the notion that Jimmy was going to skin it for a pair of boots he had been trying to make for years.

Everybody in Owensboro knew Jimmy Neal liked snake leather, made a set of black shoes when he was a teenager and had been hunting for years to find exactly the shade of brown he was hoping would match the khaki pants he likes to wear for work.

About five years have passed since that incident. No one was ever charged or arrested for sending a moccasin to J.H., and no new pair of boots were seen on Jimmy's feet. But then again, nobody I talk to recalls exactly how many snakes it takes to make a pair of cowboy boots. Jimmy Neal is known to have big feet anyway, so the fact he isn't wearing the snake rescued from the bank surely does not mean he didn't keep it for the skin.

"Lorna, what's going on?"

I realize I had gone down a big ole rabbit hole, or snake hole, as it seems to be.

"Just thinking about the package," I reply. "You remember the snake somebody sent to the bank?"

There's a pause, and I hear him breathe into the phone.

"You said it was an envelope."

"What?" I ask.

"Lorna, is it an envelope or a package?" And I think maybe Buford is considering the snake box too.

Studying it more closely now, I am fairly clear a snake could not be in this delivery. I step over to it.

"You think it was somebody who didn't get a loan or a mortgage?" I am just at the envelope.

"What?" He sounds confused.

"The cottonmouth. You think whoever sent it was not happy with the bank's handling of their finances?"

I recall Georgia's list of suspects, one of whom is Donna Jennings because everybody heard her raise up a nasty stink when J.H. didn't give her bank money to open up her real estate office when she first got her license. He said she needed to work a few years before taking out a loan, but she was mad as a bull seeing red when she was denied, spouting off all kinds of threats in the bakery for a few weeks before the snake showed up.

For the life of me, I don't see Donna successfully hunting for a moccasin and then packing it in a box and taking it to the post office to send out. Donna freaked out over a centipede that had attached itself to the hem of her designer jeans one day at the bakery, and we had to call the EMTs to calm her down. I told Georgia mailing a snake was just too woodsy for Donna Jennings, but Georgia still thinks she charmed some boy to do the dirty work for her.

She finally did get her loan, of course. And the gossip around town is that she and J.H. had a thing for a while, which seems much more her style of persuasion than a snake, but it's just one more reason Georgia doesn't particularly care for the local real estate agent.

"I don't know, Lorna," Buford answers me. "But can you tell me what was left at your front door?"

I squat down to get a closer view. "It's an envelope," I tell him, carefully picking it up by the corner. "And it's addressed to Willis."

CHAPTER TWENTY-ONE

Buford didn't come over. I told him I was fine, nothing to worry about. Afterward, I studied the envelope, wondering if I should just open it for Willis, wondering why somebody left it at my door, then I finally fell asleep.

I've been up four times since then, trying a cup of hot milk and reading a very boring book of poetry the first time I was up, scrounging around the medicine cabinet until I found an allergy pill and swallowed it down the second time I rose up, a bathroom trip the third occasion, and finally around 1:30 a.m., I went into the kitchen, found a bottle of red wine I had at Christmas, and took a big swig right from the bottle. Afterward, I was sure I was going to throw up, but I didn't. When I got in the bed, fluffed up my pillow, and pulled the covers up to my chin, I had a nice warm feeling come over me.

I slept deep, dreaming of all kinds of things but never bothered enough to be pulled out. There was brown water and a fire off in the distance, somebody calling my name, bacon popping from the skillet on the stove at Buford's. There were all manner of images moving in and out of each other, voices without anybody connected to them, sirens and nursing home patients walking in a line to the church, a boat way in the distance off the west side of the lake, and the sound of a train. The sleep was deep, but it was also fretful. And when I awoke, I wasn't sure where I was. I only know I haven't struggled out of night's grasp like that since Buford went missing overseas and we were awakened way before dawn to be given the news he was alive.

Louise, his sister, was the one who first told me when it happened. We were all in our late twenties then. Buford had been in the service for more than ten years, gotten married in the Philippines, and had Junior. We saw each other when he came home to see his mama, when his granddaddy died, when he was being honored at the state house. We were still friendly, but nothing like we were when he still lived here, and nothing like we are now.

Louise came to the pharmacy to pick up her blood pressure medicine, something I wasn't supposed to know, like all the prescriptions people turned in, but I knew everything about the medicines people took. It wasn't that I was nosy or that the Dentons couldn't keep private information confidential. I just worked there all day; you just can't keep a secret in a drugstore.

Louise had been taking medicines for her pressure ever since she had finished school. Buford always said of everyone in their family except for his father, his sister ran hottest. I guess that's how he understood her malady.

One day she came in and asked to speak to me. I walked around the counter, and she got real shaky, like she was making a confession or asking for something illegal. I could feel Mrs. Denton watching from the cash register. Their son Rodney had taken over the pharmacist job after Mr. Denton died, and he was in the back counting pills.

"I ain't supposed to tell this," she whispered.

I waited. I had no idea what Louise wasn't supposed to say.

I felt her breath, shallow and hot on my neck as she was still whispering in my ear.

"It's Buford," and I had pulled away at the sound of his name. I felt my heart sink in my chest.

She just stared at me, sad, like the news was the worst possible thing she could say.

I tried to sound out the word, "What?" but I only formed it with my mouth. I wasn't able to say it out loud.

"He's missing," she said softly, which somehow felt slightly better than hearing that he was dead. *Missing* meant *finding*. *Missing* meant *still alive*. Missing was hard and prickly to try and get my head around, but missing was not gone forever. I wavered in some small ripple of hope.

"He was with his battalion," she added. "No one has heard from any of them."

And I studied the fear in her eyes, the way she bit her bottom lip, lifted her hand to her throat. I reached for her, and we embraced even though I had never hugged Buford's sister. We had played together as children, her a few years younger than me. We had ridden our bikes around Second Town and the trailer park together all through elementary school. I thought of her as fragile because she fell a lot, needed a lot of attention from her brothers and mama. Then I experienced her as kind of standoffish when she got to high school, but I always liked Louise, always had a good feeling about her.

"He's okay," I said, not sure why I was making such a claim. "Buford's smart; he won't get captured."

And she just nodded, closed her eyes, a tear rolling down her cheek—seemed like she was trying as hard as she could to believe me.

I went to their house after work, and I must have stayed there for the entire three days while we waited for any news at all. I went to the drugstore and put in my hours, but I stayed with Louise until I heard the news with the rest of the family. Their daddy had died by then, and his mama and brother felt like kin to me anyway, so I just moved in with them like another family member, hearing all the details of Buford's life since I was in it. I heard about his Filipina wife and his son they had named Buford Jr.; the fact that she was pregnant again and how no one had ever met her. I heard that he was promoted lots of times, won service medals for the lives he had saved, and I sat with them and we all cried while one day changed to two and then three, without ever hearing anything from the government or the US Army.

Finally, and I remember like it was yesterday, the phone rang early one morning, and it was him. I still don't know the details of where he had been or how he survived, I just knew he wasn't missing anymore, and I knew I would always and only love him. Even if he did have a wife and two children. Even if I never told another living soul. Even if we were never together. I knew the moment he was not dead, not missing, the moment I knew he was alive and well, that I would only and always love Buford Painter.

I raise my head off the pillow, surprised that Buford missing in Afghanistan would be the memory that shook me awake, but it wasn't an unhappy way to greet a morning. I know how it could've been, and I know that not every man in his battalion did make it out, that some other family got an entirely different phone call that day. So, in spite of the messy night of dreams, I feel relieved to be waking up with the most important memory I have. I feel at peace even though I'm still groggy from the allergy pill and the wine and the struggle to sleep.

I check the clock: five thirty. I'm already late for work but then I remember it's Thursday, and it's generally slow on Thursdays downtown. I also remember I took out a few containers of biscuits from the freezer yesterday, and we had a batch or two leftover, so I won't have to do a lot of baking anyway.

I figure Buford won't be in until later since Willis is at his house, so it's fine if I don't get there until six. If he was already there waiting on me, I'm sure he would have called to wake me up. The fact that he didn't makes me think he's sleeping late too. But then, Buford never sleeps in.

I reach over to the side table and take my phone off the charger. There haven't been any calls or texts since I opened the door at midnight and retrieved the envelope. I really want to get that to Willis first thing, so I get out of bed and sit on the side for a minute just as the phone starts ringing.

I recognize the caller ID immediately and take the call from Buford.

"It's Willis," is all he says, and then he lets out a breath. "He's gone."

CHAPTER TWENTY-TWO

"Gone?" I ask. "Gone where?"

"I don't know. I woke up, showered, made coffee, and I didn't hear anything from down the hall, so I wasted time, fifteen minutes maybe, enough time to get ready for work, tidy things up. Finally, just now, I went to his door and knocked."

I wait.

"I stood there, thinking maybe he was still asleep and maybe I should just let him rest—it's still pretty early for most people—but then, I just had a funny feeling that something was off. I reached for the knob and the door was unlocked, so I went in." He blows out a long breath.

We say it at the same time.

"He was gone."

"He's gone," Buford repeats.

"You have any idea when it happened?" I wonder if he was awake when I called about the screen door opening, about the late-night delivery, if that's what woke him up—Buford scrambling about making plans to come over.

"I don't know," he answers, and I'm sure he's thinking about the disturbance that happened not too long after I left, how he was almost out the door and in his car when I made him wait. "Maybe ..." his voice trails off.

"Well, I'm sure he's at Evergreens, and there's nothing wrong with that. After all, we don't know that anybody's looking for Willis. We don't know that he's a suspect or that anything happened between him and Marvin, so maybe it's fine that he's out in public, seeing his mother. Maybe it even looks less suspicious."

"Maybe," Buford says after a pause.

"You want me to drive over to Evergreens?" I think about being late to work, maybe calling Georgia to come in early so the morning biscuits will get done.

"No, no, you've done enough. I'll go search for him, see what I can find out."

"You got any early appointments?" I ask, trying to help him think of everything before he sets out on the mission to recover Willis. If he has somebody scheduled to come in, I can meet them there, make a new appointment for them. These are tasks I do not mind.

"There's nothing on the books," he answers, and I know that doesn't mean somebody won't stop by first thing.

"How long you think you'll be? Will you be back in time to open at eight?"

I glance at the clock on my dresser. I've got to get going myself or we'll never be ready to open at seven.

"I don't know, Lorna. I'll drive over to Evergreens and then maybe out to the creek. I don't know where else he'll go."

"Well, I don't think he'd stay at his mama's too long. She's got to be in bed, and I doubt they'd even let him in the building at this hour. I don't imagine he'd just stand outside her window and watch her sleep since that's the way she's looked for years. I think he'd wake her up and then she'd fall asleep, and he'd leave once she dropped off. So, maybe he'd come back to your place after that. Maybe you should just stay there and wait for him. Let me drive by Evergreens to see if he's there or if he's been there."

Buford doesn't answer, and I wonder if he's listening.

"Buford, you still there?" I check my phone to make sure the call hasn't dropped.

"Yeah, yeah, I'm seeing if he left anything."

I wait a second before asking. "Well, did he?"

I hear Buford opening the closet, pulling open drawers.

"Hold on."

And I do. It's a few minutes before he responds.

"It's gone," he announces.

"What is?"

"He had a jacket. There was blood on it, so I washed it for him—along with his clothes. I hung them up on the rack in the washroom because he didn't want them dried in the dryer. And now they're all gone. He got his clothes and left."

"Well, that's a good thing, right?"

There's no response.

"He's not naked," I say, trying to lighten things, I guess.

"No, he's not naked."

"Did he have anything else with him when he came over?"

I try to think about Willis, what he might have had under his arm or in his pockets.

"I took him by his place," Buford says, something I hadn't realized had happened when they left together yesterday and then I begin to wonder about the homeless man's place.

"Out at the creek where he has his tent," he adds, since he seems to be reading my mind.

"But he didn't really bring anything with him. I'm not sure why he wanted to go out there. I thought he might just be securing all his things."

"In a tent?" I ask.

"As best as he was able, Lorna. It's his home, so I just thought he was making sure everything was put away or hidden, or that he wanted to get something to bring with him over here."

"Well, keep searching, maybe there's something somewhere that will make him come back."

"I don't know. The bed doesn't even seem slept in."

I think of something. "Maybe he didn't sleep in it. Maybe he waited until I left and then crept out."

"Except his clothes were by the kitchen. I would have seen him come out to get them."

"Oh, right."

"I guess it doesn't matter anyway, whether he left at ten or eleven or three or four. He still left."

There's a rustling sound, like maybe he's pulling away the blanket on the bed, the linens.

"Oh, Willis," I hear him say.

"What is it, Buford? What have you found?"

"Willis doesn't have any allergies that you know of, do you?"

"No, as far as what I recall Marvin was the only one, always carrying around an—"

"EpiPen," he interjects. "Marvin always had an EpiPen."

"Willis took it?"

"Sure looks like it," he tells me. "And there's something else." He lets out a sigh.

"Buford, what is it?"

He doesn't answer.

"Buford …"

"A knife, Lorna. Willis is hiding a knife."

CHAPTER TWENTY-THREE

I called Georgia, and she's able to cover the bakery shift, giving me time to drive over to Evergreens to see if Willis is there or if he's been there and gone. Buford is heading out to the creek to see if he's at his tent or if he can find out if anyone has seen him over near the railroad tracks.

It turns out Georgia was planning to go in early anyway because school is out today, and Flora would be sleeping late and then has wrestling practice at noon. Georgia had plenty to say about her granddaughter's new hobby. I quit listening after about ten minutes of the rant and just told her I needed to go.

Then she started in with the questions about what I was doing and what was going on with Buford and Willis, but I stopped her without answering, told her it would not be best to talk over the phone about a murder, and she went real quiet after that. Even though I know she wants to speculate about what happened to Marvin like everybody else is probably doing this morning, it seems like she got the notion that maybe our phone line is tapped, and when she mentioned it in a whisper before I hung up, I just let her think what she wants to think. At least she quit asking questions. I heard her rattle her dice, and we hung up.

I drive past the bakery and see her moving in the kitchen. She must have left her home right after I called, because she is there and working. I'm sure the biscuits will be hot and ready to sell by the time we open. I glance at the clock on the console of my truck and then remember it's broken, so I pull out my phone when I'm sure it's safe to glance away from the road and see that it's after six. Nobody is out. The sprinklers on the square are going, and the sidewalks are wet. I turn to see the courthouse and don't notice anyone moving around. Buford's place is dark, and all the other businesses are still shuttered. I pick up my pace and head toward the nursing home, thinking about Willis and what he might have on his mind, why he left, and where he's going.

I didn't ask Buford what he was going to do with the knife. To tell the truth, I don't want to know. And thinking about it now, who says that Willis having a knife is something to be worried about anyhow? Willis probably has lots of knives for fishing and hunting. He lives outside. Wouldn't it make sense that he would have a knife? I shake away my worries and try to focus on the things at hand.

"But why do you have Marvin's EpiPen?" I find myself asking out loud. "And why did you leave that and a knife at Buford's?" And somehow this cheers me slightly because it makes me think that maybe Willis is planning to return to Buford's. Maybe he left them and maybe he just took off to see his mama and then plans to go back into hiding. And then, this thought doesn't cheer me because I don't really think Buford needs this kind of trouble.

Before we hung up this morning, he did say he was going to call Junior again and get legal counsel about Willis and the situation. Since Willis hasn't been charged with anything and law enforcement doesn't seem to be actively searching for Marvin's brother, it doesn't seem like neither me nor Buford can be charged with harboring a fugitive or tampering with evidence or any of them other laws we might be breaking by tomorrow. I'm pretty sure we're in the clear today. I will be interested to see what Junior tells his dad and whether or not Buford will listen to him. He can be hardheaded when it comes to his practices of loyalty. It's gotten him in hot water before.

Suddenly my thoughts turn to Rooster Teal and how he came searching for his wife, Betsy, who was hiding from him in the barbershop. Buford had seen her in the parking lot behind the businesses, beat up and scared. When she refused to go to the sheriff's office because Rooster was a volunteer deputy and she didn't feel safe with Ferguson or anybody else there, Buford hid her in the bathroom in the rear of his shop until he could find somebody from a women's shelter to come and pick her up. Rooster came to the bakery first and stormed around like he thought she was in there. Georgia stood between him and me and promised him she would beat the Jesus out of him with a rolling pin if he made one step closer to the kitchen or went snooping around back.

We both believed her, and he left. Later he was arrested when he went to his sister-in-law's house, making all kinds of threats, waving around a pistol. He was locked up only a little while, but it was time enough for us to help Betsy get some of her things from their house, take her cat to her mama's, and help her make all the necessary arrangements to leave home in a hurry.

Rooster eventually found out me and Buford helped Betsy, and I worried about Buford more than I did myself because Rooster is a card-carrying member of the Klan and has never been happy about the minority-owned businesses in Owensboro. He came around a few times, tried to act all menacing, but Georgia enjoyed calling him down and Ferguson gave him a stern warning of jail time if he was seen making threats anywhere in town, especially at the businesses. He was promised that he would enjoy the full extent of the law if he made any trouble for Buford or the bakery or anywhere else that he liked to frequent.

That was a few years ago, and Rooster later died racing at the track. He liked fast trucks and always entered the race with his Ford F-150. He hit the wall going one thirty, and as far as I know, nobody misses him since he's gone. Preacher Goodlaw did a cemetery service, and a few of his racing buddies showed up, but most of us were just glad to see him gone. Betsy moved back home and now has a parcel of cats and a garden of summer flowers. She seems happy.

I drive up to Evergreens and take a long gander around the parking lot, the circle drive, the spaces around the residents' windows. I don't see Darrell. I don't see Ferguson. I don't see any FBI vehicles or any news vans. And as I scan around as attentive and watchful as I can, taking in everything in my line of vision, I don't see Willis.

I pull into a parking space and keep my engine running. I know there aren't any visitor hours for this early in the morning, so I got to figure out how I can get past security or the charge nurse or whoever it is that answers the door. I don't really have any good excuse to visit Mrs. Lemmons; I don't have family in there. As far as what they think, I'm just another nosy person from town wanting to see the miracle patient.

Then I look over at the envelope addressed to Willis. *Aha!* I can tell the person opening the door that I want to leave it with his mama to make sure he gets it. That's a fair excuse since everybody at Evergreens knows Willis shows up there pretty regular to see his mama. I think this is as good as an explanation as any, except I also know they could just take it from me and say they'll leave it in her room, so I try to consider something else.

About that time, I see some of the staff coming in for the shift change. A few workers are leaving, and I wonder if the door might be unlocked for a narrow window of time, or if I can just ease my way in with some of them I see parking and walking to the door. I jump out with the envelope.

I see a couple of girls heading to the door, and I try to appear real normal and confident. I don't recognize either of them as I get closer and then I notice that one of them, the younger of the two, is Maylynne's granddaughter, Evelyn, who just graduated from high school and is working as a nursing assistant. She temped with us last summer, selling biscuits at a booth at the fair. I like the girl, and I think she will not blink to let me in with her.

"Hello, Evelyn," I say, moving as quickly as I can to her before she gets inside. "How are you?" I ask, knowing I sound a little like Donna Jennings, and decide that's not really how I want to come off.

"Hey, Ms. Pitchford," she says, glancing behind me as if she's trying to figure out where I came from. Then she looks square at me. "What are you doing here?"

"Oh, you know, I had a delivery to make and then I needed to drop off this envelope to Mrs. Lemmons." I smile, grinning as big as my lips will stretch.

"Hmm," is all she says. "What kind of delivery?"

Uh-oh. Evelyn has always been smart, and she does love my biscuits. She ate more of the inventory at the fair booth than she sold, which is why we aren't doing the booth again this year. The sales at the county fair didn't even make up the booth rental costs. Even if we found a young person who didn't eat all the biscuits, I'm not sure it's a great financial investment.

"You know, I just wanted to stop by to see if anybody wanted any biscuits this morning. Georgia has been working before dawn, and I think we'll have a lot of cheesy biscuits and sausage biscuits to sell. I thought maybe I'd try doing a few more deliveries, to see if we can increase our market." I think it sounds true.

"Well, you have sure come to the right place!" She smiles, tosses her ponytail from side to side, her coworker not adding to the conversation. She uses her key card and opens the door. "I know we'll have lots of takers for biscuits." She turns to glance over at my truck. "Do you have 'em in there?"

"No, no," I answer, holding the door and walking in behind her, feeling like I must seem as antsy as a preacher in a strip joint. "I'm just taking orders right now. I'll come around later with the biscuits."

"Great!" Evelyn says. Then we both stop at the entryway. Her friend goes on into the building.

"I'll take orders for you in the break room and meet you out here in fifteen minutes. That give you time to visit Mrs. Lemmons?"

I take in a deep breath, feeling free and clear. "That will be perfect."

She smiles and turns to walk away. And when I glance out the window in front of me, a window that opens to the courtyard behind the front desk, I see Willis jump the wall and run out of sight.

CHAPTER TWENTY-FOUR

Well, I am definitely in a prickly pear, as my sister Cathedral used to like to say. If I stay where I'm standing or go to Mrs. Lemmons's room, I will miss Willis for good. If I leave to chase Willis, I abandon Evelyn with an order of biscuits, wondering what happened to me.

I close my eyes to think and realize that Willis is too fast to catch, so I'll just go to see his mama and find out if she knows anything. I'm doing what I got to do.

I walk the hall to where I know her room is. I'm at the door and I hear her talking, and it puts me in mind that Willis might be standing at her window. I knock softly and open the door. Willis isn't at the window, and Mrs. Lemmons is sitting up in her bed, just chatting away. When I walk in, she turns to me and smiles. I have to say, she does appear real different being awake. There's a lightness to her, an aliveness that has been missing from her for all these years of being locked away somewhere in her mind.

"Mrs. Lemmons," I say.

"Hello, dear," she responds. "Is it time for my bath?"

I realize she has mistaken me for a staff person. "No, ma'am," I answer, moving over to her bed. I close the door behind me, still holding the envelope in my hands.

"Then it's breakfast?"

I stand by her, put my arm over the bed rail, and touch her hand. "I'm Lorna," I say, and she narrows her eyes at me.

"Lorna Gayle," she replies.

"Yes, ma'am."

She pulls her hand from out beneath mine and pats me on the wrist. "You're taking care of my Willis," she says with such tenderness.

I don't know how to respond, but I like the thought that his mother is grateful for what me and Buford are doing.

"He was just here, you know," she tells me, and I want to ask her where she thinks he went, but I let her keep talking.

She shakes her head. "It's a shame about Marvin, but he's been courting danger for some time now."

This is intriguing.

"Why's that, Mrs. Lemmons?"

"Marvin always had a bad streak, like his daddy, I guess."

"What do you mean? Was he violent too?"

And she looks at me like she's weighing out the matters in her mind.

"Not violent, no," she replies softly. "Just mean and shifty. Anyway, Willis tried to tell him to watch his back." She takes her hand away from mine and touches up the sides of her hair. "But you know Marvin …"

I wait to see if she's going to say more.

"You do know Marvin, right?"

I clear my throat. "I do, Mrs. Lemmons. I went to school with both Willis and Marvin."

"Yes, that seems about right. He said you were always nice to him. You and that barber from downtown."

"Buford," I say.

"Yes, Buford." She pauses. "And Buford is going to keep Willis from getting in trouble."

I don't know what to say to that since I'm not sure anybody can manage such a thing.

She seems to be waiting for confirmation.

"Mrs. Lemmons, why did Willis think Marvin should watch his back?" I ask, since it seems this is as good as any opportunity for detective work.

"Oh, I wouldn't know," she replies, waving away the question. "You and Buford are going to keep Willis safe, aren't you, dear?"

"We are both going to do our best," I finally answer, thinking that's about as close to the truth as I can give this mother.

"Do you have children, Lorna Gayle?"

I shake my head, thinking she doesn't need to hear all the details of my mothering.

"That's a shame," she says, turning toward the window. "They can be your source of greatest joy," she explains, nodding as she does so. And then she peers right at me like she's thought this through, which maybe is what she was doing in the coma, just pondering everything. "And the source of your greatest sorrow."

I think about Marvin being murdered, Willis living in a tent at the creek, her own losses after her husband threw her down the stairs, how she'll have to hear from Willis, or anybody else that knew, the abuse her sons took at the hands of their father after she was hurt.

Here is a mother who knows about the sorrows for sure, and it leaves me wondering a bit about the joy—if she even remembers any good times in her home.

"He was just here, you know." And she points to the chair behind me. "We were talking before you came in."

"I know," I say. "I just saw him run through the courtyard."

"You did?" she answers, her eyebrows knitting together in a perplexed way.

"Yes, I was standing at the front door, and I saw Willis shoot across the rear area of Evergreens."

"Oh, I'm not talking about Willis," she notes.

I place a hand on the bed rail and lean in because now I'm confused. "You're not?"

"Oh no," she responds.

I wait.

"Then if it wasn't Willis you were just talking to, who was it?"

"Well, let me clarify. I did see Willis earlier," she notes. "He came and stood at the window for a good long time. We must have talked two hours." She motions to the door. "Bennie Longdale opened it up for us so we could hear each other." She turns to me. "Do you know Bennie?"

I shake my head. That isn't a name I recognize. "I don't, Mrs. Lemmons."

"Well, that's a real shame. Bennie is the smartest person working here. He's in maintenance, and he can work my TV remote and change bulbs in the bathroom, the real high one above the shower, do you know which one I mean?"

I nod, because it seems pointless to tell her I don't know about the light bulb.

"He can get my bed to go up and down when nobody else can operate it, takes care of the heat and air conditioner, knows just when to change one system over to the other." She pauses, closes her eyes like she's recalling all Bennie's gifts and talents. Then her eyes pop open. "And he slides out my windows when Willis comes and shuts them when he leaves. He has for years."

This surprises me, and leads me to the question I think of but do not ask. *Does Mrs. Lemmons remember Willis visiting when she was in a coma?*

"Bennie Longdale is a very good man."

"He sounds like he is," I respond.

"He's worked here over forty years," she tells me.

I nod and smile.

"Forty years," she says again and then it appears she might fall off to sleep, and I still haven't had my questions answered about Willis being there or the more pressing one.

"Mrs. Lemmons," I say, and she shakes awake.

"Hello, dear," she says, like she's seeing me for the first time.

"You said you were talking to somebody when I came in this morning, that you had already seen Willis at the window but that you were talking to somebody here in the room."

"Did I?" She places her hand on her chest, fidgeting with the buttons on her nightgown.

"Yes, ma'am. You said you were talking with somebody here, somebody other than Willis. Is it somebody who knows what happened to Marvin? Did they tell you anything?"

"Yes, that's exactly right," she notes with a yawn. She slides down on the pillow, and I think she's going to go off to sleep for good before telling me.

"Mrs. Lemmons," I lean down, our faces almost touching. "Mrs. Lemmons, who was in the room with you this morning?"

"Well, my son, dear."

"But not Willis?"

"No, not Willis."

I wait, and I hear somebody coming down the hall. I check the clock on her nightstand. I've been there for over fifteen minutes.

"Then who was it? Who were you talking to earlier?"

"Well, Marvin, of course," she says, yawns, and drops off to sleep.

The door opens, and before I can ask another question, the sheriff is standing in the doorway.

CHAPTER TWENTY-FIVE

"Lorna Gayle." Ferguson takes off his hat and holds it up against his chest. He has a furrowed brow like he can't figure out something. "What are you doing here?"

I step away from the bed and try to make up just the right excuse. I'm not sure about telling him about the delivery for Willis. I'm still holding the envelope and slowly hide it behind me. "I just came to see Mrs. Lemmons," I answer, my grin too wide, my tone too pleasant.

He waits: for more, I guess.

"I came by yesterday but there were too many folks visiting, so I decided to come by this morning before I went to the shop."

He nods, has a toothpick in his mouth, slides it around from side to side. I figure he's already had breakfast at Eugene's, and when he sees me noticing the toothpick, he reaches up and takes it from between his teeth. I guess he appears a little suspicious, too, since I thought he always got his breakfasts from me.

"You been out?" I ask him, eyeing him like he was just eyeing me.

He turns his lips down and shakes his head. "Nope," he replies like a kid caught with chocolate on his face before supper. "She talk to you?"

And I am glad he's changing the subject, though I would like to hear more about where he got his breakfast. "She did, but she said she's been up a long time, so I guess she's pretty tired."

"You think she'd slept enough for the rest of her life."

I follow his eyes to the older woman's face. Her eyes are twitching, and her lips are moving, like Buford's old dog Thunder used to do when he was dreaming. Buford always left him alone when he'd take to being fidgety, but I would wake the dog up since it was worrisome to me to see him twitch all about like that. I think about Thunder and consider poking Mrs. Lemmons just to rouse her, but I don't.

"I guess comas don't work like that," I finally reply.

"Guess not," he answers, stepping closer to the bed and to me.

I smile, keeping the envelope in one hand behind my back.

"You come alone?" Ferguson glances around the room.

"Just me," I say. "Taking orders from the staff for a delivery," I add, making it sound like the real reason I'm at Evergreens at six thirty in the morning.

"Smart," he replies.

And I think it is brilliant, not so much as a business plan but as a rationalization.

"She tell you anything?"

"About?"

"What she knows, who she's seen." He reaches up with both hands and grabs the bed rails.

I shake my head, deciding not to tell him what she just said, about seeing Willis and Marvin.

"She thought I was here to give her a bath," I respond.

He nods, drops his hands from the rails. "You haven't seen Willis around, have you?"

I clear my throat. "I have not," I answer.

"She mention him?"

I shrug, not quite sure how to answer. Then I decide. "She was talking to somebody when I came in."

This seems to get his attention. He scratches his chin, nods like he wants more.

"But there wasn't anybody in here," I tell him.

He motions toward the window since I guess everybody knows Willis stands there for his visits. "He out there?"

My eyes follow where he's gestured, glancing out the opened window. I turn to face him, shaking my head. "Not that I saw."

"So, what? He left when you came in?"

"She said she was talking to Marvin," I say, hoping that will change the direction of this conversation, namely his questions about Willis.

He folds his arms across him, nodding like he's trying to understand what the sleeping woman knows and doesn't know, how alert and oriented she is now that's she out of her coma. "Marvin?" And he smiles.

"That's what she said," I reply, raising my eyebrows like we're sharing a juicy secret.

"Well, you never know what deficits a person comes out with after a long-term brain injury."

"Or gifts," I add.

And he glances away from Mrs. Lemmons to me. "What?"

"Maybe there are gifts from beyond a person gets when they've been unconscious for a long time."

He's still holding the toothpick, and I know he wants to stick it back between his teeth but he doesn't. I realize I got an upper hand here, and I have to admit I like this position. It's almost as if I caught him cheating or something, which is kind of what I've done. Ferguson always says he doesn't like the food at Eugene's, and seeing him act all guilty makes me want to ask him how often he gets his breakfasts there. But I should probably just enjoy his discomfort and my upper hand, and not press matters. "Well, I suppose seeing your dead son could be considered a gift."

"Maybe he might tell her who killed him," I reply, watching him close to see if he seems to have any new insights or information, seeing if he might let me in on what's he's been working on.

"Seems like I should ask her when she wakes up."

"Maybe," I reply. "You still on the case?"

He shifts from one side to the other. "FBI working their angle; I'm working mine."

"They aren't the same?"

He shakes his head. "Not right yet they aren't."

"You got suspects?"

"You are inquisitive this morning, Lorna Gayle. You get the law-enforcement bug since you were at a crime scene yesterday?"

"Could be," I respond with a grin. "You need a new deputy?"

He studies me. "What I need actually is to find Willis; got some questions for him."

My face reddens slightly. I just lost my upper hand.

"What kind of questions?" I figure I might as well try, even though I don't sound nearly as confident as I did earlier when I noted his infidelity when it comes to my biscuits.

He shakes his head, puts the toothpick between his teeth. "Just his whereabouts at the time of the murder." He rocks slightly front and back. He glances from Mrs. Lemmons and then to me. "You wouldn't be his alibi, would you?"

"Not an alibi, no. Well, I mean, I don't know. What time did Marvin die?"

Ferguson cocks his head. I guess he sees what I just did. "That's not confirmed," he answers. "But that sounds like you've seen Willis recently then—maybe yesterday morning or the night before?"

I'm shaking my head way too soon, and you can almost hear me sigh with great relief when there is a knock at the door and it suddenly opens.

CHAPTER TWENTY-SIX

"Oh good, Lorna, you didn't leave." Evelyn walks into the room. "I was worried you forgot me." She's holding out a piece of paper. "I've got six orders." She then notices the sheriff, turns to me, then to Mrs. Lemmons, and then to him again. "Sheriff Gentry," she says, sounding slightly surprised. "Everything okay in here?"

I hurry around the bed to stand beside her, to get away from Ferguson and the direction of our talk, and start to make my exit. I stuff Willis's mail behind me in my pants so I don't appear so suspicious and can use both hands.

"It's all fine," he answers, watching me as I take the slip of paper from the nursing assistant.

"This is great, Evelyn." I unfold the paper and read the biscuits the staff have asked for.

"It's mostly sausages," she notes. "A couple of eggs." She reaches into her front pocket and pulls out a wad of bills. "Most everybody wanted to use their debit cards, but I told them cash only for this deal." She smiles and hands the money to me.

I take it. "That's really great. Thank you, Evelyn. This is so much easier." And I hold the money up, happy not to have to keep up with credit card sales and receipts.

"Just be sure that all makes it to your cash register," Ferguson says, and both Evelyn and I turn to him. He rolls the toothpick around inside his mouth.

"What?" I don't understand.

"Cash business," he replies. "IRS always snooping around cash businesses."

And I don't know why he's telling me this, making me wonder if this is some sort of veiled threat. I start to respond, but Evelyn interrupts.

"Like the car wash on *Breaking Bad*?" She suddenly sounds all breathy, and I'm not sure why.

And even though I recognize the title of the hit series, I'm not onboard her thought train since this wasn't a television show I followed. I know a lot of people are fans, but it was a bit on the violent side for me and Buford. We tried a couple of episodes because I have to admit I was intrigued by the premise of a high school chemistry teacher choosing a life of crime. But I don't know anything of the details of the show, like the kind of business she's talking about.

"You think she's washing cash for the drug cartel like they did at A1A?"

I smile. Now I understand even though I don't recognize the name of the *Breaking Bad* car wash.

"At a biscuit bakery?" And Evelyn laughs. "You know how much cash she takes in a day?"

I would rather Evelyn not share everything she remembers about working with me and Georgia last summer. Even though I'm not engaging in any tax or drug schemes, I would rather not have her telling all my business to the county sheriff.

I stop her before she breaks down my daily sales to law enforcement. "Thank you, Evie, I will get this order to Georgia and have those biscuits to you in an hour." I pat her on the shoulder as I try to move toward the door.

"Hello, dear." Mrs. Lemmons suddenly wakes.

We all three turn in her direction, and Evelyn and I respond at the same time, "Hello, Mrs. Lemmons."

"I'm sorry," I say, realizing she's speaking to her nurse.

"Is it time for my bath?"

"It is just about time, but I got a few errands to take care of first." Evelyn moves over to the bed, reaches to the control pad on the rail, and pushes the button to raise her head. "How did you sleep last night?"

"Like a baby," Mrs. Lemmons answers, sounding even more animated than she did during our conversation. "A perfectly healthy, happy baby."

Evelyn smiles and smooths down the linens across her patient's body. "That's exactly what we like to hear, Miss Martha."

"Did you meet my guests?" the patient asks.

Evelyn turns to look at Ferguson first and then me. "I did meet them. You are quite the popular lady this morning, to have the baker and the sheriff in your room."

"Who, them?" she asks and motions for Evelyn to lean down so she can whisper in her ear.

"Yes, ma'am?" Evelyn bends at the waist to get closer as she is being summoned.

"I didn't invite them," she says loud enough for us to hear.

The young girl stands. "But you know them, right, Miss Martha? This here is Sheriff Ferguson Gentry, and that's Lorna Gayle Pitchford, makes the best biscuits in town."

The patient motions for Evelyn to lean down again, and she does.

"I know Lorna Gayle; she's friends with my Willis. She's welcome anytime."

And I quickly turn toward Ferguson, who glances in my direction.

"But I don't remember inviting him in."

He clears his throat to answer for himself since we all can hear her. "Sheriff Ferguson Gentry, Mrs. Lemmons. We've met a few times, but maybe you don't recall. You were sleeping when I came in."

She doesn't respond.

"Anyway, I came by to ask about your son, Mrs. Lemmons."

"You find him?"

I'm more than a little confused about which son she's talking about, so I wait to hear how Ferguson is going to answer.

"How did you know I was looking for him?"

I wonder that, too, and I turn to the patient now sitting up in the bed, the covers up to her neck like she's hiding.

"Cause you were here yesterday and had the deputy sitting out there in the driveway all day, and now you are here again."

I am astounded at what Mrs. Lemmons is grasping about her situation, especially since she just acted like she didn't know Ferguson. I'd say she's returned from the great beyond with more gifts than deficits since I don't ever recall her being that astute to the goings-on around her. Not that I ever really knew her that well. She just seems extra sharp right now, extra sharp and maybe even slightly evasive.

The sheriff scratches the top of his head and then puts his hat squarely on his head. "It is true. I was here yesterday and now today."

"And had somebody watching my room."

He grins, slides the toothpick around from side to side, then reaches in and pulls it out. "We were just patrolling the facility, Mrs. Lemmons, making sure you and the other residents are safe."

"He told me you were trying to find him."

All three of us turn to get a closer look at her.

"Willis told you I was searching for him?"

She shakes her head, and I raise my eyebrows at the sheriff. *Here you go,* I want to say to him.

"Not Willis!"

And we all wait before speaking to let her finish, even though I know the name she's about to call out. The sheriff glances over at me.

"My other son," is what she says.

"Marvin's visited you today?" he asks.

She pulls the sheet over her face. "Marvin's dead," she explains, her voice muffled.

Evelyn, who is still standing next to her, pats her on the leg. "Miss Martha, you don't need to talk about that to anybody unless you want to."

Mrs. Lemmons drops the sheet, smiles at Evelyn, and pulls out a hand from beneath her covers, placing it on top of the young girl's. "I don't mind, dear." She squeezes the hand still resting on her leg. "Marvin's dead, but he still visits for now. He explained about Willis."

And I feel myself holding my breath.

"He explained the sheriff is trying to find him." And she turns to me. She opens her mouth like she's about to say more, like maybe she's about to tell Ferguson that I know more than I've let on, that I've been helping Willis, that I know where he is. And then, just like that, her face softens. "Hello, dear," she says.

I exhale. "Hello, Mrs. Lemmons."

And then to Evelyn, she asks, "Are you here to give me a bath?"

I feel as if I have suddenly been given a pass to get out of a pop quiz on a book I didn't read. "I'm going to go and get those biscuits," I say, holding up the piece of paper with the orders and trying to make a quick exit, sort of sidestepping so I don't expose the envelope sticking out of my pants.

"Miss Lorna," Evelyn calls out just as I reach for the door handle.

I turn.

"Isn't that something you brought for Miss Martha?"

I reach behind me and pull out the envelope and notice the sheriff is watching my every move.

"Oh this?" I ask, holding out the envelope. And before I can explain or lie, the walkie-talkie on Ferguson's belt goes off. "Nuh-uh," is all I say, and I hurry out the door.

CHAPTER TWENTY-SEVEN

I jump in my truck and speed out of the parking lot before Ferguson can get out there and stop me. I pull out onto the road so fast, I think I might leave some tire marks in the circle driveway, but I'm in too much of a hurry to stop and check out things behind me. I take the first turn and head toward town.

The sun is up, and I can tell it's going to be a hot one. There is a haze settling across the horizon, and even driving faster than I should be, I can hear the cicadas stirring in the tall grass, the long, busy sounds of late spring. Buford told me this year is remarkable for the insects because two broods are emerging simultaneously. He explained that there's a brood that surfaces every thirteen years and a brood that rises up every seventeen years, but two specific broods of different life cycles co-emerge only every two hundred and twenty-one years. Then he said some more stuff about seeing all seven named periodical cicada species as adults in the same year, but he started sounding like my algebra teacher, talking in a voice that does not register in my head except to sound like the adults in Charlie Brown's comic strips, and I quit listening.

All I know is that it is very loud around town, and there are shells of insects covering light poles and mailboxes, dropping from trees and fence posts. I told Buford that I preferred the creatures to stay underground, and when Georgia heard what we were talking about, she made the suggestion that we're being punished with a plague, that God is fed up with human shenanigans and is filling the earth and skies with locusts like He did in Egypt when Moses was taking the slaves and leaving.

Buford tried to explain that cicadas are not the same as locusts, that locusts are the swarming phase of a short-horned grasshopper. When he said that, she just threw a biscuit at him, which he dodged sufficiently. I told her I was going to dock her next paycheck if she was going to hurl the inventory at our customers. She replied that a bug can still be a plague, to quit challenging her prophetic capabilities, and that Buford was family and not a customer, and the inventory she pitched at him was too old to eat anyway. Then she took the broom and swept up the biscuit from where it had landed and stuck a dollar in the cash register to cover the loss.

I come to the edge of town, pull into the alley behind the bakery, and notice Buford's car is already there. I wonder if he found Willis, but I need to give Georgia the order from Evergreens before I head over to the barbershop. I walk in the rear door and hear Georgia talking to a customer in the front. My phone signals that I have a text, and I pull it out of my pocket and read it.

You find him? is what is written. It's Buford asking.

I type a reply. *No.* I assume if he's asking me the question, he didn't see him down at the creek, and it makes me wonder where Willis has gone.

I head into the kitchen, hang my keys on the hook, and take down an apron.

"You do what you need to do?" I hear the bells on the front door jingle, and I assume the customer is leaving. Georgia is standing in the doorway. She watches me as I pull the apron strings around and tie them in the front.

"I got a breakfast order from the nursing home." And I hand her the piece of paper. She unfolds it and nods like she approves.

"You gonna start driving around town first thing every morning to beg for orders?" She sticks the paper in her bra. "We hurting that much for business?"

I shake my head. "Just went there to see Martha Lemmons."

She narrows her eyes at me like she's reading my face for a better understanding.

I raise my eyebrows, waiting for the next question, but before she can ask anything, the front door jingles again. This time someone is coming in. Georgia makes a noise and returns to the dining room.

I head to the sink and wash my hands, remembering that I left the envelope for Willis in the car and wonder if I should go get it to take over to Buford. I decide to wait.

I peek through the glass on the oven door. Georgia has two pans of biscuits baking. I glance over at the table, but she's wiped that clean, so I don't know what she made for the morning rush. Then I hear her telling the customer what's about to come out fresh.

"We got blueberries today, and I found some Canadian bacon in the freezer that I fried up. Those are here on the serving line."

"Blueberry biscuits?" I hear someone ask and realize it's not a voice I recognize right away.

"Yes, sir," Georgia answers. "Like city muffins but not so sweet."

"Uh-huh," the voice replies.

I try to think who it might be.

"Just give me three plain biscuits and three with Canadian bacon," I hear him say. "I don't think anybody on the team really likes fruity breakfasts."

It's the voice of the young FBI agent from Marvin's house.

"You got coffee?"

"We got coffee," Georgia answers.

"Four coffees, too, then."

I figure I should go into the dining room to help. I take a quick look at the timer to see there's about five minutes left on what Georgia put in the oven, then I touch up the sides of my hair and add my morning smile.

"Well hello," I say as I walk my way next to Georgia.

She moves aside to give me room.

The young man simply nods in response and then stares at me, trying to remember where he saw me before, I imagine.

"I'm Lorna," I tell him, thinking that might jog his memory.

Clearly, it doesn't.

"We met yesterday at the …" I think for a second. "At the scene of the crime," I add in a kind of whisper.

He doesn't respond.

"So, they put you in charge of breakfast this morning," I say, then immediately recognize how that must have been offensive to the agent. He bristles at the suggestion.

"We left the hotel before they starting serving," he answers.

"Early then," I say, the smile still plastered on my face.

He doesn't answer.

"You all still working up at the victim's house?"

He waits, like he's trying to decide how much he should be talking to us about the carryings-on of the FBI. "We've got a temporary office at the courthouse."

I glance behind him like I'd be able to see it from where I'm standing. He turns to follow my eyes as if he thinks somebody might be coming in. And I think this is a good development. Maybe they'll curb the sheriff's investigation since they're working in the same building.

"Well, I'll get those drinks started." And I turn to the coffeepot and pull out four cups and lids.

I hear Georgia wrapping up the biscuits and then rattling a bag to put them in, letting me know she's taking care of the rest of the order.

I pull out a cardboard tray from a shelf and line up the cups. Then I find a small paper bag and fill it with sugars and creams and stirrers. When I turn around, Georgia is ringing up the sale. She is unusually quiet.

"Ya'll gonna be here long?" I ask.

And he smiles like he's pocketed a secret. He pulls out a credit card and hands it to Georgia. "Just till we find a murderer," he answers, pauses, and then stares at me hard. "You don't know where we might find one, do you? You don't have one stashed in the kitchen?" He peeks over my head like he's checking things behind me.

Georgia glances over at me. I get the feeling she's about to say something when the bell rings on the timer, and she just shakes her head, holds out the bag of biscuits, and walks into the kitchen.

"I do not," I answer. "But you are welcome to take a peek around before you leave."

He takes the bag and the drink tray. "Well, you never know. We may just do that."

Georgia clears her throat in the kitchen, and I understand we have suddenly reversed roles. She is trying to stop me from oversharing with the customers.

"Okay then," I reply. "We'll be waiting on you."

He walks out the door without a response.

"You sending out an invitation for trouble?" Georgia asks from behind me, and for a second I wonder if that's what I have done.

CHAPTER TWENTY-EIGHT

After the Rainbow Day Care children leave, Georgia and I are both spent, but she decides to deliver the order to Evergreens and then pick up some milk from the Piggly Wiggly. We're supposed to have an order from Dreamland Dairy later today, but we ran out of milk when the children came in for a field trip and everybody wanted a glass of milk with their biscuit. We had not expected the run on dairy products so soon in the day.

I always ask Trina Meacham, the owner of Rainbow, to let us know if she's bringing the kids into the shop so we can make sure we have ample inventory, but she never calls, just shows up with fifteen out-of-control preschoolers. We were lucky today that Georgia had baked an extra tray of mini biscuits, since that's really all the wee ones like to eat. She said she threw her dice and just had a feeling they might show up. Hearing that made me think maybe Georgia is spiritually gifted, but I wasn't about to let her know. She'd be spouting off prophecies without hindrance if I encouraged her. But it does make me wonder how she knew.

Buford stops by to tell me all the places he has driven trying to find Willis, but there was no sign of him anywhere. I explain that I saw him run past the window at Evergreens but that once the sheriff arrived, I was not able to chase him down.

Buford thinks he'll return, and he seems real calm about both Ferguson and the team of FBI agents conducting separate searches for the murderer. He says that they're likely to miss things as long as they're all strutting about like barnyard roosters, one trying to outdo the other, but I don't think doubling up is a good thing, and I hope the FBI orders Ferguson to stand down. I figure as long as the FBI is in charge, Willis has a better chance of not being the lead suspect. I worry if Ferge stays in charge that he'll zero in on Marvin's brother and focus only on that line of investigation. Buford considers my theory and finally agrees. Ferguson seems a little too eager to find Willis; neither of us thinks that's good news.

Buford leaves the bakery when Junior finally returns his father's call about ten a.m., saying he wanted to have the conversation in his shop in case I got more customers and he wouldn't be able to talk freely. Of course, I'm curious as to what Buford confesses to Junior and even more interested in what his son advises. But I know it's a private call and needs to be treated as such. Georgia may have had the premonition about the five-year-olds coming in but I've got my own prophetic musings—and I'm pretty sure Ferguson isn't finished with me yet and will be making a call to the bakery sometime before the end of the business day. It's best he doesn't overhear a conversation between Buford and his lawyer son.

With Georgia gone and the morning rush subsided, I decide to clean things. The Rainbow children left milk spills on the tables and crumbs on the floor, so I get out the broom and start sweeping. I've just finished wiping down all the surfaces and dumping the dustpan when the bakery phone rings. I head into the kitchen to take the call.

"O Biscuit," I say, letting the receiver rest under my chin as I walk to the sink to wash my hands.

"Yes, hello."

It's a voice I don't recognize and there's a lot of background noise, like the person is standing outside where there's a lot of traffic. "Yes, who's this?"

"You don't know me."

"Okay," I say, thinking this is a weird way to start a conversation. I wait for them to continue, trying to make out whether this is a woman

or a high-pitched man. I need more material to be certain. I find my
pad of paper and a pen, thinking this will likely be some order to fill.

They clear their throat. "My name is Lucy."

So at least I know I'm talking to a woman.

"I'm calling from Nashville."

"That's a nice place." I'm not sure what else to say to Lucy from
Tennessee. I put away the pad of paper since I hardly think this is
someone making an order from the next state over.

She clears her throat again, sounds more nervous than clinical.

I walk into the dining room with the cordless phone, glance out
the window, and wave at Rainey Harper walking by, dressed for a
funeral, black suit, starched white shirt. He raises his chin and smiles
but keeps walking.

"I met your sister."

And the phone slides out from under my chin and almost falls to
the floor. I scramble to catch it.

"Cathedral?" I say, trying to understand how this person from
Nashville somehow knows my sister, has spoken to her when I suppose
it's been more than a couple of decades since we last talked.

"Cathy," she replies, sounding a little surprised about the name I
just called out. "I don't know a Cathedral."

I walk into the kitchen and stare at my reflection in the mirror above
the sink. It was another of Mae's ideas, having a mirror in the kitchen
so that you can check yourself before meeting customers. She found
this one at the Walmart, and Buford nailed it up years ago. Mostly I
forget it's even there, never bothering to measure how I appear, but
now, watching myself talking to someone about my estranged sister,
I'm struck at the way surprise pinches the resting look on my face.

"Where is she?" I ask.

"Memphis," Lucy answers. "I mean, she was in Memphis."

"Tennessee?" I try to imagine how old she'd be now. I start to do the math. *If I'm fifty*, and I commence counting the years between us, forty-nine, forty-eight, forty-seven … but I don't get very far.

"Yes, she roadied for a country music band, selling T-shirts, taking down microphones, about anything they need." She pauses. "I work at the bar where the band played."

"You met Cathedral?"

"Cathy, yes."

"Is she okay? Is there something wrong?" And then I realize there is so much wrong. A stranger is calling me with recent information about my sister, whom I haven't seen since she was a teenager … I would say there's a lot wrong with that.

"Oh, God, you don't know, do you?"

"I don't know what?"

There's a long pause, a full breath pouring across the line.

"When we met, she was okay."

"What does that mean, she *was* okay?" I ask, and she doesn't answer right away.

I try to imagine my sister as a grown woman, wonder if we resemble each other, and I take a long gander at myself in the mirror. I remember that our baby pictures were similar, that there wasn't much to tell us apart early on, but it didn't take much time to realize that Cathedral was a lot prettier than me, a lot prettier than anybody. She was popular from the time she was old enough to play with other children, charming everyone with her big blue eyes, cherry-blond ringlets, rosy cheeks.

I don't recall who her daddy is or even if I ever knew, but Draymond and I always said he must have been the most handsome of all of Mama's baby daddies. It's not that I see a thing wrong with either of us, but Cathedral was just better looking. She always got the attention, which was part of the problem for her, I think.

I get back to the caller, this random call. "So, is she all right?"

"Well, Cathy …" she stops. "Cathedral told me where to find you."

And this surprises me. I don't for the life of me know how my sister would know anything about my business, my bakery, my phone number. "Okay," is about all I can think of to say.

"There was an article about Marvin Lemmons a few months ago, maybe a year," she explains. "About his business in computer rooms. I was reading it when the band was here, when we met. It turns out Cathy knew him too."

And here there is another surprise, since I didn't know Cathedral knew anything about Marvin and Willis. She was quite a bit younger than all of us, and she left Owensboro before she even finished high school. I had been out of school a few years at that point. I was still working at the drugstore and had decided to go to community college, maybe study chemistry; maybe transfer to State or Carolina; maybe become a pharmacist. The Dentons were encouraging, thought I had real talent for helping folks, running a business—said I could learn the science. Rodney was even going to help me with my studies, even the tuition.

And then Cathedral disappeared. And I realize now that she was sixteen—same age as Marvin when she left, just a bunch of years after him and not to attend some fancy college. She left with no warning, no explanation. I missed the first semester of school, then the second, and then I just resigned myself to being a clerk at the drugstore, nothing more.

She pulls me from my memories. "And then today I saw that Marvin was dead, that he was …" She pauses. "It's on the internet," she adds.

"Yeah?" And I notice that the look in the mirror, this way I am feeling, has changed from surprise to confusion. I don't understand this phone call, this connection between Marvin and Cathedral and this woman from Tennessee contacting me out of the blue.

"They went out a few times," she says.

"Who?"

"Marvin and Cathy," she answers, and I don't even know what this is I'm seeing now on my face. *Where did my sister run into Marvin? Why did I never know this?*

There is a long bit of silence, and then the bells on the front door ring. Someone is coming in.

"I did too," Lucy adds.

"Did too what?" I ask, trying to follow this conversation, trying to understand what I'm being told when everything seems so strange.

"But later, I suppose."

I don't respond.

"Cathy told me about her family, about you. She said you were a good person."

"And did she also say that we haven't talked in decades? Did she also tell you that she just up and left and never told us anything, never called, never wrote? Did she tell you that we searched for her for years, that we all thought she was dead? Did she explain anything to you about where she's been and why she left?"

Lucy from Tennessee doesn't respond.

I can tell someone is standing at the counter. I hold the phone away from my mouth. "I'll be right there," I say. And then I put the receiver to my lips again but realize I don't have anything more to say.

"I'm sorry. She didn't tell me anything specific about you or how she left home. She was real nice, that's really all I remember."

I squint my eyes, trying to put aside what is haunting me.

She goes on. "And then yesterday when I saw the newsflash about Marvin, I remembered Cathy noticing an article I was reading one time about Marvin's enterprises, how she laughed and said Marvin was from her hometown, that she knew him."

"Okay." I really don't understand what this woman wants from me.

I hear a throat clearing in the dining room and know I need to check on my customer.

"I just felt like I should tell someone there, in Owensboro, something about Marvin, since I heard about his murder. I just thought somebody needed to know that he wasn't who he said he was."

"Marvin said he was somebody else?" I am really confused now. "He say who he was?"

"No, no, not like that. He said he was Marvin Lemmons. That part was true."

I stick my head out the door to tell my customer that I'll be there just as soon as I get off the phone, but I don't see anyone, which is strange since I didn't hear the bells on the door jingle again on their way out. I step farther into the dining room, but no one is there.

"He was just, well, you see, I did some work for him, computer stuff, saved files, made copies, that sort of thing."

"Uh-huh." I walk around the counter and don't see a soul, even anyone outside walking on the sidewalk. I think maybe I'm hearing things and return to the kitchen.

"I just think someone needs to know that he was into some stuff that could have got him into trouble."

"What are you talking about?"

"Some of the files I copied and deleted weren't exactly aboveboard."

"What?"

"I can't say anything else right now, not like this, but maybe I can call you later when I can talk? I left Memphis. I'm staying with a friend in Nashville, and I'm just laying low for a little while."

"Okay," is all I can think to say.

"There's something else."

I wait. Surely, this has been enough … but I'm wrong.

"There's something else I need to tell you. Something I see now that you don't know. Something I should have told you right off."

There's another long pause, and I'm about to ask if she's still there.

"It's Cathy."

"You already told me she was in Memphis."

"It's something else."

And I feel myself start to grow impatient. I got things to do.

"Cathy ... Cathedral, your sister, is dead."

"What?"

"I'm sorry. When I realized you didn't know, I wasn't sure how to tell you. I've never done this before."

"Lucy, I don't understand."

"There was a wreck on the interstate a couple of months ago. Several members of the band were hurt, and Cathy didn't make it."

I pull away from the mirror and drop onto the stool at the center table. "Who are you again, and why are you calling me now?"

She doesn't answer.

"You said you spent time with her. You said she was doing fine."

Still, the girl from Tennessee doesn't reply.

"Are you trying to tell me that her accident had something to do with Marvin's murder? Is that why you're calling? Is that why you left Memphis? Is there something I'm supposed to do?"

But she doesn't answer.

"Lucy, are you still there?"

But there is only silence. The call was disconnected.

CHAPTER TWENTY-NINE

"So she died, what, sometime this month?"

I phoned Draymond to let him know about the call. When I hear his voice, I realize I haven't talked to my brother in a while. He lives less than an hour away, and we just never talk. We were close when we were young and later when we worried about our little sister, but once we gave up the search—once we realized nobody was going to help us because everybody just assumed Cathedral ran off with some boy—me and Draymond drifted apart.

"Guess so," I answer.

"Huh," is all he says, but then again, Draymond was never very chatty. "Well, mystery solved."

"It took a long time," I reply.

"Yep."

"Did you really think she was dead a long time ago?" I ask.

"I don't know. I guess not. I mean, Cathedral was always a wild child. After Mama left, I mean, she went really off the rails."

"Yeah, I remember all too well."

"She definitely resented you."

I think about the fights we had when I tried to get her to be more responsible, to stay in school, try to get her to help around the house, do her homework, keep a curfew. She was incorrigible as a child; when she hit puberty, she became undone. I was trying to keep a low profile for the three of us so Child Protective Services didn't come in and separate us, put us into foster care, even though we were old enough to stay on our own and even though Grandma Lawton moved in until she died. Still, even with Grandma there, when it came to Cathedral, I half expected to come home from school to be told she was in jail or knocked up by some older boy.

"I was just trying to keep her out of trouble," I reply.

"I know, but I also know that made her jump in deeper."

I think about the three of us being left alone, how we were just trying our best to get along. Draymond and me trying not to call attention to the family while Cathedral seemed like she wanted the whole world to know what happened.

Images of my childhood flash before me, images of hiding at school from the guidance counselors, teachers a little too curious about me and my siblings, running home in the afternoons to lock the doors. And always searching for Cathedral; always trying to cover up what was going on in our home; always trying to care for her, comfort her, be there for her, but always coming up short. It was as if she blamed me for everything bad that happened. And even though Draymond and I became a little closer and I had Buford as a friend, there just always seemed to be a fracture in our family, a gulf between us, a hole in my heart that never got filled.

"She took the most after Mama. I don't think there was nothing any of us could do about her."

And I don't know if he's talking about Cathedral or our mother, but I decide not to ask.

"I guess you're right."

"I know I'm right."

And I realize he's talking about them both.

"Did you know she dated Marvin?"

"Marvin Lemmons? Isn't he dead too?"

"Yeah. He was murdered."

"How would I know they dated?"

I consider his response and realize he wouldn't know anything about our sister's dating life since neither of us has heard from Cathedral in so long. "Yeah, you're right, I don't know why I asked you that."

"Was that the reason she left?"

"What?" This is not a notion I've considered.

"Is that why she left Owensboro? Something happen with Marvin?"

"I don't know. I got the feeling that this woman who called, meant she had dated him more recently." But then I also don't know this for sure since nothing about the call today made sense, and nothing was explained. Maybe she did date him when she was fifteen or sixteen; maybe she did leave because of him, but that doesn't seem right. Marvin had finished college by the time she was in high school. But then, I wonder, how did they meet? Where did they meet? And that just makes me think that maybe Cathedral never really went so far away when she disappeared—maybe she was right here under our noses and we never knew it. Then I recall how Marvin stared at me that day around Christmas when he stopped in the shop. He did remember me, because he remembered Cathedral.

"That's strange."

"It is that," I reply.

"Huh. Cathedral and Marvin. What is that between them? About a twelve- or fifteen-year difference?"

"I don't know," I answer. "I don't think it's that much." But I don't do the math.

"What did this woman say?"

"About Marvin?"

"About Cathedral?" I can hear people talking in the background, and I assume my brother is at work. He still sells tires, does automotive work. Like me, never married; always seemed content to be alone. We never really talked about our dating lives.

"She said she traveled a lot, worked as a roadie with a country music band." I pause, thinking about the call that still has me in shock. "Lucy said when they met that she was good, that she seemed happy."

"Even though she ran away and never let anybody know where she was, if she was alive or dead," Draymond replies. "Even though she upended the two of us?"

"I guess."

"Well, thanks for letting me know," he says.

And just like that, we've run out of things to say.

"Be careful around there. Sounds like Owensboro is getting to be as dangerous as the big towns."

"Yep, okay, I will."

There's an awkward silence. I can tell he's about to hang up.

"We should get together sometime," I finally suggest.

"Sure," he replies. But then it becomes pretty clear that won't likely happen.

Another pause.

"What happened to us?" I ask.

"What do you mean?"

I shrug even though I know he can't see me.

"I mean, we don't ever see each other. Mama died. Grandma died. Cathedral left, and we just ..."

I hear him breathe.

"I don't know, Lorna. I just always felt like you didn't really need a big brother. You seemed pretty all right on your own."

"But I don't think brothers and sisters have to stay together because one needs the other. I think they stay in touch because, well because I guess they like each other."

"I guess."

I hear a car's engine revving up.

"You were a good brother, Draymond. I never held nothing against you."

"Yeah, I know."

"It was always just so crazy with Mama and then Cathedral, Grandma dying like she did. I guess we just never had much of a chance to get to be close. I just felt like we limped from one emergency to another."

"I suppose."

"I guess I felt like you wanted to leave too. I figured you would."

"And yet, here I am just forty miles from where we grew up."

"Yeah."

I am standing in my house. I'm going to have supper at Buford's, and I'm already a few minutes late, but I don't want to end this call. I feel an ache I haven't felt in years, and I don't want to hang up. I don't want to say goodbye to Draymond. I am swallowed up by grief or sadness or—now that I think about it, it's something else. Something I've never claimed or acknowledged or named.

It's the longing I've had my whole life, this longing to be connected, to be a part of a family that loves and cares for each other, the longing to be close to my brother, my sister, my mother. This longing that we should be more than what we are, what we were. There was just so much chaos in our house, so much that didn't work, I finally gave up that anything we had could work. I finally just accepted that there was no real bond between any of us, and none would ever magically appear.

And the truth is, just talking to Draymond, just remembering Cathedral, hearing that she was alive for so long and we didn't know and that now she's dead, brings up so many bad memories, so much water rushing beneath the bridge that I can't see as we can ever get beyond everything that went on at the Dixie Crossings Trailer Park. I can't really imagine we can be more than all that did and didn't happen to us.

He pulls me away from my thoughts. "Maybe I'll come to the bakery next week. You always did make the best biscuits," he says.

My throat tightens, and the tear rolling down my cheek is an even bigger surprise than the call about my sister.

"That'd be nice, Draymond."

"Okay then. Thanks, Lorna, for letting me know about Cathedral. I'll see you."

"Yeah, I'll see you too."

And when he hung up, I clutch my phone to my chest.

CHAPTER THIRTY

"What does that mean, 'he was in stuff that could have gotten him into trouble'?"

I shake my head. Buford and I are cleaning up the dinner dishes. He made spaghetti and meat sauce. He had meatballs in the freezer, and he fixed a salad when he got home from work. He has jars of tomato sauce lining the shelves in his basement. We have spaghetti at least once a week.

"She just said he wasn't who he said he was and that she saw papers and files that weren't aboveboard, that she did secretarial work for him, and that's how she knows so much about him."

"How did she know he was dead so soon?" He hands me a bowl, and I dry it, place it on the shelf where it belongs.

"Said it was a newsflash or something. She must be following him, maybe on social media."

"Hmm," he replies, hands me the other bowl.

"You don't believe her? You think she found out some other way?" I watch him closely for an answer.

"I didn't know he was so important that his murder would show up on the news in ..." He turns to me.

"Memphis," I say, understanding what he's asking.

"Tennessee," Buford adds. "Just seems suspicious."

"You think she had something to do with his murder?"

He shakes his head like he's not sure.

"Well, the fact that she claimed to talk to Cathedral right before she died sounds suspicious to me." I take the tea glasses, dry them, and place them on the shelf with the others that match.

"It's odd, that's for sure."

We talked a bit about the phone call when we sat down to eat. I told him everything this Lucy said and that I had called Draymond, who knew nothing about our sister either. Both of us had no idea she dated Marvin.

"But if it's true, that his death shows up on a newsflash, I guess that does let us know he ran in powerful circles, explains the FBI poking around. And not just poking around, but actually taking over the case," I add.

"Right." Buford feels around in the bottom of the dishpan, searching for what else might be left to wash.

"You think it was drugs or something with the mafia?"

"The mafia? In Owensboro, North Carolina?"

"Well, it's as good a hiding place as any, and Ferguson said they have lots of overdoses in the county. Maybe Marvin was a drug pin and worked with the Mexican cartel—might explain why he doesn't hire anyone around here, why he's so secretive."

Buford finds, washes, and hands me two forks and a spoon, and then he turns over the dishpan and empties the soapy water down the sink. I wipe the flatware and place them in the drawer. I wait to see what he thinks of my idea about Marvin manufacturing drugs in his warehouse or selling them for some gang out of Mexico. It seems plausible to me. Lord knows, the television programs like this theory of murder a lot. Maybe it's happening in real life, right here in Owensboro.

He wipes down the counter, dabs the cloth around the sink, places it over the faucet, and takes the towel from me, dries his hands, and kisses me on the cheek. He folds the towel and hangs it on the bar across the stove door. At first the kiss on the cheek felt dismissive, like a pat on the head of a child, and I'm about to say something, but then I see it's a sign of affection. It's just Buford being Buford.

He smiles. "Well, it does give us more evidence that Marvin could have made enemies somewhere along the way, that there are more leads to follow. I think that, actually, this is good for Willis; gives another path to take."

"Mr. Denton always said somebody was giving folks drugs from prescriptions that he didn't fill. Maybe Mr. Lemmons started a family business that Marvin simply took over."

I lean against the counter while he reaches on a shelf above the stove and grabs a toothpick. The question comes to me why so many men use toothpicks, but I don't ask. I just watch him stick it between his teeth and think of Ferguson from earlier in the day.

"The Lemmons cartel," I say dramatically, hearing how it sounds out loud. "You think they use little lemons for their drug logo?" Then I think about what Buford might have noticed but not paid it any attention. "You ever see a lemon tattoo on Willis? You think he's in on it?"

Buford doesn't answer.

"I bet I could ask Mavis some things about Mr. Lemmons. Hey, maybe I could check out tattoo parlors to find out if there's been a run on fruit tattoos in Owensboro."

I think Buford must be giving real consideration to my new theories. He's not commenting, and he seems real serious listening to me.

"We could talk to some employees at the warehouse. Do you know where Leo Landry lives? Maybe you could go see him and get him to spill the beans?"

Buford pulls out the toothpick. "You want me to check him for tattoos?"

I'm thinking about the possibility that Marvin made his employees get branded to show their loyalty to the cartel when I realize that Buford's just making fun now. I grab the dish towel and pop him with it.

He winces and rubs his arm. "Ouch!" He places the toothpick in his mouth.

"Oh, don't be a baby," I say. "It won't leave no mark."

"Well, maybe not like a tattoo," he replies.

This puts me in mind of the last wound we treated together. "So, any thoughts of where Willis is hiding?"

Buford takes the towel from my hand, returns it to the rack. "I don't know if he's hiding. Maybe he's just holed up somewhere taking a nap."

"Come on, Buford, you searched everywhere. He didn't tell you where he was going. He's been gone all day. You might not want to admit it, but Willis is hiding." I walk into the dining room, pull out a chair, and take a seat. It's just a few seconds before he joins me at the table again.

"You want some ice cream? Something sweet?"

I shake my head. "The dinner was plenty."

He nods, pulls the toothpick from his mouth again.

"What did Junior say?"

He shrugs. "That the fact Willis was at the scene of the murder, has an injury of unknown origin, has a record and a history demonstrating contention between the brothers—it doesn't look good for him. But he said it appears worse if he's hiding. He said we should take him in to talk to Ferguson, get on the record as being compliant, and for him not to stay on the run, which makes him seem guilty, even if he isn't."

I watch him closely. "But you still don't want to do that." It's easy to see Buford's resistance to the idea.

"I know what will happen to him."

"You can't be sure they'll charge him," I say, not certain I believe such a thing.

Buford looks uneasy.

"What?" I ask, sensing there's something else to be said.

He just shakes his head. "There's just precedence," he answers.

"Precedence?"

He waves the question away. "Doesn't matter. I can be sure this is bad for Willis. He was at the scene of the crime at a place he wasn't supposed to be and can't remember what happened. And I know what being in jail will do to him." He rests his elbows on the table, drops his head. "He won't survive in there."

"You tell that to Junior?" I ask, knowing that part of being in jail would break Willis. I know we got to figure out some things fast.

He glances up, shakes his head. He takes the toothpick and picks a little at his front teeth.

I lean in, holding out for more.

Buford bites his lip. "There's that other thing," and he gets up from the table and leaves the room. When he comes back, he has something in his hand. He hands it to me, and I take it.

"The EpiPen," I say. "But we already knew about that."

"Yeah, but it's one more piece of evidence that implicates Willis." He drops down into his seat. "There's just too much circumstantial evidence that isn't good for Willis. And I haven't even mentioned the knife."

"It doesn't mean anything," I tell him. "Everybody has knives. I have a ton of knives, and I didn't kill Marvin." Then I pause. "What did you do with it anyway?" I ask.

He shakes his head, and I think of something before he answers.

"Wait! The envelope!" I jump up from the table. "I completely forgot about it. With the call from Lucy and the news about Cathedral, I just forgot. It's in the truck," I say. "Maybe it'll have some answers, maybe there's something in there to help Willis!" I head toward the door but then turn around. "And maybe Marvin gave him the EpiPen," I suggest, searching for an explanation. "Or maybe he keeps an extra with him like he did when they were young. Or maybe he took it because he just wanted something to remind him of his brother. I get that," I say, thinking about my call with Draymond, my longing to be connected to my family.

Buford opens his mouth to speak, but before he can get anything out and before I can get outside to my truck to retrieve the envelope, we are interrupted by a knock at Buford's door.

CHAPTER THIRTY-ONE

Buford takes the toothpick from his mouth, glances up at the clock on the wall. It's after nine, the sun dropped low on the horizon. Days are getting longer, but in my opinion it's still too late to be calling on someone.

He stands up and walks to the front door, pulls aside the curtain on the small window. I notice how he suddenly straightens up, his shoulders raised. He unlocks and opens the door.

"Evening, Buford."

I recognize the voice and feel my own shoulders tighten.

"Sheriff," he responds, still standing in the doorway.

"It all right if I come in?"

Buford hesitates but then steps aside, and Ferguson walks in after dusting off his shoes on the mat, then he notices me at the table for the first time. He nods in my direction. He's holding his hat in his hands. "Lorna Gayle, didn't expect to see you." He grins like he knows some secret. "That's two surprise visits in one day."

I smile. "Ferguson." And then, I glance over on the table, at the spot in front of where Buford was sitting and realize the EpiPen is still there. Right there in plain sight for the sheriff to see. I quickly stand up and move over to block the sheriff's view. I step back a few steps and reach behind and feel on the table for the pen, collect it, and hold it tightly in my hands, just like I did with the envelope this morning. I feel like I seem way too jumpy to be innocent.

Ferguson doesn't seem to notice. He's facing Buford who is standing at the door. There hasn't been an invitation to be seated, and I know it isn't my place to offer hospitality. There is an awkward bout of silence between us.

"You're a hard man to catch, Buford," the sheriff says, smiling like he's trying to be friendly but sounding more like he's disappointed.

"That so?"

Then Ferguson turns to me. "And you sped off this morning before we had a chance to finish our conversation."

"Had to get that order in," I say, still clutching the pen behind me. He studies us both.

"Not that hard to find me. I've been at the shop all day," Buford says and seems to relax slightly. "What do you need, Ferguson?"

The sheriff has his arms to his sides. "Well, I'm looking for Willis Lemmons," he answers. "I thought you might know where I can find him."

Buford shakes his head before he replies. His arms are also at his sides, but I can see his fingers twitching a bit, and this makes me nervous for him. "I can't say as I can help you."

Ferguson nods and then faces me. "How about you, Lorna Gayle, you were out awful early this morning to Evergreens, in his mama's room—you seen Willis today?"

And I am so relieved I don't have to lie, well, I mean if you don't count me seeing him jump the wall. "I have not talked to Willis today," I respond, feeling the tightness in my throat. It's not really a lie, but it falls down the slippery slope of deception, that's for sure.

"Well, okay," Ferguson replies and seems like he might take his leave but then he doesn't. "You see, it's just I think you may have some information about where he could be." He seems to be saying this to Buford.

Buford turns his head ever so slightly as if he might, just a tiny bit, be offended at this statement. "Yeah, Ferguson, what makes you think that?"

The sheriff shakes his head. "Well, it's the strangest thing, but Clara Smiley, your neighbor ..." He waits and Buford doesn't react. He scratches his cheek and then rests his hand on the gun on his belt, like he always does. "Turns out, Clara has insomnia, has had it for years. She gets up and apparently likes to stare out the window."

He leans back on his heels. "If I had a dime for every time she calls 911 to tell us she's seen a raccoon taking off trash can lids and wants us to send an officer to trap it or that she heard an old barn owl screeching and she knows that means somebody's about to die. There was even the time she called at three a.m. to report a boy skateboarding down the middle of the street. She thought that was a crime, to be outside after midnight."

Ferguson laughs. "I'll be honest and tell you that we don't always take her calls anymore." He glances over at me and points his finger in the air. "But I'll deny that if it ever gets out."

I don't respond, but I do wonder if Georgia knows about the barn owls and think to ask her in the morning.

"Is there a point to this, Ferguson?" Buford has gone serious.

"Oh yeah, sorry. Well, anyway, she called this morning, but we let it go to voicemail. Mavis apparently left the message on my desk, which got covered up with papers and things, and I just saw the message about dinnertime. I've been over there talking with Clara." He stops again, turns to me. "Have you ever eaten Clara's pecan pie?"

I shake my head even though I know I have many times. Clara wanted me to sell them in the bakery when I opened, but I explained that O, Biscuit only specializes in biscuits, not desserts.

"You, Buford?"

Buford blows out a breath. "Clara does make good pie."

"With vanilla ice cream, warm." He smacks his lips together. "Mmm-mmm-mmm." He pats his belly.

I watch Buford's fingers twitch a bit more.

"So, it seems like she was up last night, like always, and saw a light come on in one of your rooms, a bedroom most likely, since it's that side of the house. And well, we all know Clara is a bit nosy . . ."

And I think that's the greatest understatement of the day. Clara knows everything about what happens not just on this street but in all of Owensboro. She has been accused on more than one occasion for stalking people because she likes to follow folks around and make up stories about what they're doing. We all know to take what Clara says with a measuring cup of salt.

Buford and I gave up a long time ago trying to hide our relationship from Clara. She worried us to death about why I was over there every night until I just told her Buford and I were studying the Bible together so that we could grow in our spiritual lives more strongly. I think it embarrassed her so much that she might be standing in the way of the Lord, she left us alone after that. Buford did say she dropped off some pamphlets on his front door from the Freewill Baptist Church where she goes regularly, and she does sometimes want me to pray with her at the shop, but she doesn't pester either of us anymore about our nights together.

"Anyway, where was I?"

"Clara saw something last night," Buford says as a reminder.

"Oh right, right. So, she saw the light come on and knew it wasn't your room." Ferguson stops again. "I guess she watches here frequently."

Buford doesn't change his expression.

"And that's when she sees somebody open the window and jump out."

He studies Buford closely.

"And she recognized who it was?" Buford asks.

"She does. Ain't that the craziest thing?" Ferguson turns to me. "She recalls you leaving after it was dark, Lorna; thinks you were having one of your prayer meetings." He has an expression on his face that reminds me of Cathedral when she used to say something she knew would get me in trouble with Mama.

He continues. "So anyway, when she saw the window open, she says she knew it was Willis jumping out because he looked right at her when he saw he was being watched. And you know, Clara knows everybody."

I can see the wheels turning in Buford's head, and I have no idea what he's about to say, so I jump in and do what I got to do. I say the thing no one expects.

CHAPTER THIRTY-TWO

"Willis came for dinner last night," I say.

Ferguson watches me closely.

"He wanted to rest a while after we ate, so Buford let him shower and sleep in the guest room."

Buford is staring at me. I wait for him to jump in, but he just stares.

"We had ham and beans."

Both of them just seem stunned.

"Tomatoes."

Nothing from Buford, so I keep going. "Had strawberry shortcake for dessert. Willis ate good. Seemed like he was hungry and looked like he could use a shower."

Ferguson narrows his eyes at me. I turn to Buford, hoping he'll chime in at some point.

He clears his throat. "He comes here from time to time since he doesn't have access to clean running water out by the creek. I also cut his hair for free. We give him money for food. Don't see any crime in that."

Ferguson doesn't respond.

"But Clara's right, he left sometime in the night. So, like I said, I haven't seen Willis today."

We got us a strategy going now. We're telling just enough of the truth to satisfy the questions without giving anything more than what's being asked. Those *Law & Order* folks don't have nothing on Buford and me.

"You care if I take a peek in the room?"

Buford doesn't answer right away. I can see he's weighing his options. He glances over at me and seems to notice my hands behind my back, realizing I'm covering up the EpiPen, but he doesn't seem to notice that I'm shaking my head, not grasping that I think it's a bad idea for him to let the sheriff roam around his house.

"Sure, Ferguson."

And he steps from the door and walks near me while I take a few steps backward away from the table, the pen securely in my right hand. Ferguson doesn't look in my direction, he just follows Buford as he heads down the hall.

I hear them talking but don't make out the words. I hurry into the kitchen and hide the pen in the drawer with the silverware, get back to the dining room table before they return. They aren't in the bedroom long.

"He didn't leave anything with you?"

Buford shakes his head. "What do you think a homeless man takes with him to visit a friend?"

Ferguson doesn't answer, just waits.

"No, Sheriff, Willis came for dinner, took a shower, a nap, and like Clara said, left sometime in the night. I haven't seen him since."

"She said you left about dark." Ferguson is talking to me.

I shrug. "Not sure," I reply.

"But you said you hadn't seen Willis." He studies me. "This morning, I particularly asked you if you had seen him yesterday."

"Is that right?" I ask. "Oh, I thought you asked me if he had been to the shop yesterday, if I had seen him downtown at the shop. I am so sorry, Ferguson. I didn't know you meant had I seen him here, at Buford's. I just said no because Willis hadn't been to the bakery."

He's nodding at me, a gesture of goodwill, but I don't think he believes me.

"Well, I'm glad that we know Willis is safe, or at least was last night. That he's full after supper and I reckon since he showered, clean."

Buford smiles and nods.

"If he stops by again, is there something in particular you need from Willis?" I ask.

Ferguson takes in a breath. "Just tell him I'd like to talk to him about Marvin, see what he knows about his brother's demise. You know, just ask the standard questions."

I step closer to him. "But why would you think Willis knows anything about Marvin?"

Ferguson doesn't answer, so I go on.

"Marvin and his lawyer made it very clear to Willis not to talk to his brother. I doubt Willis would know anything more than either one of us."

"Well, see, that's the problem." Ferguson leans against the wall near the hallway where he's been standing since they returned from the guest bedroom.

Buford and I both wait for more.

"We think Willis saw Marvin sometime this week."

"Yeah?" Buford asks.

And I remember the report from the guard shack when I went to Marvin's lake house—Maynard telling me that he had seen somebody at the Estates. I remember he knew that somebody suspicious had been around, and I can only guess that he figured out it was Willis.

"Maynard White saw him," I say before Ferguson can elaborate.

He turns to me, stands up straight. "How do you know that?"

"When I brought breakfast yesterday, he told me."

Ferguson nods. "Maynard never could keep his mouth shut. That's why he's a security guard and not a deputy."

"Guess it isn't a state secret," I respond. "But he doesn't have any video of Willis coming to the gate, just thinks he saw him down by the fence. And when I asked a few questions, he didn't have any details about anything." I take a seat at the table. "I don't think Maynard's all that reliable."

Ferguson waits a second before saying more. "Well, maybe not, but you know, Lorna Gayle, I'm still curious as to why you're asking so many questions about this case. I've never known you to take that much of an interest in my work. Well, except …" And he doesn't complete the sentence, but I know what he means.

Buford and I share a glance.

He means the time Cathedral went missing and I was at his office every day for about a year trying to get the latest on the search. He was young, new at his job, a deputy at the time, but he remembers.

And so do I.

"And I can't say as I remember you being that curious either," he notes, eyeing Buford.

"We care about Willis," Buford answers. "That's no surprise, so yeah, we're interested in his welfare, in his grief process. He and Marvin may not have been close, but they're still brothers. We just want to make sure he's okay, gets the answers he needs about what happened to his brother."

"And then there's his mother," I note, though I'm not sure how Mrs. Lemmons waking up from a coma is relevant.

Both men glance at me like they're not following.

"How she suddenly sprung back to life," I try to explain. "How that might affect him, too, like maybe he'll want to take her somewhere else to live, take her out of Evergreens. I just think Willis is going through a lot." I smile. "With me and Buford being about his only friends, we just want to make sure he's okay."

Buford turns to the sheriff as I keep talking.

"And we're nervous, being business owners and all, that there's a murderer wandering the streets of Owensboro. This could hurt our bottom lines, people choosing not to go out. Well, we're just trying to be good citizens, find out what we can." I pause. "To help law enforcement, you know." There's a big grin plastered on my face.

Ferguson nods, like he's considering all I've just offered. He takes a step toward the door. "You just let me know if you see him again," he says, and I guess he's talking to us both.

Buford follows him to the front door, opens it wide.

Ferguson turns to make a final observation. "You might want to check that bedroom window. Willis more than likely left it unlocked."

Buford nods. "I'll go and see to it right now," he answers.

Ferguson gives me a final look. "Lorna Gayle, I'll stop by the shop in the morning, probably get the office breakfast since everybody's working extra hard on this case."

"We'll be open as usual." And then, I can't help myself since I'm still a little put off that Ferguson went to the diner instead of the bakery this morning. "'Course, Eugene has an earlier shift than me and Georgia. You might want to get something from there."

He smiles, understanding the gist of my suggestion. "Eugene doesn't have biscuits," he says, reaching for the screen door. "But he has started baking cinnamon rolls." Then he turns and winks. "You got some new competition." He opens the door and walks out. We hear him from the porch. "I'll be in touch."

And just like that, he's gone.

Buford closes both doors and then joins me at the table. "Can you believe that?" he asks.

"I know," I reply, thinking we're talking about the same thing. "When did Eugene Bullard start baking cinnamon rolls?"

CHAPTER THIRTY-THREE

"The envelope," I say, as I stand up from the table.

"In the truck?" Buford asks.

"In the truck," I reply, feeling around in my pocket for my keys. I head toward the kitchen door.

"I can't believe you didn't open it," he says, keeping his seat.

I shake my head. "It wasn't addressed to me," I say. Sometimes I can be as nosy as Clara, so I don't feel too offended. I go out to the truck. I don't really know why I haven't opened it except there's been more activity going on in Owensboro than at the bingo game the first weekend in the month when everybody gets their government checks.

Buford's in the same place when I return. I set the large envelope on the table in front of him.

"I still don't understand why they left it at your house," he says. He picks it up, turns it one way and then another.

I shake my head, take my seat across from Buford. "I don't know, except I think maybe they knew I had been with Willis. Maybe somebody saw him at the shop when he first showed up, whoever that was we heard at the front door when we were in the hallway with him."

He sets it down, folds his hands together. "I don't know, just doesn't make sense."

"Well, let's face it, Buford, none of this makes any sense." I lean against the chair, drop my hands on my lap. "Willis showing up like he did, saying he doesn't remember anything, Marvin's murder, Mrs.

Lemmons waking up from a decades-long coma, FBI suddenly in town, Cathedral in Tennessee, Cathedral dead."

He glances up at the name of my sister. "We didn't get much of a chance to talk about that."

I put my elbows on the table, rest my chin in my hands.

"You sure you're okay finding out she's dead?"

"I don't know," I answer. "It was such a surprise after all this time."

Buford reaches for my hand. "You searched a long time for her," he replies, like he knows I feel guilty for giving up on her, like he's remembering how it was for us back then.

"Maybe I could've searched more," I say softly.

"Lorna, don't do this to yourself. She left. She made it clear she didn't want to hear from you or Draymond. She made her choice, and you couldn't save her. You were never going to be able to save her. Besides, I think I was the one who told you she'd come home, to stop searching and that things would be fine." He glances away. "And she didn't." He adds softly, "And they never were fine."

I nod and turn away and know he feels as bad as I do about what happened so long ago, then I think about what's going on right now. "Then maybe we can save Willis," I say. "Maybe I couldn't save her, but maybe we can save him."

There's a pause between us. And I think this is why I do suddenly care so much about clearing Willis's name, why I am so interested in solving this case. I'm not all that religious and not even sure I understand it but all this feels a little redemptive, like I've been given a do-over; and I feel myself making a vow that this time I won't quit just because the law says quit. I'm staying in this thing until the mystery is solved and we have the answers we need.

This time, I'm not giving up.

I turn to Buford. "You know it's funny, but I quit ruminating about her like I used to. I mean, I still think about her and Mama a lot, but I've not been obsessed like I was when she left."

He glances up.

"They were bad days," I say, not telling him anything he doesn't know. Buford was with me every step through that dark valley. "And I don't blame you for telling me to stop."

"It was hard for you," he responds, and I see the tenderness in his eyes.

"Probably the worst," I answer. "Not knowing if she was dead or alive, not getting any help from the police. All those nights I cried myself to sleep, all those searches, stupid wild-goose chases when somebody would call and say they thought they saw her in Raleigh or Asheville or Lumberton." Tears well up. I clear my throat and glance across the table at Buford. "And off we'd go."

He looks down.

"I never thanked you properly for what you did for me during that time, what you did for me and Draymond, how for years you searched as hard as we did, how you believed me, how you took care of me."

"You weren't that much older than her, Lorna, just a few years. You were practically still a kid too."

"I was at least twenty, and you were the same age as me. You were a kid, too, and you acted like a grown-up, acted like the only grown-up who cared that my sister was missing."

He doesn't respond.

"But then, finally, I believed everyone. I just got used to her being gone. I don't even remember exactly when I stopped searching for her, when I decided she was either dead or chose to be gone. It just suddenly died down, you know, that desperation, that fever of always searching."

"And I still feel bad that I left you."

"What?" I sit up in the chair. This feels new.

"When I left for the army. I still feel like I shouldn't have gone."

"Buford, you put off going for almost two years. You wanted to go into the army for as long as I've known you. It was your way out of Owensboro, out from your father's house. I still feel bad that you deferred your signing on because of me and my drama at home. First just trying to take care of Cathedral and then when she left. There was always something going on at the Pitchford trailer, and you were always there to help me."

"I didn't see it that way."

"Well, it's the only way. If I remember correctly, I was the one who made you go when you did. If I hadn't, I don't think you'd have ever joined up."

"And then I met Mel and she got pregnant and we got married—"

"And it's ancient history," I interrupt him.

"Until it's not," he replies.

I don't follow at first but then I think about the call from Lucy from Tennessee. "Until it's not," I repeat.

"So will there be a service?"

"For Cathedral?" I ask. "I don't know. I didn't ask Lucy, and I haven't had time to even think of that."

"You know, if she worked for a band that was in Memphis, if there was a big accident, there would be news. It couldn't be that hard to find out which band and where they are now, find out where they buried her, if they buried her."

I shake my head. "I'm not sure I can even search for her anymore," I tell him, thinking that sounds somewhat harsh. "I mean, dead or alive, I'm not certain I have it in me to go looking for her again. As much as I have missed her, as much as I wish we could've been a family, as much as I still miss her, I'm not sure if I want to find her now. Maybe I'm just done with that part of my life."

"Like Marvin was done with Willis?" he asks, and we both stare down at the envelope.

"I don't know about them," I answer. "But maybe I just feel like the past is the past, and it makes more sense to take action for the living than for the dead."

He nods, understanding I'm talking about Willis, but I think he sees how much hearing about Cathedral has affected me, how he knows I'll probably try to find her again.

"You want to open it?" I ask, ready to talk about something other than Cathedral and her sudden reemergence into my life, the recent news of her death, thinking that I'd rather be involved in something that I might actually fix or help or change, feeling satisfied that maybe Willis should have my attention right now.

He picks it up and shakes it, turns it over from end to end. "It's up to you."

"We may never see him again."

"I can't imagine Willis would leave now, not with his mama awake."

He has a point, but I never thought Cathedral would leave when Grandma Lawton got sick. I never thought she'd leave any time, and I was certainly wrong about that.

"Maybe you're right," I say. "But maybe there's something in there that can clear his name, and he won't have to be on the run. Maybe it's information about the stuff Marvin was into. Maybe it's news about the Lemmons cartel."

Buford rolls his eyes. "I don't know."

"Then don't open it. Leave it in the bedroom, maybe he'll come over later tonight."

"I don't think he's coming back."

"Why not?"

"I think he's spooked."

"Well, we know he goes to see his mama. We could leave it in her room."

"You said yourself she isn't completely alert and oriented. She could give it to someone else or forget where it is." He's shaking his head, still holding the envelope. "I don't think that's the best answer either."

"Then I don't know what to tell you, Buford. Maybe it's nothing. Maybe it's just a letter telling him to pay the court fees from the case.

I'm sure he's way behind on that. Or maybe it's just mail he hasn't picked up from the post office. Maybe it's a doctor's report." I interlock my fingers, place my hands on the table. "It could be nothing," I repeat myself.

"You're right," Buford replies. "Or it could be damaging evidence that somebody is trying to use as blackmail."

"On Willis? What do they think they can get from him by black-mailing him? He doesn't have two nickels to rub . . ." And then, I don't know, something comes over me, and I reach over, take the envelope, and tear it open.

"What are you ..." This was not what Buford was expecting.

We both glance down and see what falls out. There are photographs.

I start sifting through them, and then I slide the glossy papers across the table to him.

He just shakes his head.

"This is not good news for Willis," I say.

CHAPTER THIRTY-FOUR

"But who would have had access to Marvin's security cameras?" I ask, taking a long look at the pictures of Willis first entering the mansion, then leaning over the body. Photograph after photograph of damaging evidence. "And how come there's no pictures of the murder happening?" I slide them back to Buford. "Doesn't make any sense."

"Could be blackmail, like we said." He studies them closely.

"But Willis doesn't have anything," I say, repeating what I said before we knew what was in the envelope.

"Well, not now, but Marvin doesn't have any other family. Unless he had a will and left all his money to somebody else, Willis will inherit it all." He puts down the paper and shrugs. "Maybe somebody figures that to be the case, has the other photographs of the murder, and this is just a veiled threat letting us know what somebody else knows."

I close my eyes. "What about Mrs. Lemmons?"

He waits for me to explain.

"She's his mother, wouldn't she get everything?"

"Maybe," he answers. "But how much longer do you think she really has? As long as she goes before he does, Willis would still end up with it all at some point."

I nod. It makes sense. What doesn't make sense is who sent these pictures to Willis, and why they put them at my doorstep.

I sit up, a new thought racing across my mind. "Do you think it was somebody that saw us with Willis when he first showed up? You think that's why they left this with me?"

He shakes his head. "I don't know. Why not me?"

"He came to the bakery, not the barbershop."

"True."

We both glance down at the envelope and the photographs.

"What should we do with them?" I ask, remembering I stuck the EpiPen in the silverware drawer. I walk into the kitchen and retrieve it, then place it on the table next to the envelope.

"That was smart of you to hide that," he tells me. "You're becoming quite the criminal mind." He winks. "Maybe I should be afraid ..."

"Maybe you should," I respond.

"You got a fruit tattoo?" he asks.

"You want to check?"

He raises his eyebrows like he's considering it.

Then we both smile.

"Who would have been able to get these pictures?" I ask, returning to the matters at hand, wondering who visited the murder scene after Willis left. "How did they get in the mansion and why?"

"You said the guard at the gate had no record of anybody else visiting Marvin?"

"That's what Maynard said, but he said he didn't have video, so I don't know."

"Somebody found Marvin, found the security tapes, made photographs, and left?"

"Sounds about right," I say.

"But why?" Buford asks the question neither of us can answer.

"Seems like blackmail is the only thing that makes sense," I finally respond. "Maybe it was the murderer?" I add.

"Guess it could be," Buford replies. "Maybe they killed him and then were trying to find whatever evidence they thought he had." He pinches his forehead, something he does when he's thinking hard about a problem or situation that requires focus.

"So, somebody kills Marvin. Willis shows up." I wrap my arms around my waist. "And what?"

"Well, he did have a wound on his head. Maybe he caught the person, and they hit him and then stole the tapes." Buford is following along the scenario I'm presenting.

"But if Willis blacked out and then went in the house to do this …" I hold up the photograph of him kneeling next to the dead man. "Did the murderer hang around, hoping for Willis to do something incriminating?"

Buford sighs. "No, you're right, that doesn't make sense."

"Marvin is murdered. Willis shows up, for reasons we don't know or understand, gets knocked on the head, goes unconscious, finds Marvin, kneels beside him, takes the EpiPen, maybe the knife?"

Buford waits a beat. "I threw the knife in the river," he finally tells me. "I don't know if it was the murder weapon or not, I just thought I should get rid of it."

His confession surprises me. "Did anyone see you?" I have to ask.

He shakes his head. "No."

I think about what he's done, what evidence the knife might have been. It seems reckless that Buford got rid of it but, regardless of why he did it, it seems like it doesn't matter now. Unless we want to go dragging the river bottom.

"Well, anyway, back to the murder scene and these pictures."

"Willis finds Marvin, kneels beside him, takes the pen, and runs off."

Buford jumps in. "And somebody else is there, the killer maybe. He knows about the cameras and removes the tapes that recorded everything, getting the pictures of Willis at the scene."

And we both blow out long breaths together.

"I mean, it could be a setup," Buford acknowledges. "A setup to frame Willis by the real killer." He pauses. "Maybe they lured Willis there, hoping for pictures like these. But it still doesn't explain why someone killed Marvin."

"Maybe Marvin had something they wanted, or maybe there was an argument and a knife fight."

Buford puts his hand on his head. "Somebody must know it isn't Willis but wants him to know that they have something that makes it look like he did it." He pauses. "And wouldn't the murderer do that? Why would somebody else send photographs to you?"

I shake my head. I'm so confused, I'm thinking of Andy Griffith sitting with us at the table in a seersucker suit, rubbing his chin. Georgia would like this vision, I think.

"I wonder if Ferguson has any information about the security cameras, the footage, what is missing." Buford interrupts my thoughts of Matlock.

"He probably wouldn't tell us if he did."

"Yeah, especially now."

Buford purses his lips together, cocks his head to the side.

I explain. "He knows we were with Willis, that we've been acting ..." I pause, searching for the right word.

"Suspicious?" He gives it to me.

I nod. "Well, we have been avoiding the sheriff, or at least that's what it seems he thinks of us."

"Yeah, he does act like he believes we know more than we're letting on."

"Which we do," I note.

"We do," he agrees.

I tap my fingers on the table.

"I'll keep the photographs," he tells me, sliding them back into the envelope.

"And the pen?" I ask, noticing it still on the table between us.

"And the pen," he replies, taking it and sticking it into the envelope.

"You know, when I was at Marvin's house, I thought about asking Darrell who found the body," I say. "But I didn't get the chance. But maybe, if I can uncover that information ..."

Buford catches on. "That might tell us who took the tapes and who made photographs. Could at least let us know who was in the house right after the murder."

"It's a start. I bet I can ask Mavis, and she'd tell me what she knows."

Buford folds the top of the envelope and sets it down in front of him.

"Where you going to hide it?" I ask.

He shakes his head. "Somewhere that Clara can't see from her window," he answers and smiles.

I glance at my watch. "Speaking of Clara, I should probably get going. We've had a long prayer meeting tonight."

Buford grins.

"I'll walk you out," he says as I push in the chair, feeling in my pocket for my keys. "You got your phone?" he asks.

I feel that too.

"Call me," he says. "When you get home. When you're safe."

We walk to the kitchen door, and he moves aside so I can get out. He touches me lightly on the shoulder as I pass, and I turn to him and we kiss. I stick my head out cautiously, just making sure there isn't anyone out there, and then hurry to my truck. And even though we have more questions than answers and we still haven't found Willis, I feel like we've made a little progress.

CHAPTER THIRTY-FIVE

I don't know that I'm being followed until I pull into my driveway. That's when I see the dark sedan driving past and realize it's been behind me the entire way home. It's too dark to see a license plate, so I wait as it passes, jump out of the truck, and hurry into the house. When I get in, I lock the door and move to the front, pull the drapes closed on the big living room window, and stand in the corner to see if they drive by again.

It's been fifteen minutes, and I haven't seen the vehicle on the street. I decide not to tell Buford when I call since I know he has enough to worry about and now that the car didn't come past or isn't sitting outside my house, I think maybe I'm imagining things. Maybe it's just a coincidence that somebody was leaving Buford's road and happened to travel to mine. I don't know. I just realize I'm tired, the doors are locked, and I have my phone in hand. There's a baseball bat near the back door, and Buford is still restless and will answer a call from me no matter what time it is. Besides, if there is someone watching the place, following me, I doubt it's helpful if I'm murdered too. I suspect if there is someone casing the joint, my joint, it's the person who left the envelope, and if that's the case, then they'll want me alive to do whatever they plan to do next … send more photos? Ask for money? I don't know. But murdering me seems a little unlikely.

I get a glass of water, stand in front of the sink, and think about the activities of this day. I think about the early morning visit with Mrs. Lemmons, the day care children, how it felt like a hurricane touching down in the bakery, the sheriff's need to talk to Willis, the FBI agent stopping by, the dinner with Buford, and again the call from Lucy of Tennessee and the news that Cathedral is dead.

I finish my drink, wash out the cup, and begin to get ready for bed. I change my clothes, brush my teeth—all the usual activities I engage in when I am at the end of the day. Finally, I lie down.

"What were you doing with Marvin?" I ask the question out loud, as if my sister was in the bed, her head on the pillow next to me. "And why did you leave and not say goodbye?"

Cathedral and I shared a bedroom and a bed until I was in middle school. Finally, Mama bought us twin beds and even though we weren't that much farther apart than we were in a shared double, we both appreciated having our own space. We were fighting pretty steadily by then.

I reach over and pat the empty place beside me, remembering how it was when she was little and would find my hand under the covers and hold it until she fell asleep. I can almost feel her tiny fingers in my palm, the smell of her hair, washed in lemon juice, her small puffs of breath as she slept. Cathedral was many things during the waking hours—cantankerous, selfish, loud, obnoxious—but when she was asleep, she was actually loveable. I would stroke her arm, rub her head, even pull her into a spoon with me if she was upset and crying.

"Hush, little baby, don't say a word, Mama's going to buy you a mockingbird." I would sing softly in her ear as she settled down.

"Mama ain't never buying a bird," she said once, and we both giggled at the thought of our mother keeping a bird.

Mama was scared of anything flying. She'd spray wasp spray at mosquitos and gnats, even honey bees and hummingbirds. Draymond hid the can one summer when he saw her trying to get rid of a nest of house wrens that had hatched near the trailer door. My brother had always loved animals, and he hated when Mama would start trying to kill anything that flew or crawled around the place.

With everything our mother is guilty of—leaving us for days on end without providing us with anything to eat; not paying the bills, which meant the electricity and gas would be off for weeks at a time; the violent episodes when she'd just throw everything we owned out into the front yard; bringing home men we knew were no good, forcing the three of us to go stay anywhere we might be welcomed or out of trouble until they left—with all of that and more, Draymond hated her most for what she did to the birds. He never forgave her for that, and when she died, he put a little ceramic brown wren he painted in art class on her grave just to spite her.

I close my eyes and think about the three of us, how any of us survived her parenting, how it is we haven't turned out as addicts or convicts. But then again, I don't really know how Cathedral turned out. She could very well have been an addict or convict. It's been a long time since I knew my sister, a lot of time for stuff to happen. Who knows how she spent her young adulthood?

And then I think again about her and Marvin dating and wonder if they met at some place close by or if their paths crossed somewhere on the road. Or maybe they dated before she left and it was just one more thing I didn't know about her when she ran off.

I think about the stories Draymond and I heard when we tried to garner attention and sympathy for her when she left. There was the one that she had stayed with a boy from Burlington in a hotel off the interstate when she told us she was going to church camp when she was thirteen, the one that the girl told us about her saying she was sleeping with the boys' basketball coach late in the afternoons before she'd come home from school, how she seduced young boys in middle school and told the high school ones she was older than she was just to get them to buy her alcohol, take her out on dates.

We heard stories of her stealing, bullying—terrible stories that never felt completely true. Cathedral could be a real pain, but she wasn't a bad kid. She was just wanting attention and trying to find her place.

We all do that the best ways we know how. And even when the teachers would tell us she was unmanageable or a terror in the classroom, we also heard from the librarian that Cathedral read more books than anyone else and that she liked to stay and help reshelf the loaners and write letters when the books were overdue.

There were other stories, not as many of course, but other stories of how Cathedral was helpful and attentive and kind. But no one really believed those. It was the ugly ones that most everyone accepted, and it's those stories that solidified for anybody who knew Cathedral that she was not dead or kidnapped, but that she had simply left town when she got kicked out of school, that she had taken up with some boy or even some man and was living the life they all knew she would take to—a life of running around, of manipulation, of crime, of promiscuity.

"She's not in danger," the sheriff at the time told me and Draymond when we had shown up at the station for the better part of a year, demanding they keep searching for her, that they give us some update. Ferguson was standing behind him, nodding in agreement with him.

"Your sister is living exactly like your mama taught her."

And with that, we had gotten up and left, and we never asked for help from law enforcement or teachers or counselors or adults again. We understood that the police weren't ever going to help and most everyone else was more willing to spread gossip or look the other way, and we would need to figure things out for ourselves. We recognized then that any work that was done on my sister's behalf, any search, any determination and strategy and work to find her, wasn't going to come from anybody but us. And along with Buford, who promised everything was going to be okay, we searched for Cathedral by ourselves, on our own, everywhere we knew to look.

Until we didn't. Until somewhere along the line we just didn't. We picked up the lives we had put aside and we moved out of the trailer into our own adulthoods and we didn't search anymore.

And now here she is, this time really dead, having given out my contact information like she used it herself, telling strangers she dated a murdered man. It's all beyond me. It's all more than I know what to do with. I throw my arm across my forehead and try to let the thoughts and memories sail past, understanding that what I feel about Willis, what I think is needed to clear his name, is very much akin to what I felt about Cathedral when we searched alone, when we gave up on law enforcement.

Only this time I won't stop until I find the answers. This time I will not be managed or handled or patted on the head and sent away. This time I will stand by the one I care about until I have the answers, until I know everything has been done that can be done.

I let the thoughts go, and I'm just about asleep when I hear a storm settling down on us in Owensboro. There are long rumblings of thunder, cracks of lightning, wind blowing the limbs of the old oak in the back yard, the branches tapping on the window by the bed, the rain heavy, the noise on the roof so loud I can't hear myself think.

"Summer storm," my grandmother used to say when Cathedral was petrified and hiding in the closet, me and Draymond trying to act like we weren't bothered but still feeling our hearts beating wildly in our chests. "It's just a way of God clearing out the hubbub and the trash. Children are never harmed in storms," she said, trying to reassure us, none of us actually believing what she said but wanting so desperately for it to be so.

"That mean she's dead?" We heard the tiny voice behind the closed door.

"What, child?" Grandma Lawton leaned in toward the closet.

"Mama," she answered. "She ain't no child and she's out there somewhere ... I heard my teacher call her white trash."

Draymond and I glanced at each other and then quickly looked away.

"It's all going to be okay," Grandma said. Even then I could tell she knew—just like Buford had when we couldn't find Cathedral—that it wasn't true.

I steady my breathing and will myself to sleep, and just as I drop off, I think I see Willis standing outside my window.

CHAPTER THIRTY-SIX

I am awakened by the chirping of my phone. It takes me a minute to find myself since I was lost to deep sleep and ghoulish dreams. I shake away the night and the flood of memories that seem to have barred me from reality. I reach for my cell that I left charging on my nightstand.

"Hello," I say before checking the caller ID. It was almost ready to go to voicemail. I check the clock, it's just after six. I'm late and it's Friday, which means we make more biscuits for those wanting a half dozen or more for the weekend, which calls attention to the fact that I'm really late.

"You sleep okay?" It's Buford.

I sit up a bit, get my bearings, know I need to hurry.

"I did," I answer.

"That was some storm," he says.

I recall the rain and thunder, the flashes of lightning that pulled me in and out of unconsciousness. "It was," I say.

"You coming in?" he asks, and I realize he's at the bakery or the barbershop, not really sure, just know he's downtown and I'm still in bed.

"I overslept," I confess.

"You probably needed the sleep," he tells me. "I can start something for you if you want. Georgia isn't here."

I throw off the covers so that I can sit on the side of the bed. "I'm not sure what we have," I answer, trying to recall what our plans were for the weekend. I think we still have blueberries from yesterday, sausages in the freezer. Everything feels like a blur.

"I can just make some plain ones."

My mind clears, and I think about Buford standing in the kitchen at the bakery, pulling out the trays and an oven mitt, making coffee, starting the day for me.

"Thank you," I reply. "That would be nice." I scratch my head and decide not to shower. "I'll be there in about thirty minutes," I add.

"You take your time," he responds. "I'll have your breakfast ready when you get here."

This makes me smile. "Don't make them too big."

"What?"

"The biscuits, no catheads."

I hear him laugh. "I remember," he responds, since I'm always getting on him when he bakes because he won't use a biscuit cutter, which means he makes the biscuits way too big, which means I run out of inventory before day's end.

"You know the public loves my biscuits," he says.

"The public loves getting two for the price of one," I reply.

"You mean it's not the flaky, tasty way they come out?"

"Sorry to burst your bubble, but no, it's the size, not the quality."

"Dang," he says, and this makes me laugh.

"Make sure there's enough Crisco. Seems like we were running low."

I hear him humming, figure he's standing near the refrigerator. We keep the cans of shortening on the shelf above it.

"You got plenty," he notes. "But you know I prefer lard."

"I got bacon grease." I head to the bathroom.

"Yep," he replies. I hear the refrigerator door close. "Still not as good as lard."

I like pork fat too. It does make better biscuits, but Leonard Sweet, the town butcher, started charging me more for the animal product, claiming the rendering takes too much time and he needs to be reimbursed for his efforts. I went along with him for a while, but he just kept raising the price until I decided bacon grease and vegetable shortening gave the same results. No one has seemed to notice any difference except Buford, and I think he's just teasing. He claims it ain't a biscuit without a pig.

"You got cheese?"

"Block of cheddar in the vegetable drawer."

There's a whooshing sound over the phone, and I know he's opened the refrigerator again. He's humming.

"You hear from Willis?" I don't even know why I'm asking. He'd have led with that if it were so.

"No, but Clara wants us to study the book of James for our next prayer meetings."

"She call you this morning?"

"She phoned after you left, wanted to know if there was another murder, since the sheriff was visiting."

"What did you tell her?"

"That as far as I know, there hasn't been another murder in town and that we are still in the Old Testament but when we get to the gospels and the New Testament, I'll let her know."

"You know you can go to hell for lying," I say.

"Well, I 'spect there'll be a long line for us to wait on if that's the offense sending us to eternal damnation."

"Liars will be just behind the fornicators and the heretics," I reply, playing along. "And they'll be right in front of the murderers."

And then it strikes me what has happened in our city and that there is, in fact, one of them sinners still walking our streets. One of them sinners is still a threat.

Buford doesn't reply. I think he's considering the same thing.

"Okay, I need to get ready," I say, changing the subject.

"And I got to get baking. I'll see you when you get here."

I do all the morning things in my daily routine except make coffee. I usually like a cup while I'm getting ready, have a thermos to take for the drive to work, but I don't have time for such luxuries this morning. Besides, I always get plenty of coffee at the bakery.

I brush my hair, tie it back with a bandana, wash my face, brush my teeth, take a pill, drink some water, and throw on a pair of jeans and a T-shirt. I'm out the door fifteen minutes after the wake-up call from Buford but know I need some gas since the fuel gauge reads empty.

I stop at the convenience store between me and the bakery, and I'm the only one around. I step out of the car, find my credit card, place it in the reader, and start pumping.

The sun has not yet risen on the horizon, but the sky has that blue tint of morning. I'm not usually standing outside at this time of the day, and I forget how still and restful it feels at dawn. A raven flies above my head and lands on the power line across from the gas pumps. He bobs his head up and down like he's giving me the day's greeting, and I lift up my hand to say hello. He nods once more and flies off, and I wonder if there's a gathering of the black birds somewhere and what it means for more than one raven to be together.

I'll work late, I tell myself, *bake a few extra trays so that we'll have enough for lunchtime.* We close at one on Fridays, and we're open only for a few hours on Saturdays and closed on Sundays. I have to admit I'm looking forward to this weekend. These last few days have felt like an eternity, and I wonder if Buford has plans or if we'll spend our off time together.

Sometimes he visits family on the weekends in Raleigh, New Bern. He has people all across the state. But most of the time we just cook out on his grill, play a few hands of cards, go to garage sales and flea markets, and read from the stack of novels we both keep on shelves in our living rooms and on our bedroom dressers. Turns out, Buford and I don't need much entertaining, although this weekend I doubt either of us will have much in mind regarding leisure or hobbies—unless trying to solve a murder is considered entertainment.

I screw in my gas cap, and I'm getting in the car when I see Ferguson drive past, slightly above the speed limit. Darrell is close behind him in the deputy's truck, and I feel a slight uneasiness about the direction in which they are heading.

CHAPTER THIRTY-SEVEN

"Buford?"

The rear door is unlocked, and his car is in the parking lot.

"You aren't eating all the day's inventory, are you?"

There's no answer.

The lights in the kitchen are on. The mixing bowl is filled with dough. The ovens are off but the door is warm to the touch, which tells me they've been turned on and then off sometime within the hour.

I head to the dining room, which is dark. I switch on the overhead lights.

"Buford?"

Nothing.

He's probably next door, I think, but still find it odd that he would've turned off the ovens just to run an errand at the barbershop, and I didn't see any sign of life at his place when I drove up. Still, he must be somewhere close. I decide it's a little soon for worry.

I hang my keys on the hook by the door, grab an apron, turn the ovens on again, and pick up where I can tell he stopped.

I turn on the large mixer and the dough begins to move. It's gotten a little lumpy and dense, so I grab the buttermilk from the fridge and add half a cup or so for softening. When it's mixed through, I turn off the machine and empty the bowl onto the wax paper I've placed on the table and covered with flour.

I roll out the dough and cut the biscuits regular size, place them on the trays, and put them in the oven. I spin the timer for thirteen minutes and decide to walk over to his shop, just to see if Buford is there. I consider the notion that maybe he left for a bit and then got held up with a call or somebody stopping by. I wipe my hands on the apron and head out.

The door is locked, but I have my keys and I open it.

"You in here?"

There is only silence. I nose around just to make sure he isn't in the restroom or out front sweeping, but Buford is nowhere to be found. The place is quiet, and the chairs are still covered in the towels he always puts over the back when he leaves at night. It doesn't appear as if he's been in here.

When I return to my place, I see I've missed a call. It's a number I don't recognize, so I choose not to call it, deciding I'll wait to see if there's a voicemail, thinking it's just spam, some bank trying to get me to make a business loan, or some tax relief services claiming I owe the IRS. I get a couple of these a day.

When the timer rings for the biscuits to come out, I've already finished making the coffee, taken the chairs off the tables, opened the blinds, and prepared the dining room—and there's still no sign of Buford.

I finally hear the rear door open after I've taken out two trays and put in two more.

"Where you been?" I ask, feeling my pulse slow. *He's okay. He's back.*

"Am I late?"

It is not Buford.

Georgia walks in the kitchen. She's carrying a Styrofoam cup, probably a Diet Coke since that's how she likes to start her day, and a bag of groceries. "You expecting me to come in early again? Did I miss something?"

I shake my head, my relief slipping away as my heart beats faster. "I just thought you were Buford. He was here before me, and now he's disappeared."

"Hmm," she says and puts the bag down on the table. "You didn't come together?"

I glance at her. "We don't live together, Georgia."

"Well, that's up for debate," she replies. "And maybe you should anyway."

"What?"

"You're always with each other. None of us understands why you don't just go ahead and get married."

"Okay." And then I'm stopped by what she has just said. "Wait, who is 'us'?"

"Huh?" She's put down the bag and the drink and is putting on her apron.

"The 'none of us,' you just said, who is the 'us'?"

"Everybody."

"Everybody is talking about my and Buford's relationship?" And even though I know what it means to live in the fishbowl of a small town, I am so stunned by the news of Owensboro's gossip that I almost forget Buford's gone missing.

"For years," she replies.

I shake my head. I don't even know what to say now that I'm just finding this out. "Why are people talking about me and Buford?"

"Well, I expect it has to do with the fact people love to talk about anybody but themselves. Just more interesting to consider other people's troubles than work with their own."

"Is that what me and Buford are, trouble?" I ask.

She waves away the question. "Did you check next door?"

She's changed directions.

"What?" I'm still trying to find my way out of the notion that people think me and Buford would be categorized as "trouble," trying it on to see if it does in fact fit. *Are we trouble together?*

"For Buford, did you check the barbershop?"

"Yes."

"Maybe he went for a newspaper."

I hadn't thought of that. Sometimes Buford goes to the newspaper desk and picks up a copy for us to share. The thought of him walking up to Frank's office cheers me for a moment, but then I remember that I've been here almost forty minutes and it doesn't take more than five to walk down the sidewalk to the Owensboro newspaper office and walk back.

"I don't think so," I respond, and I know I appear worried.

"You sure he was here?"

"He started mixing the dough, turned on and then turned off the ovens, left the door unlocked."

"Huh. That doesn't sound like Buford."

I shake my head. It doesn't.

"No note?"

I glance away, find the spatula, and start scooping the biscuits off the tray, sliding them into the serving dish.

"His car is out there," she says, telling me something I already know.

"Yeah. And he called me when he was here starting the biscuits."

"Well then, he can't be far. I'm sure somebody just stopped by for help or needed something, and he'll be here in a second."

This is possible. Maybe Thelma needed him to bring in a box of beauty supplies or Robbie wanted help taking dead flowers out of the cooler at the florist's shop. Mavis could have needed assistance opening a door or getting rid of a mouse. There's a hundred and one reasons somebody might have asked for Buford to assist them and it's just taking longer than he thought.

But none of that seems right.

Buford is dependable and wouldn't have left in a hurry without leaving a note or giving a call. I pull my phone out of my apron and check the calls. Then I try to phone him, but it just goes to voicemail. I text him as well but no response.

"You want me to call upon the prophecies? Give the dice a toss?"

"What?"

Georgia reaches into her purse and pulls out her two dice. "You want me to go to the broom closet and pray for insight?"

"I think I'd rather you put another tray of biscuits in the oven," I say, not interested in the prophetic signs or the meanings of numbers. I take the serving dish into the dining room and walk over to the front door to turn the sign to Open.

I hear Georgia make a "*Pffft*" noise. I probably hurt her feelings.

I open the door and step outside. I look all around the town square, walk over and peek into the barbershop window. I glance in every direction. There's no Buford. There's really not anyone out and about yet.

I turn and walk into the shop, and when I do, my phone buzzes. I pull it out of my apron and swipe right.

"I'm sorry I left in a hurry," is what I hear, and before I can ask a question, he continues. "I'm at the police station."

"What are you doing there?" I ask, considering the scenario I previously imagined—a mouse and Mavis asking for help.

There's a long breath pouring across the phone line.

"I've been arrested."

CHAPTER THIRTY-EIGHT

"Arrested?" I almost drop the phone. "Lord, have mercy, Buford. For what?" I sit down at the first table, the one by the window, the one we always share in the mornings.

"Well, it seems Judge Farley gave Ferguson a search warrant for the house."

"Yours?"

"Yep. He had the decency to come by and pick me up before going in without me present."

"I don't understand." I place my hand across my heart.

Georgia walks into the dining room. She takes the dice from her apron pocket and holds them in her hands.

"They found the photos," he answers.

My stomach drops. I hear the dice bounce across the counter, and I wonder what a pair of numbers is going to tell her about Buford being in jail.

"Why did they get a search warrant?" I'm having a hard time understanding why Ferguson would have continued to think Buford was hiding something when he was over there last night, even took a look around.

"Seems there was an anonymous call to the station late last night."

I think for a second. "Clara?"

"I don't think she knew anything about the envelope; besides, I doubt she's even anonymous."

"Then who?" I can't imagine who would have given this information to the sheriff. Then I think about the sedan driving past my house last night, the conversation Buford and I had about where the photos came from, the possibility of blackmail. And I think the killer may have put a plan into action and is now pulling the strings to frame Willis.

"Maybe the person who took them," he answers, seeming to read my thoughts.

There's a pause as we both wrestle with the circumstances. I hear someone talking in the background, somebody at the station.

"What have they arrested you for?"

"Hiding evidence," he replies. "I guess the official charge is obstructing justice."

"How long can they keep you locked up?" I ask. I don't really know anything about search warrants and arrests and booking. Any information I know mostly comes from the television shows, and it seems to me like folks are always getting out not long after they've been caught. Well, the rich ones anyway. The white ones.

"I think Ferguson is under the impression that either I am aware of how to contact Willis or that Willis will find out I'm at the jailhouse and show up."

"So you're just a way for him to find Willis?"

"That's my thinking," he replies. "Darrell as much as said it when we rode to the station."

My mind is a whir.

I find myself whispering. "Did they find the pen?" I ask.

He doesn't respond.

I let out a long breath. This is not good. Ferguson has photos of Willis at the murdered man's house kneeling over a stabbed Marvin, and Buford has personal property of the dead man. I'm already imagining visiting Buford in prison, sitting across from him, talking on a phone, a glass partition between us—the kind of visits you always see in the movies. I turn to the window and place my hand on it like I'm sitting across from him.

"Can you call Junior?" he asks.

"Oh … yes, of course. I definitely will call him." I pull my hand away when I see Donna Jennings and Miss Abigail walking in the direction of the front door. I guess we'll be watching the older woman for the morning.

"And I need my meds," he tells me. "In the bathroom, I have a pillbox, but I need the bottles so they can see what I'm taking and how much."

"Blood pressure," I reply, nodding my head. There's a new pill he started when his blood pressure stayed high last summer. I try to think of what else there might be. "Vitamins?"

"Those aren't really important. Just the carvedilol," he answers.

Donna opens the door. "Well, hello, Lorna." She sees I'm on the phone and whispers to her mother. "Come on in, Mama, and let's be quiet. Miss Lorna is talking on the phone."

Miss Abigail walks in and stops at the door and stares at me like she's not sure who I am. I hold up my hand and smile. She stays at the door while Donna walks to the counter and then she steps closer to me.

"There's one more," Buford says in my ear, and I drop my hand.

"One more what?" I ask.

"Zytiga," he says.

"Zy-what?"

Miss Abigail reaches over and puts her hand on top of mine. It seems like a gesture of consolation.

"Zytiga," he repeats.

"What's that?"

Miss Abigail pats my hand now like she's hearing the conversation between me and Buford, like she knows before I do, like she understands I'm getting ready to hear something hard.

"It's new," he replies.

"And what's it for?" I know I sound nosy.

Donna and Georgia are talking over at the counter. I can't hear what they're saying because there's a dull buzz now rumbling across my thoughts.

I hear him breathe; he's stalling.

"It's for prostate cancer," he finally replies. And Miss Abigail shakes her head, takes her hand off of mine, and heads to the table across from where I'm sitting, giving me some privacy.

"What?"

"I saw Dr. Henry about three months ago," he responds, and I suddenly don't know which is worse, Buford in jail or Buford with cancer.

"What?" It seems like this is all I can say.

"I have the test every six months," he replies. "My PSA number has been going up for a couple of years. This last time it was very high. Dr. Henry ordered a biopsy ... I have cancer."

"You had a biopsy?"

"When I went to Raleigh a few weeks ago."

"When you went to Junior's birthday party?"

"It wasn't really a party," he answers.

And then, I just feel numb ... then, angry.

"You didn't tell me you were having a biopsy? You lied that you went for a party and you were in the hospital? You have cancer?"

Donna and Georgia turn in my direction. I'm talking louder than I thought.

"It's in the early stages," he tells me. "I could have taken a shot once a week, but I wanted the oral dosage."

I am shaking my head. I hear someone talking to Buford in the background, and I hear him say something in response, but he sounds muted.

"Look, I'm sorry, Lorna. I've tried a hundred times to tell you and it just never felt right. But I can't really talk about it now. I'm sorry. If you can just bring my pill bottles—not the box, has to be the bottles so they know what I'm prescribed—and call Junior. That's what I need right now. I have to go."

And before I can even form a word, ask a question, tell him I'm sorry, the call is over.

CHAPTER THIRTY-NINE

"Everything okay, Miss Lorna?" Donna is asking.

I glance over in her direction and see Georgia slipping her dice into her pocket. She turns and walks toward the kitchen, leaving me alone with Donna and Miss Abigail.

"Hunky-dory," I respond and walk around to the other side of the counter. "You get your breakfast?" I ask as I see what Georgia has placed in the serving dishes. It appears as if we have plain biscuits and sausage biscuits. I wonder if she's going to finish up the blueberries.

Donna puts out her hand and holds up a bag. "Georgia took real good care of me," she replies.

I nod. "You want coffee?"

She holds up a cup to show me she has her drink as well.

"What about your mama?" I ask, trying to regain the cheer in my voice.

"Georgia's getting her some milk," she answers just as Georgia comes from the kitchen.

"One cold milk," she says, and Donna takes the cup being handed to her.

Donna smiles. And we're all three silent for an awkward minute.

"You sure everything is okay?" Donna asks.

Georgia clears her throat.

I don't respond except with a fake smile.

"You know, with everything going on, with Marvin being killed and all this craziness, I think we'll take our breakfast and sit at the office while I make some calls," Donna says, standing there like she's hoping me or Georgia will tell her it's okay to leave her mama in the dining room.

Neither of us replies.

Donna, still smiling, manages to take her coffee and the cup of milk and the bag of biscuits and then she stands there for a few more seconds. Georgia and I don't move. I don't know if she's changing her mind about that decision or hoping I'm going to answer her question with some story she will probably repeat before she even makes it to the office.

"Let's go, Donna," Miss Abigail says from the front of the dining room, surprising us all. We all three turn in her direction. She places a loose strand of hair behind her ear and walks to the door. She seems like her old self, like the Abigail Jennings I remember from the piano bench. Tall, chin held high, shoulders squared. It's astounding how different she is.

Donna raises her eyebrows and then turns to face us again. "Well, thank you so much," she says, the big realtor grin plastered across her face. "I guess we'll be going. You all be blessed," she adds.

And she joins her mother at the door. Miss Abigail opens it and then turns to me. She opens her mouth but then doesn't say anything. She just nods, keeping the door open as Donna walks past.

When they're both gone, Georgia places the lid on the serving dish and faces me. "What kind of cancer does Buford have?"

"What?" I realize I'm asking this a lot this morning.

"Cancer," she repeats herself. "What brand?"

"You get that from your dice?" I ask, pointing to her pocket.

"I did not," she replies, and I can tell she sees the confused look on my face. "You were talking loud enough for Thelma from the beauty salon to hear you," she adds.

"Oh."

"So?" She waits.

"Prostate," I answer her, picking up the cloth at my hands and wiping the counter.

"*Pffft*," she says. "That's nothing."

"Nothing?" I hold the cloth tightly in my hand. "It's cancer. That's not nothing."

She doesn't respond.

"And he didn't tell me."

"He told you today."

"Because he had to," I say, feeling the red-hot heat of anger color my neck and face.

"He didn't have to," she answers.

I exhale sharply, deciding to tell it all. "He's in jail."

"Wait, for having cancer?"

I just stare at her. "For having some of Marvin's property at his house."

She takes out the dice and shakes them in her hand like she's going to toss them. She returns them to her pocket, keeping her hand there. "How did Ferguson find out what Buford has at his place?"

"Search warrant," I answer, wiping another part of the serving area. "Seems an anonymous caller let the sheriff know Buford was hiding something." I shake my head. "I need to go. He needs his pills, and I have to call Junior."

"Junior going to represent him?"

"I guess that makes the most sense, doesn't it?"

"What are the charges?" she asks. "What can they lock him up for?"

"I don't know." I check my phone to see what time it is. "Obstruction of justice, hiding a fugitive ..."

"He was hiding a fugitive?"

"Ferguson knows Willis stayed the night with Buford after the murder." I close my eyes and finally tell her the truth. "He was here."

"Buford?"

"No, Willis."

Georgia is studying me. "I know that. But there's no arrest warrant, so he ain't no fugitive," she responds.

"Except that he remembers Marvin was murdered."

"Does he recall it being him who did it?"

I shake my head.

"Then again, he ain't no fugitive. He's just addled."

"He is that," I note.

"So then what?" she asks.

"And then we helped him, and Buford took him to his house."

"And Ferguson found him?"

I shake my head. "No, Willis left sometime in the night, but that's how come Ferguson came over."

She shakes her head, sucks on her teeth. "Let me guess, Clara told the sheriff that she saw him."

I nod.

"That woman always got her nose in other people's business. One day somebody's going to lop it off." She picks up the knife she was using to slice the biscuits and strikes the counter with it. "Lop it right off."

I feel slightly unsettled at the knife in her hand and think how I might take it from her. "Well, anyway, what's done is done. Ferguson is holding Buford in jail, hoping Willis will get wind of it and turn himself in."

As if she understands my thoughts at the moment, Georgia puts the knife down, removes the cover of the serving dish, and takes out a biscuit with the tong. She wraps it up in foil and puts it in a bag.

"That for me?" I ask, realizing I haven't had anything to eat.

"Nope. That's for Buford. He's going to need his strength."

"For jail?"

She shakes her head. "Nope, for facing you when you drop off his pills." She clucks her tongue against the roof of her mouth. "The way you're wringing that rag makes me a little worried that it ain't going be cancer or prison that takes Buford down." She eyes my dishcloth. "It's going be you."

CHAPTER FORTY

"They can't keep him in jail for that." Junior took my call. "Well, the sheriff has him, and I only know what your dad told me. They arrested him after they found incriminating evidence at his house."

"Incriminating evidence about what?"

I pause.

"I know about Willis, if that's what this is about," he says as if he has read my mind. "I was coming up this weekend to talk to him about it all, find out more. I guess there's more?"

"Ferguson knows that Willis was at Buford's after the murder. He came over last night, had a little search for himself."

"Well, that's not legal."

"Buford invited him inside."

"Still not legal."

"Which I guess is why he got the search warrant."

"Who signed off on the search warrant?"

"Judge Farley," I respond.

"What was there?"

"Photos of Willis at the crime scene, the victim's EpiPen."

Junior doesn't reply.

"Marvin had bad allergies," I say to explain about that piece of evidence.

I am driving to Buford's to pick up what he needs. I'm also eating the biscuit Georgia wrapped up for him since I know I will need stamina for this day. I'm swerving a little since I have the phone in one hand

and breakfast in the other. I check my rearview mirror to make sure I'm not being followed by the police even though I don't know why they'd be following me. It makes not a lick of sense, but the way I feel about the law at the present moment, I'm not sure what Ferguson might do. So I'm just being careful. We don't both need to be in jail.

"Where are you going now?" he asks.

"To your dad's. I need to pick up his medicine. I guess he thinks they plan to keep him in there overnight."

"Well, that's not happening." I hear papers being riffled, and I wonder if he's packing up to come to Owensboro.

"You coming?" I decide to ask. Biscuit crumbs fall into my lap.

"Yes," he answers and blows out a breath. "Is he okay?"

I make the turn onto Buford's street. "He sounded fine," I respond. I pull off on the side of the road and put the car in park. "Well, I mean, I guess he's fine …" I sense an opening here. "Why didn't he tell me about the biopsy?"

There's not an immediate reply. I watch a car pull around me. It's a dark SUV, and I don't recognize the driver. When Junior still doesn't answer, I check the phone to make sure we haven't been disconnected.

"Lorna, that's not for me to say. You need to talk to him about that."

"I want to know what you know," I respond.

Another long breath. "I found a doctor here in Raleigh to do the procedure. I told Dad to come have it done here and stay with me for a couple of days when it was over."

"When did he tell you?"

"What?"

"About the cancer? When did you know?"

"Lorna, I don't want to be in the middle of this. You need to talk to him."

"Just tell me, Junior. I just want to know how long he's known."

"A year."

The entire biscuit falls out of my hand and onto the floorboard.

"A year?"

"Well, not that he had cancer, just that his PSA was getting higher. We talked about options, about doctors, plans of action, being in a place where he can get the best care." He pauses. "That's not Owensboro."

I start to argue but realize he's right. We aren't exactly known for our state-of-the-art medical facilities or our renowned health-care providers. Dr. Henry's clinic is in a strip mall next to the mayor's mattress store and a tanning booth. Although everyone agrees he is a lovely man, treats and cares for everybody in town, has the kindest disposition you'll ever find, can spot an infection as soon as he takes a look at you, and will send you to Winston when you need a test—Dr. Henry is still just a country doctor. He is certainly not a specialist. He's not an oncologist, and he doesn't do biopsies. Junior is right to have gotten his father to come to Raleigh. I would have probably suggested that if we had talked about it.

If he had told me. And he should have told me.

"Look, he asked me not to tell anyone. He hasn't even told Odelia or his sister. He was waiting to find the right time. Besides, the doctors are optimistic about the hormone therapy."

I don't argue with Buford's son about the choices his father has made. I understand that I have no reason to be angry. Buford and I are not married. We're not even engaged. I don't know what we are. But I do know finding out this secret stings. And I do know that I thought we were close enough that we tell the big things to each other.

I do know that.

"So, I need to make some calls before I leave," he says, pulling me back to what is most urgent—what must be priority number one—getting Buford out of jail and then clearing Willis's name. "Pick up what he asked for, take it to him, and see what you can find out," he tells me. "I'll phone Judge Farley's office and try to get a better understanding about why there was a search warrant. I'll find out about the charges and when bail is set." I hear something close and lock, like a briefcase or desk drawer. "We'll get him out as soon as possible. They can't keep him jailed for finding photos of Willis."

I think about telling him about the photographs showing up at my door and about the sedan I think was following me, but I figure Buford will fill in the details. Besides, I can't seem to get my mind off finding out about the cancer.

"I hope you're right," is all I can think to say.

"Lorna, we'll talk about all of this together, later, when he's out."

I know he's waiting for a response. I watch the cars coming and going, and I just stay where I am, parked on the side of the road. It seems like the world is just moving on all around me while I'm stuck in this place of shock and anger. And sadness. I don't know why, but there's a little sadness.

"Are you okay?"

"Yep," I answer, nodding as if he can see me, as if I'm trying to convince someone, myself. "I'll get his things and check in with Ferguson. And I'll try to see if bail is set, and I'll keep looking for Willis."

"A town that small and you don't know where Willis is?"

Somehow we didn't get to this part.

"No, he's been missing for about two days. We searched in all the usual places but nothing. I actually think that's the real reason Buford's been arrested."

"Trying to get Willis to turn himself in?"

I shrug. "I guess."

"That makes sense, but that is not legal."

"This is Owensboro, Junior. You should know that the sheriff doesn't generally do everything that's legal." I check my rearview mirror again.

"You got proof about misconduct?"

I think about the question. I think about some of the stories I hear from time to time.

"No, no proof," I answer.

"Well, doesn't matter anyway, he will play by the rules on this case," Junior replies, and I smile a little to hear the bravado, the confidence. I know Buford is so proud of his children.

"I'm glad he has you, Junior," I say.

"And I'm glad he has you," he replies.

I feel a softening inside.

"He does have you, doesn't he?" Junior asks.

And I close my eyes to consider the question. "Of course, he does," I respond quietly.

"That's good. You do what you got to do, and I'll see you in a couple of hours."

"Thanks, Junior," I reply, thinking he sounds just like his father.

"Bye now."

CHAPTER FORTY-ONE

After picking up the medicines, his toothbrush, and a few snacks from Buford's house, I get back on the road to head toward the courthouse. Just before making the turn into town, however, I decide to drive over to Evergreens just to see if Willis is there. It's not too far out of the way, and I think I have a few minutes to spare. I want to find Willis so that I might ask him if he knows anything about the security cameras at Marvin's house, or if he has any new ideas about who might be the killer. I want to know if he's thought of anything new that would add to the case.

And I suppose, to be honest with myself, I'm also hoping that Willis might see the light and go and talk to Ferguson, tell him what he knows; or if Buford's right and it's not safe to talk to the sheriff, then at least come with me to be close by when Junior arrives.

I know Buford would be upset that I would choose to tell Willis what has happened, and I worry, too, that it might cause him to turn himself in and be arrested as soon as he does, but I think Willis needs to know the state of things. He needs to prepare himself for questions, and he needs to do what he has to do to get Buford out of jail.

"It's just not right to have Buford rotting in there for something he hasn't done," I practice out loud, as if Willis is sitting next to me in the car. "I know it's scary, but you need to do the right thing. You need to go and talk to Ferguson, tell him what you know. We'll get it straightened out," I say, but I'm lacking the confidence I will need if I do tell Willis about this. "We'll find Marvin's killer," I add, trying to bolster my resolve.

Buford will not be happy with me if this is the plan I put into place. He will tell me what he has already told me: Willis is a dead duck if Ferguson finds him. There's too much circumstantial evidence for them not to arrest him. And then he'd launch into why Willis can't be in jail.

Then I recall something he told me about "precedence" with Willis and wonder if there's some story I don't know about Willis and the law. I decide that I'll still just take a quick look around at the nursing home, and then once I get to the jailhouse, I'll try a little snooping to see if there's more to the investigation, more to the information of how Marvin was found, and something more to Willis's background that somehow establishes "precedence."

"Maybe Buford's right," I say, thinking more about it. "Maybe it would kill Willis to spend a night in jail and maybe I just need to leave things with Willis well enough alone." I slow down and put on my blinker. "I need to find the killer, not make Willis turn himself into Ferguson."

I'm about to turn around in the circle parking lot at Evergreens when I suddenly spot the dark SUV parked there. I see now it was the same government vehicle that pulled around me when I was talking to Junior just a little while ago. Instead of driving off, I turn in and park a couple of spots away from it. I change my strategy, and I think that I'll talk to the agents and tell them my theories, see if I can't make a case about an alternate killer or motive, or at the very least, find out what they know.

I'd rather approach the agents in the parking lot if it's possible rather than inside the building. After all, I don't want to get the old people all bothered and concerned. I adjust my rearview mirror so I can see if they're about to make their exit from the facility and wait.

Minutes pass, and nothing happens. The only one going in the nursing home is Mr. Clyde Dawkins, to see his wife, I'm sure, and the only ones I see coming out are a couple of nursing aides who walked around the corner to smoke. I'm about to get out and go inside, strategizing how to be nonchalant but also effective. I reach down to get my phone that has fallen off the front seat, and when I sit up, there is a knock on the driver's window. It scares me so bad I scream and honk the horn. I reach for my chest, to keep my heart from jumping out.

"I'm so sorry, Lorna," I hear the muffled voice and see Pastor Goodlaw standing next to me.

I take a few deep breaths and roll down the window. It's an old truck, so I use the handle.

"I didn't mean to startle you there," he says, a warm smile on his face.

"It's okay, Reverend," I reply, my hand still across my chest like I'm making some oath but then drop it when I notice he seems to be waiting for me to say something.

"No, no, I shouldn't have come over here." He moves back a few steps. "You're on your way out."

I don't respond.

"Were you visiting Mrs. Lemmons?" he asks.

I shake my head, but then I wonder why he wants to know if I visited her. I could be there to visit anybody.

"Is that who you saw?"

He smiles again. "I did stick my head in to see her, but I have a couple of other members who live here. I come weekly."

This makes sense.

"Is she doing okay?" I ask.

"Well, I didn't really get a chance to talk to her." He turns to glance behind him, in the direction of the SUV I'm watching. "She has company."

I follow his gaze.

"I think they're from out of town," he says, turning to face me.

I just nod.

"You've seen her though, right?" he asks, leaning in. "I mean, since she's awake."

"I did," I answer, thinking I really need to be going but also feeling very curious about the FBI visiting Willis's mother, about why the preacher seems so interested in my visits to Mrs. Lemmons.

"It's a miracle," he says as he inches closer, "like we said yesterday at your shop. You really do see that, don't you?"

And I suddenly feel like the clergyman is just a wee too close for my comfort. I feel myself leaning slightly away from him, in the direction of the passenger's side.

"Yes, yes, of course," I answer. "It's a miracle." I slide a little more away from the door.

"I just think it's important that we see God at work here, see how God can step into our lives and make a difference. And if we do anything to help someone or benefit someone, it's really God's hand upon us, guiding us." He leans in closer. "Because not everyone sees it that way," he adds.

He is acting mighty peculiar. "Well, how else do they see it?" I ask, watching him closely.

He pulls away and laughs slightly. "Oh you know. People don't always recognize God's leading upon our lives."

I shake my head. "Well, most everybody I hear talking about Mrs. Lemmons and what's happened are calling it exactly what you just did—a miracle."

"Well, that is good to know. Good to know," he repeats himself. But somehow, I don't think we're talking about the same thing, and I decide to let the miracle topic go.

"You didn't see Willis when you were in there, did you?" I ask.

His face softens. It's easy to see he likes Willis. "Not today, no," he responds. And it seems like he has more to say, but the front door of the facility opens and we both turn to see who's coming out.

"Well, what do you know?" Reverend Goodlaw says, an edge of worry in his voice. "Seems like he was here after all."

Willis is walking out the door with two FBI agents.

CHAPTER FORTY-TWO

"Should I tell Ferguson?" I whisper the question to Buford.

Darrell let us have the sheriff's conference room to talk. There's a big whiteboard on one wall and lots of flyers and papers on a bulletin board on another wall. There's a coffee maker that needs cleaning and paper products on a table beneath the bulletin board. There's a refrigerator in the corner, and a microwave and toaster oven.

It's a room that feels like it's used more for eating lunch or sharing snacks than having meetings, but as I sit with Buford, I think maybe they do both. I don't imagine there's a lot of necessary strategizing for the Owensboro Sheriff's Department, probably more conversation about who's covering what weekend shifts and a fair amount of gossip about the calls they've been on, but I don't know. Maybe they have fancy meetings in here with PowerPoint presentations. Then I spot the magazine rack in the corner next to Buford and a stack of paperback books and newspapers, and I think there's probably not too many PowerPoints going on in this entire office, much less in this room.

"Did he seem distressed?"

Buford seems fine. In fact, he seems the same as he does every morning. It feels like us just sitting in a room talking. I don't know what I expected since his arrest—a black eye or broken bones. I really have to quit watching so much television.

"Well, it was weird how he leaned in the truck like he had a secret, and he seemed pretty set on knowing if I had visited Mrs. Lemmons, but I wouldn't really say 'distressed.' Do you think he had something to do with Marvin's murder?"

Buford looks confused. "What?"

"What?" I repeat.

And then I see. "Oh, wait, you're talking about Willis."

I realize what happened here. I was talking about the preacher, and he's talking about Willis. I'm still ruminating on the minister's odd behavior. Seems like I'm imagining everyone is a murder suspect, even the preacher.

"He just walked out with them and got in the SUV. I couldn't tell if he was distressed or not, but he seemed fine. It didn't appear as if he was being arrested or even detained, just walked to the car."

"Was he handcuffed?"

I think back on what I saw, and Buford must think I'm trying to decide if he's asking about Willis or the preacher.

"Willis," he clarifies.

"I know," I answer. "I'm trying to recall."

He waits, still sitting upright in his chair.

I shake my head as I remember Willis pulling himself into the vehicle; there were no cuffs on him.

"This is a real new development," Buford says.

"I know, Willis with the FBI."

Buford nods.

"Ferguson is going to be mad," I tell him, and he nods again. "Mavis said the sheriff was out trying to find Willis." I glance around. Buford glances around too.

"You talked to Mavis?" he asks.

I nod. "When I first got here, and …" I glance around again. This time he doesn't follow suit.

"And?"

"And I saw a file," I add proudly.

"On Marvin?"

"On Willis," I answer.

He waits. "Well, what did it say?"

"Well, I didn't get to look at it yet," I answer.

He nods, appears slightly disappointed.

"So I took it," I reply and lift up my blouse to show the file stuffed in my pants.

"Lorna!" he says, a bit too exaggerated if you ask me. "You need to put that back."

"I will," I tell him, like I've been caught by the teacher with the answers for a test. "As soon as I have a look."

We stop talking when we hear the door open to the conference room. It's Darrell. "Oh, I'm sorry. I forgot you were in here," he says and seems awkward that he interrupted. He stands there a minute while we wait.

"I was just going to get my drink," he tells us, like he's asking for permission.

"It's fine, Darrell," Buford responds.

Darrell turns to me. "You don't have any biscuits, do you, Lorna?"

I put my hands over my belly, hoping to cover up the file.

I shake my head. "Sorry, I haven't been back to the shop since I went to Buford's for his medicines."

Darrell's face falls. He wanted a biscuit. He just stays at the door.

"Well, come in and get your drink," Buford tells him, watching my hands.

The deputy walks over to the refrigerator and takes out a soda. He pops open the can and just stands there like we're a family in the kitchen. Buford and I don't continue our conversation.

Darrell decides to join in. "I told Buford that I don't know why Ferguson has him locked up. Don't make any sense to me. Seems wrong, in fact."

"It's okay, Darrell," Buford says. "We'll get this all straightened out soon enough."

"You got Junior coming in?"

Darrell and Junior are about the same age, but I don't know if they ever ran around together. Junior went to school while Buford was in the service. He didn't grow up here.

"He is."

Darrell nodded, took a sip. "I hope I get to see him," he says. "Been a minute."

"You and Junior friends?" I ask, trying to act all innocent and at the same time interested in Darrell and Junior.

He glances over at me and smiles. "We were; played ball together—summer league, that time he came home."

And just like that, I remember that year. Buford separated from his wife and returned to North Carolina. He brought his children with him, and they lived in his grandmother's house. It was the first time we had seen each other for years. I remember how it felt to know he was home, how it was to see him walking down the sidewalk on Main Street, how my heart seemed to open again. That was when he ended up staying, and that was when I knew I still had all of my feelings for my old childhood friend.

He bought the barbershop not long after that. Junior went to college, Odelia finished out high school and joined the service, and I never really heard what happened to their mother, Buford's ex-wife, how they ended things. I never asked a lot of questions, and Buford didn't share a whole lot about his experiences in the service, traveling across the world, getting married.

I realize now, with the knowledge of the cancer and the way he held that information from me, there's probably a lot of things I don't know. As I sit here with him, I wonder if I will ever ask, if he will ever tell.

Darrell walks over and shuts the door, comes closer to us. It's like he has something he wants to tell us without anybody else hearing.

"Ferguson ain't gonna keep you long," he tells Buford. "He knows he ain't got nothing on you."

"Then why did he arrest him in the first place?" I ask, feeling like we have the right to know.

Darrell shakes his head. "He's got it in his mind that you can get Willis here," he answers. "He's convinced that you know more than you're letting on."

We know this, of course, but don't say so.

"What exactly does Ferguson have on Willis?" I ask, deciding it would be easier to hear an answer than try to find it in the file stuck in my pants. "He got a motive? He found something else at the scene? Shouldn't he be investigating other theories than just Willis?"

Darrell stares at me like he might think I'm hiding something or asking too many questions. I start to wonder if Darrell is smarter than I think, that he's figured out I'm trying to solve the case, and maybe he even knows I took Willis's file from Mavis's desk.

Then he just laughs a little, puts the soda on the table, and pulls out a can of chewing tobacco. He sort of sways from side to side and then turns over the can of tobacco in his hand like he's studying it. "You know they're selling peppermint leaves now in chewing tobacco tins?"

Buford shakes his head.

"Who on earth would want to chew peppermint leaves?" And he takes a wad of the tobacco and sticks it between his bottom teeth and his lip. "That's the dumbest thing I ever heard. Sucking on peppermint leaves. Disgusting."

And I think, nope, Darrell is just about as smart as I figured.

CHAPTER FORTY-THREE

I leave Buford and go to the bathroom to look at the file, but it turns out nothing is in there except the old police record of Willis being arrested for the fire at Marvin's, the court findings—nothing we didn't already know. As I come out, Mavis comes in, so I hurry out and put it on her desk before she returns.

Before I take my leave, I tell Buford that I'm going to try and find out where the FBI has Willis. I tell him I almost tailed them from the nursing home, but then I got worried and wanted to see him, make sure he was okay, get him his pills in case he needed them right away.

I decide that before I go on my snoop for the SUV, for the FBI and Willis, that I would run by the shop, and make sure Georgia is handling things okay. I know how busy Fridays can be and even though I have a murder to solve, I also need to make sure there's enough biscuits on the line.

When I walk through the rear door, I hear her talking to somebody out front.

"I can bake you a dozen if you give me an hour or two," she says.

"That's not too much trouble?" comes the reply.

"Not for you," Georgia answers. Her voice sounds as soft and gooey as the biscuit dough, and I'm curious as to who it is that has her talking like this.

"You know you're my one and only," the customer responds, and I can't make out the voice. It's familiar, but I can't call up the name.

"Me *and* your wife," Georgia says, and I hear a slight giggle.

"She don't hold a candle to you."

I am almost alarmed. *Is Georgia having an affair with a married man? And ... Georgia giggles?*

Then I can't make out the rest of the conversation because Georgia seems to have walked around the counter to the front. The bells on the door jingle as it opens and closes. She is humming when she walks into the kitchen.

"Jesus, Mary, and Joseph," she yells, surprised that I am standing next to the baking table.

"'My one and only'?" is all I say, and I give her the same look of admonishment she usually gives to me.

She reddens. I don't think I've ever seen Georgia blush. She has a dish towel in her hand, and she waves it at me like she's sliding off my comment.

"How long you been here?"

"Long enough," I respond.

"*Pffft.*" She twists the towel. "You get your morning duties taken care of? Buford okay?"

"Uh-huh," I answer, not letting her off the hook. "You want to explain?"

"What? That?" And she points her chin toward the dining room. "That's nothing," she says, sounding like a girl with her hand stuck in the jar of cookies. She pushes past me to the shelves near the freezer. "I've got an order for a dozen butter biscuits."

"So I heard," I respond, waiting for more details.

She returns with flour, stares at me while I watch her. "You gonna get out of my way, or do you want to bake them?"

I step aside, and she starts pulling out bowls and ingredients from the refrigerator.

"Georgia?"

She hums a little more, starts adding the flour and the shortening, pours in the milk.

And then, I just decide to let it go. I got to figure this FBI thing out. I'll circle back to this later.

"Willis got picked up by the FBI," I tell her as I head into the dining room, just to get a look around.

"I know," she answers.

"You know?" I stop at the doorway. "How do you know?"

And I swear she reddens again. She shakes her head.

"Georgia," I turn around and move closer to her. "What do you know?"

She puts down the spoon and slaps both hands on the table in front of her. "It's Judge Farley, all right? He's been sweet on me for a while now, and I thought I could make use of it."

I know I have that look of surprise spread across my face.

"For you and Buford," she explains. "I figure I can get some information from him about what's happening over at the courthouse."

"From the judge?" I ask, unable to mask my amazement. *Georgia is a whore-spy?* I am washed in a wave of guilt but also a little intrigue.

"He knows more than anybody," she tells me. "So I just ask him."

"And he tells you?"

She smiles and then touches up the sides of her hair. "He tells me everything."

That's when I notice she's also wearing makeup. I lean in to get a closer look, and I smell perfume.

Georgia never wears perfume. She always smells like flour and dough. It's nice, like how you want home to smell. This is different. This is flirty and flowery.

"What?" she asks as I'm taking a sniff.

"Perfume?"

She closes her eyes and turns away like she's insulted. "It's an old bottle," she informs me. "I thought I'd just add a splash." And then she fans herself with the dish towel.

"Georgia, Judge Farley is a married man." I say it in a kind of shocked whisper, and even though I know I am in no place to judge others and their relationships, I swear I sound like Miss Waverly, the Sunday school teacher at the Baptist church.

She snaps her neck around. "They are separated." And this is news to me.

"Like divorced?"

She clears her throat. "Well, not exactly."

I raise my hands. "Well, then like what?"

She glances away again and mumbles.

"I can't hear you."

"She's away for the summer." She then clarifies, "She's gone to take care of her sister in Little Rock."

We stare at each other.

"That ain't a real separation," I tell her.

"That ain't none of your business," she replies. And she stares me down like she's challenging me to arm wrestling.

"You're right," I admit.

She puts down the towel and returns to her mixing. This conversation is over. For now.

"Well, what did you learn about the FBI?"

She smiles and stops stirring. She glances around like somebody might be listening, and for whatever reason, I do it too.

There's nobody here but us.

"They asked Willis to go to Marvin's house. It's not about him being a suspect or even a witness. They just think he can help them get into a safe or on his computer. Wayne isn't sure about that."

I start to ask about the first name of the judge being used—a first name I didn't even know, to tell the truth—but I just close my mouth. No need to say anything. I'll just let her finish.

"So, they went up there this morning and Wayne …" She watches me. "Judge Farley said Willis didn't know any passwords or combination numbers, so they just drove him to the creek."

I lean against the sink behind me, wondering why the judge didn't tell the sheriff where Willis is and why he signed a search warrant for Buford's house if he knew what the FBI is doing.

"Well, this is mighty good intel, Georgia," I tell her, wanting her to know I appreciate her intelligence gathering tactics and that I recognize her solid investigative skills. "The FBI's looking into whatever Marvin is keeping at his house … maybe they have a better suspect than Willis."

"There's more," she says, and I watch her puff up like a flat tire getting air. "They found something that Willis showed them. Something they didn't know about before." She stops like she's waiting for a question.

I don't ask anything.

"Marvin had a secret room," she says, bringing her hand to her chin. "Apparently, Willis knew about it when the mansion was being built."

"And?"

"And they found it."

"And what was in there?"

She rolls her eyes. "Well, that part I don't know, but Wayne is meeting with them later, and I'll find out what he knows when I take him his biscuits."

"You going to the courthouse?"

She turns that same shade of red as before and shakes her head. She starts humming again and mixing the biscuit batter, and I suddenly understand what's going on.

Georgia is going to Judge Farley's house. And it dawns on me: Georgia is not just a good investigator; Georgia is a world class whore-spy.

CHAPTER FORTY-FOUR

Junior is in town. He's at the jail getting Buford out. And while that's going on over there and Georgia is doing her spying with the judge, I'm driving over to the creek to see if Willis is home and find out what he knows.

We closed the bakery early. Traffic was slow, and we were out of fresh biscuits anyway. Georgia took a dozen for her espionage get-together, and Thelma wanted everything on the serving line for a family dinner she's hosting tomorrow for lunch. I don't usually like to leave the shop without something in the freezer for next week, but there're more important things to do than bake right now. We need to find the killer, get some answers and Buford out of jail, and clear Willis's name.

I take the road that heads out of town and meanders near the creek where Willis likes to camp. I know where it is because I've been out there with Buford on a few occasions. Sometimes he just likes to drive out there to see if Willis is okay, especially after a hard rain or the once-in-a-lifetime winter storm. I take the turn beyond the trailer park and past Second Town, head up Blankenship Road, and stop just before crossing the bridge. There's a turnoff where I can park, so I pull up, glance around, and get out.

It's muggy this afternoon, sort of like moving through Jell-O, and I pin up my hair with a few bobby pins I find in the ashtray, open a few buttons on my shirt, and start walking. I don't see anyone around. I cross the road and start down the incline near the creek bank where Willis keeps his tent. When I get to his campsite, everything is gone.

No tent, no clothes hanging in the trees, no trash, no fire ring, not a single sign that he's been here. It's all cleared out. I wonder if Ferguson has taken everything to use as another means to try and get Willis to turn himself in or if Willis has made a real disappearance.

"Willis!" I call out his name, thinking that if he's still around that maybe he moved farther down or is sitting somewhere close by. A duck flies out from the water near where I'm walking, and I'm so startled, I almost fall down the bank. A car crosses on the street where I parked, but it crosses the bridge and keeps going. My heart is pounding from the heat and the scare from the water. I watch the duck lift itself high above my head and fly to another spot on the creek.

"Willis!" I yell again, walking a little deeper into the woods.

It's cooler in the shade, and I stop to catch my breath and get my bearings. There's a dog barking up ahead, but it seems far away. The only other things I hear are the water hurdling over rocks and a light breeze in the oak trees. I see a large granite rock on the path I'm walking and I get to it and sit down, to rest, to watch the water, to breathe—to think about what to do next.

My phone buzzes, and I reach into my pocket and pull it out. It's a number I don't recognize, but, unlike the last occasion, this time I decide to answer it.

"Hello," I say, the rock suddenly a bit uncomfortable. I try to find a better way of sitting, hoisting up on one side and then the other. I land in exactly the same spot.

"Hey," comes the voice on the other end.

I pull the phone away and check the number again. I don't even recognize the area code.

"Who's this?" I ask.

"Lucy," she answers.

The girl from Tennessee. The one who met Cathedral before she died. The one who went out with Marvin. The one who knows some things.

"Hey," I say, deciding to keep her on the line long enough to see if she might have more to tell me this time, wondering if the signal is strong where I'm sitting or if I should try to get out from under the trees.

"Look, I don't have long to talk. I buy these throwaway phones, and they don't last long."

"Okay."

"I want to apologize about the way you had to find out about your sister, the way I broke the news. I know that must have been hard, and then I just hung up." She pauses. "After I read about Marvin, I guess I'm a little nervous that somebody will find me."

"I don't understand. Are you in trouble?"

"Hard to say," she sounds faraway. I hear trucks passing, highway noise.

"Has somebody threatened you?" I ask, thinking about the envelope at my door, the dark sedan driving past my house. An anonymous call to the sheriff. "Are you worried about your safety?" I'm not sure what makes me ask this. It just seems like I should.

"I think everything is fine, just wanting to be extra careful, you know."

But I don't know.

"Lucy, what's going on? What does your being careful have to do with Marvin's murder?"

"No, that's mine," she says, her mouth away from the phone. "I'm leaving soon." And I don't know if she's now talking to me or to whoever might be wanting to know about her belongings.

"There's a record," she says, her voice soft.

"Like an album? From the band in Memphis." Cathedral's band, I think.

"No, like a computer drive or maybe a folder of papers."

"Where? About what?"

"About Marvin ... what he was doing."

"And this has you on the run? Why don't you go to the police?" I ask.

"I'm not sure I can trust the police," she replies.

"So what's on the drive or in a folder? What did Marvin keep that could be dangerous?"

"Look, I'm sorry to bother you with this but you're the only one I know in Owensboro."

"Okay," I answer, realizing she must have gotten my number from Georgia at the bakery, glad that I brought my phone with me when I left the truck.

"It's damaging stuff," she says, and I hear a sound break behind me, like someone stepping on a stick. I turn to see if someone's walking near, if Willis has returned. I don't see anyone except I do notice that the duck has returned to this side of the creek. It stares at me like it knows I don't belong.

"Is this why somebody killed him?"

I keep my attention on Lucy and the call. I know this is important information, information that could be the key to unlocking everything. I feel lucky that Lucy has reached out to me. I know she was spooked when she hung up during the last call, and I'm grateful she had the nerve to call me again. I don't want to lose her this time without asking what it is she knows.

"It shines a bad light on some people. Marvin showed me a couple of years ago when I was doing some work for him. He was bragging about it, but I knew even then it wasn't something he needed to keep and certainly wasn't anything he should be showing me."

"What was it, Lucy? What was Marvin into?"

"I don't want to say this over the phone. I've been laying low, worried that the wrong person would remember that I worked for him, remember that I was in his office and in his home. I just finally thought I should tell somebody, so I called his mother at the nursing home first. I thought maybe she might know who to trust, but then some preacher took the phone from her and I hung up. I don't know what she told him."

I remember Reverend Goodlaw at Evergreens earlier, how strange he acted, and I wonder about his place in all of this.

"I can tell you where Marvin used to keep the files," she says. "I don't know about now, but I can tell you where he stashed it before. It's not where he works; it's at his house."

"In the secret room?" I ask.

"What?"

"Marvin had a room built into the mansion on the lake. I guess that's what rich people do with their secrets."

She doesn't reply, and for a second I think I've lost the connection. I pull the phone away from my ear, but it appears as if we're still connected.

"I don't know about that."

I wait.

"It's out in the field behind the house, where his brother used to stay in a camper."

I try to recall Marvin's house. I haven't ever been in the rear of the property. But I thought that when Willis left, it was because there had been a fire. I didn't expect there was anything still there. Even if there was, I can't imagine that Marvin didn't move these scary files inside. It only makes sense that he would have built the secret room for something like what she's talking about. Besides, unless he'd changed a whole lot, Marvin wouldn't keep anything outside. All those allergies ...

"There was a fire," I tell her. "That's been years ago."

"This is since the fire," she says, and I wonder if Lucy was here in Owensboro in recent times. I wonder if we may have even crossed paths and didn't know it. I try to remember if I ever saw Marvin with a woman.

"I don't know what you want me to do," I say.

I hear her breathing.

"I think somebody knows that I saw Marvin's files," she says. "I think they may be after me. I don't know who to talk to because Marvin seemed to have some relationship with somebody on the police force there," she says.

"Ferguson?" I ask. *Could he be behind all this? And is that why he won't let go of the case? Could he be trying to frame Willis because he's involved?*

"I don't know anything for sure," she tells me. "I just had a feeling that he has friends in high places."

I think about his mansion and the new zoning laws he made happen at the lake. I think what she says could have credibility. Maybe Ferguson wants this case, wants to pin it on Willis so that things that he might know about don't come to light.

"I just don't know who to trust, but if somebody can get the files and show them to the right police officers—if somebody can catch the people he's got stuff on—they'd find his killer, and then I wouldn't be nervous."

I don't respond. I check my watch and see that it's almost five p.m. I want to call Junior and make sure Buford is out of jail, and I need to leave the creek bank. The mosquitos are trying to find dinner. I swat one that has landed on my neck. I look at my hand and see I'm too late. There's a small patch of blood on my fingers.

"I'm sorry, but I gotta go. I got a ride to take me farther south. I'll call you again, when I can."

And just like that, the line goes dead and the duck flies out of the creek like someone else is approaching, splashing me in the wake.

CHAPTER FORTY-FIVE

I wait, but I don't hear anyone coming in my direction. I'm holding the phone in my hand, my arm lifted above my head, and I'm not sure what protection a cell phone would give me. I figure I would throw it hard, aim for the person's head, and try to run away. Then I think that I should probably keep the phone and throw a rock. I start searching around for something big enough to cause a little damage or at least a distraction but small enough that I can give it a good heave.

I got good arm strength, all that stirring of biscuit dough, but I haven't thrown anything with intention for a long time. I'm not sure how close somebody would have to be before I could actually make contact, and then there's the getting-away part. I may have stout and sturdy arms, but I can't run more than a few yards.

I turn in the direction where I would escape and all I see are obstacles and elements that I'm quite sure would trip me up in a minute. I glance toward the creek. The duck has returned. I still don't hear anything, so I watch the waterfowl for clues and suddenly it shakes its head, flinging water. I take it as a sign that the coast is clear.

By the time I get to the car, the sun has dropped low enough to cool things off. I pull out my phone and am just about to call Junior when I see that my battery is way down, 10 percent in fact, and I figure I may need it more later than I do now. I turn it off and throw it on the seat near the passenger's side.

I find a stack of napkins in the glove compartment, and I use them to wipe the sweat from my face and neck. I didn't bring anything to drink, and I am almost tempted to jump in the creek just to cool off, but the bank is high and I already experienced the mosquitoes and spotted the poison ivy. Plus, I need to get moving. I roll down the windows for a little natural air-conditioning. I see the duck again, this time flying above the bridge, heading toward the mouth of the river, out to Marvin's, out to Whitman's Lake. I nod in its direction, like it's now my partner, and follow its path, driving in a hurry, in hopes that the breeze from the open windows will be enough to cut into the stifling heat.

I take the turn to the Lakeview Estates and then put on the brake, remembering the guard shack and knowing I don't really have a reason to be driving in there. I stop before I get there and glance around the truck. There are no biscuits to say I'm delivering. I know some folks who live up here, but if the security guard calls anybody I name as a customer ordering biscuits, they'll surely report that I am not expected.

"Think, Lorna, think," I say to myself, tapping my forehead as if that will clear out the cobwebs and give me an idea. I'm just sitting at the intersection, the truck idling, when I see a car coming from the Estates. It's Maynard, and he waves as he pulls past. I realize it's a shift change and that maybe this is where I can find my story. I wait until he's driven around the corner, me no longer in sight, and I make my way to the entrance. I drive up slowly and see someone coming out of the gatehouse. I'm surprised to see it's Leo Landry, the one Buford told me worked security at Marvin's warehouse, the only one from Second Town employed out there. And I realize how lucky I am that he's there. Here's my chance to ask him about the warehouse.

"Miss Lorna," he says. He comes in for breakfast once in a while, usually when he's getting his hair cut at the barbershop.

"Mr. Landry, I didn't know you worked here." I feel myself relax. Maybe I don't need a story after all.

"Just started. In fact, today's my first shift alone." He glances behind me, and I follow his gaze in my rearview. I don't see anybody. "It's nicer than walking around outside that old warehouse."

I know now that he's just taking in the view. Seeing the lake every time you look up is a world away from an industrial park.

"I would imagine that's so," I reply.

"Law closed up Marvin's place, and I need work. I can't sit around and wait on them to decide when we can return to our jobs."

"Why did the law close up Marvin's place?" I ask.

"Above my pay level," he answers. Then he leans in the window. "But that place was always a little sketchy. I'm not sure anybody but Marvin knew exactly what went on there. Well, him and a few others."

This catches my attention. "What others?"

He pulls away, shakes his head. "Hard to say."

I wonder just what Mr. Landry knows, or what he suspects, was going on at the warehouses. Seems like he might know more than he's letting on.

"You ever see anything that might point to somebody having a beef with Marvin?"

He shakes his head. "Nah, nothing like that," he answers, and then pauses, like he might have more to say. "Anyway, that's all over now." He glances around the area. "Maynard told me about the night position over here, and I got hired just yesterday."

I'm hoping he might have more to say about Marvin's business, so I wait.

He holds up the clipboard he brought out with him. "And it's nothing too hard. Just need to learn who lives here and who's visiting. Residents have remotes that open the gate, so I don't have to worry much." He smiles. "And you know rich people and their love of gates." Then his face goes all worried looking. "I don't mean no offense, Miss Lorna."

I'm not sure of his reason for an apology, and I'm trying to think of another question to get him talking again about his former job, not the new one.

"You live up here?"

And then I get it, and the thought of me living in a house in the Lakeview Estates suddenly makes me laugh. "Mr. Landry, there ain't enough biscuits in the county to afford me a place up here."

And he takes in a breath and nods like he understands completely.

I clear my throat. I guess he's not saying anything more that might be helpful. So it's time for the show, time for me to get through the gate. I grasp the steering wheel with both hands.

"Speaking of, Maynard just stopped me and asked me to come up and get my serving trays from the boathouse. Guess somebody wants to decorate for an event, and my catering stuff is in the way."

He flips through a few pages on the clipboard, bites his lower lip, and I'm prepping for the fact that Leo Landry has me busted. I can only hope he doesn't want to call Maynard to confirm.

I smile, try to clear my face of worry or that twitch I get sometimes when I'm not completely truthful, like when I tell a customer we're closing in an hour just to get them out of the shop.

"Oh, right, right," he says, and I lean over to see what he's seeing since I know I'm telling a big fat lie and that the last meal I brought up here, and not to the boathouse, was on the day of the murder, and that was all in paper bags and cardboard trays. I don't even own a serving tray.

"The wedding," he announces, and I know I appear surprised. "Says right here, wedding on Sunday, and that means caterers and florists and preachers and musicians. That starts tomorrow morning, so it makes sense they're trying to get it all cleaned out today." He glances away from the clipboard and looks me square in the eye. We hold the stare for a good long minute, and then I swear he winks.

"You do know where the boathouse is, right?" He steps back, giving me a long view of him.

I nod.

He heads toward the guardhouse, pushes a button, and the gate opens.

I smile. "Thank you, Mr. Landry."

"I don't expect you'll be there very long?"

I shake my head. "Just in and out," I respond, wondering how much time I have to check out the area behind Marvin's house, wondering if Leo Landry really knows what is going on and is simply playing along because he knows I'm a friend of Buford's or he likes my biscuits, and trying to guess just how long I have before he may come searching for me.

He turns to glance behind me, and I see a car pulling up. It's a Mercedes-Benz, a sports car, so low to the ground that now that it has come up on my rear bumper I can't even see it.

Mr. Landry just waves at me, and I drive on through the gate like I belong. I watch in the rearview mirror as the sports car follows right behind me, turning off onto a side street as I make my way to Marvin's.

CHAPTER FORTY-SIX

Since Lucy wasn't all that specific about what kind of files Marvin had, I don't know what I'm searching for. And I don't think I should park in Marvin's driveway. I'm supposed to be at the boathouse, so I decide to leave my truck there and walk to Marvin's. It's still hot, but the sun is setting now and it's not too far.

I hurry, hoping not to run into anybody, hoping no one sees me walking in the Estates, clearly a place I don't belong. I hear a car coming in my direction, and I quickly jump behind a bush, just at the corner of a lot where a large house looms. There's a gate and a tall iron fence wrapped around the entire piece of property. I gawk at the place, wondering how many fences a person needs to feel safe, or superior. "Rich people," I scoff, recalling Mr. Landry's comment about their love of gates.

I peek through the fence and notice the perfect landscaping, the neat flower beds, not a weed to be found, the lawn so green and plush I almost think it might be store-bought, like the greens on a golf course, the ones that Buford says keeps the balls rolling forever. Newly planted geraniums are in the biggest pots I've ever seen, and the colors are as rich and bright as the lipstick Donna Jennings wears: pink, red, even something that looks a little purple.

I count eighteen pots as I squat behind the bush and figure that many geraniums must cost about as much as my groceries for a month's till of biscuit dough. But I must say, it does look fine, all of 'em together with another plot of rose bushes and a row of bulbs comming up, likely tulips and the green, green grass. I just want to drop down in the middle of it all, drop down and make snow angels. It's as pretty as the gardens I see photographed in the *Southern Living* magazines that show up from time to time in the barbershop, some mother leaving them there after she's waited for her son's haircut.

Buford always brings them over to the bakery even though Georgia and me have both told him that's not reading for us. She prefers the tabloids, and if I've got time to spend reading, it's usually a good mystery book, not a magazine for rich people loyal to a region.

I'm still admiring what this house owner hides behind their fence when I see a garage door open on the side of the house. I hurry across the street, make a right, and head toward Marvin's. I feel slightly hungry and check my watch. It's now after six o'clock, and I figure Buford may be searching for me, if he's out of jail and if he's not all tied up in knots answering all of Junior's questions about what's been going on in Owensboro and how his father got pulled into Willis's misadventures. I decide not hearing from me is the least of Buford's worries.

When I get to Marvin's house, I stop. There's a car in the driveway, one that I recognize although it's not the FBI mobile, the black SUV, not a sheriff's truck or van. It's the Mercedes I just saw at the entrance, the one that came in behind me. I creep across the driveway, then move from shrub to shrub, like I used to when Draymond and I played hide-and-seek or when we just played hide-from-Mama-or-Cathedral. Even as I move, I think about how we giggled at each other, as one jumped behind the bikes leaning against the trailer and the other leaped and hid behind the garbage cans.

"You know I can see you," Mama used to say, yelling at us through the screen window by the kitchen table. "Either you play with your sister and get her out of the house, or I'm locking the door and not letting either of you hoodlums in."

I would meet Draymond's eyes across our scrappy yard, him behind the dented silver trash can, me at the corner of the trailer. We'd both let out a big sigh. We'd have to take Cathedral with us to the empty lot where we played football with the other kids or out to the street where a group was always playing kick the can. We knew we had no choice; Mama had locked us out before.

I run to the next shrub and peek around to get a better view of the inside of the house. I see a person in there, but they're standing with their back in my direction, so all I can see is a suit, narrow hips, short brown wavy hair. I can't even really tell if it's a man or a woman. When I see them shift as if they're turning around to face the front, I slip down behind the bush. When I raise up just enough to peek, they're gone. I wonder who it might be, wonder if it's the murderer returned to the scene of the crime as they sometimes do on the television shows, but I decide against trying to figure out who it is and get back to my plan at hand, to find what Lucy suggested was hidden out in the field behind the house, before the daylight is gone. If it's the murderer and they're in the house, then maybe they don't know about a hiding place outside. Maybe I can find it before they find me. Maybe I can find it and then see who it is in Marvin's house.

I hurry to the side of the house and slide along the brick walls, trying to make myself small and nimble. Just as I make it to the corner, I trip over a water hose and land in an anthill. I jump up and catch myself before letting out a scream, but slithering against the walls is no longer an option. I feel like I have ants crawling all over me and I make a dash from the back of the house to a big silver maple tree in the southwest corner of the lot. I drop down, my spine poking against the trunk, and start swatting and brushing off the ants still walking up and down my legs. Luckily, they aren't fire ants or I'm afraid the person in the house would likely know there's a prowler outside, and one with their limbs burning. I can only imagine what I would look like dancing to the sting of fire ants.

I flick one last ant from my ankle and watch it sail over the roots of the tree. I take in a few breaths and lean around the trunk to see if

I can find the person through the rear windows and make sure they haven't come outside after seeing me playing my own personal game of hide-and-seek. It appears dark in the house, and I take that to mean the person is gone or still in the front, hopefully still standing in that window, not knowing of my whereabouts. I slowly get up and check out the rear of the property, the part separated from the manicured lawn around the house by a barrier of loblolly pines, a neat row planted before the house was started, a way to mark off the lots when the wealthy decided this was a good spot to build. Originally listed as two separate lots, Marvin had bought them both, telling J.H. at the bank he didn't want a family of yuppies and teenagers living in his backyard.

The area remains undeveloped, and I can make out a spot where the weeds are shorter than the others, a spot with what looks to be a worn path around it. This is likely the spot Willis used to stay in the camper Marvin bought for him, the one that burned and that Marvin claimed had been set afire by his brother. This is likely the area that Lucy said Marvin hid files.

It's green and gold in the late afternoon sun, with horse nettle and dog fennel, alligator weed and tall sneezeweed growing across the large expanse. All the bees and mosquitos make this place an allergy attack waiting to happen. I can't imagine Marvin ever stepping foot behind his house. Just to think about Marvin and his allergies and to see all that's growing up back here causes my throat to start itching and my nose to stuff up.

But I hurry to the overgrown lot anyway. I think I'm far enough from the house and the pines are tall enough and the weeds vast enough that the person in Marvin's house won't notice me. I try to steel myself against the weed onslaught. I find the narrow path I could see from the maple tree and follow it to the worn spot, a spot where I can still see the remains of an old grass fire, a scorched earth, the grass cleared.

There is no sign that a camper was ever parked there. In fact, as far as what I can see, there isn't anything: no vehicle, no tent, no outdoor chairs. It sort of reminds me of where I just was, out at the creek near Blankenship Bridge, the more recent residence of Willis Lemmons. I think of the instructions we used to be given when we took a science hike near the elementary school, out in the woods by the teacher's parking lot.

"Leave no trace," Mr. Sneadly, the fifth-grade science teacher, used to say. "Pack out what you pack in."

We used to make fun of him after those trips. Buford would pull his pants almost up to his armpits, take my glasses and put them on, puff out his lips, and put his fists on his hips, looking a lot like the teacher he mimicked. "Leap no face," he would say, sounding like the old man who had a slight lisp. "Back out what you back in," and he'd turn around and stick out his butt and walk into me.

Have mercy, we did love to make fun of our teachers. But Willis must have paid particular attention to these rules for being outside, since I haven't found a trace of him here or by the creek. Or maybe it's not Willis leaving everything untouched and empty. There's certainly been a big gap of time since he lived behind Marvin. Willis's brother could've hired somebody to tow away the camper, clear out Willis's things. I'm confident Marvin didn't do it himself, but he probably wouldn't have thought twice to pay somebody to do it for him.

I walk around the spot where the camper was more than likely parked, the burned spot of land, and realize I would only know it was here if I had seen this patch of land from the tree near the house, if I followed the path, if I knew about the camping arrangements. There's no sign that anybody ever lived, or anything was hid out, here.

Lucy, you can't be right about this being a hiding spot. And if you're not right about this, then maybe you're not right that Marvin has any secret files. I'm about to turn around, since it's now closer to seven o'clock and I am a bit worried that Leo will come searching for me or somebody will report my truck just sitting in the parking lot—clearly without the proper residential sticker on the windshield—when I see something out of the ordinary to my right.

It's a collection of rocks, a big one, like the ones we used to sunbathe on when we could walk around the whole lake. It looks like an outcrop, but I don't think it's natural to the area; it's just too different from the rest of the landscape. It's like a gathering place or resting spot. The rocks appear intentionally placed, and I think if I were taller or gazing out from an airplane, I might even see a design.

I step near it and notice that one rock is loose. I squat down to pull at it to see if I can lift it. I yank and push, able to get my fingers beneath one edge, but it doesn't budge, and I'm about to give up, when suddenly the whole rock gives way. As it topples way out in front of me, I'm almost pulled into a large hole in the earth. I lean over it and can see it's not a hole but rather a large black safe, the front of it facing up, with an electronic lock that was hidden just under the now-shoved-aside rock. It's nestled in the outcrop, almost as if the rocks were cut and placed around it to stabilize it in the earth. It's buried so deep and so well, I doubt a person could ever pull the safe out. I don't guess anybody would want it out anyway. What they would want is to get inside.

"Lucy, what do you know!"

I reach into my pocket to get my phone to take a picture or call Buford and remember that I left it in the truck and don't have it with me, when I feel a heavy blow to the back of my head. There's a flash of light, and for some reason I sneeze. The last thing I sense is sliding down rocks.

CHAPTER FORTY-SEVEN

There is a sweetness to this sleep, like the nights when it would rain lightly, the drops like somebody tap dancing across the metal roofing of our mobile home. Draymond hated the sound, said it seemed like somebody was banging on the trailer, somebody trying to get in. I found it soothing, rhythmic, like the way it would feel riding the school bus with Buford.

I breathed long and steady when it rained because I knew it was unlikely Mama would go out and bring home some new boyfriend. Her car was an old canvas-top convertible with gaping holes, and she never had any wipers that worked. Usually when it rained, she'd either stay at home and watch television with us, or if she decided she had to go, she'd call a friend. But she never brought anybody home when the ground was wet and soggy, puddles around the front steps. I never asked her why that was, but I always loved the rain.

My eyelids are so heavy, and I feel a sharp pain every time I try to move my head. I feel darkness, which I know people say can't be done, but I know it. I've hidden in it. I've tried to lose myself to it. I understand darkness, and that's what I sense around me.

I also feel a tightness around my legs, down at my ankles and also around my wrists. I think of being tied up when I was a kid, Cathedral and Draymond playing a joke on me. One of them would pin me down while the other wrapped tobacco twine from feet to hands, pretending I was a calf they were roping in the rodeo.

It was never my favorite game.

I feel divided. Part of me feels an urge to break the ties and sit up, open my eyes, and steady myself in the place where I have landed; part of me just wants to sleep, to fall deep into that rhythm of breath and plunging deeper into whatever this is.

"Lornie." I hear a voice, a tinny voice. I feel a punch in the arm, my shoulders being shaken. "Lornie G."

Nobody calls me that anymore, I think.

"Lornie, you have to wake up. Open your eyes. Lornie!"

And then I recognize the voice of the girl, the tinny voice that sounds so small, so far away. It would be easy to dismiss it, to refuse to listen. It's so small, but it's also so familiar.

"Lornie!"

And it is very persistent.

"Lornie!! Get up."

"DANG IT, CATHEDRAL. CAN'T I SLEEP LATE JUST ONE MORNING?"

And then, I don't know if it's the memory of my sister waking me on Saturday mornings to walk with her to the skate rink and wait for her while she tried to talk someone into paying for us to skate, or if I'm just not able to sleep any longer, but I decide to open my eyes. It takes a lot longer to do so than I ever thought it could.

"Whh …" I can't form the question word I'm searching for. Is it *what* or *who* or *where*? I can't think of the information I need to know, and I still can't open my eyes all the way.

I try to listen, try to see if something I can hear will help me ask the question I want to ask. I hear night sounds, the cicadas, I think, but then wonder if it's crickets or thunder. None of it makes sense. There's popping and clicking and sounds of a scurry. And I try to concentrate, try to focus, to understand … this.

The voice is gone. I think it's because I'm more awake and she'll leave me alone now, or maybe she's pestering somebody else. *Think,*

I say to myself. *Think of what it is you want to know.* And then, just like that, my eyes pop open.

"What the hey?" I finally ask and lift my head. It hurts, and then I have to turn to throw up. I lie down again. And I know I'm outside, on the hard ground, with things poking into my spine and neck. I try to raise my arms to touch my head where it hurts so bad, and I think maybe I have been dragged across the ground.

I don't hear any voices, not Cathedral's waking me up or Georgia's or Buford's. It's dark and it's quiet, but I have a distinct knowing that it won't stay this way. Whoever hit me, whoever tied me up, will surely return.

I try to think of where I am, where I was when this happened. I remember driving through the gate at the Lakeview Estates. I remember Leo Landry's face, the gate opening in front of me, the sports car behind me. I remember the giant geraniums behind the iron fence and Marvin's house and the lot behind it. Then I recall the outcrop of rocks, the one stone I loosened, the safe underneath it. And then I remember the pain on the back of my head.

I reach around as far as my hands will go and feel for anything to help me know where I am, other than just outside. I touch something hard, and as I lean over and try to move my hands, I can tell it's tall. Pieces of it fall into my hands. *Bark*, I think. *Pine bark.* And I remember the row of loblollies. I remember how they marked a separation between two lots, how the south side of Marvin's property was cleared but not landscaped, the manicured lawn ended first by a silver maple and then in a row of pine trees. This is where I have been left.

I swallow and taste the sour taste of vomit, and it makes me queasy again. I try to turn onto my side, but it's hard to turn myself over. Everything either feels tethered or heavy, but I keep trying and finally roll all the way over and land on my belly. I drop my face on the ground and feel something wet on my brow and nose. I don't know if I've landed face down in water or ... and then I decide to quit thinking about that.

"Rain," I whisper. "It's just puddles of rain."

I think I might be able to wiggle in a sort of sliding movement on my stomach, but that proves to be too difficult. I have to try and stand up. I have an idea that if I can roll over again and lift my torso, I might be able to lean against the tree trunk and use it for support and get to my feet. So I give this a try. After getting sick one more time after having rolled over, I push myself up and feel the tree behind me.

"Use your core," I hear Melanie Jones telling the exercise class Georgia and I signed up for a couple of years ago.

We were given two free passes from Melanie for her weekend classes, and we went on a Saturday evening since we worked in the morning and Georgia had church on Sunday. Georgia was wearing long polyester pants, pink ones that stretched across her hips and dropped low when she started exercising, her wide belly falling across the top.

We both did okay with the warm-up, the walking from front to back, then side to side. We even managed the little steps she handed out, going up and down, but when she passed out the yoga mats and the instructions about sit-ups, neither of us could stay with the rest of the class.

Georgia farted every time she tried to lift the top part of herself up, and then I'd get tickled and she'd elbow me in the side and fart again. Melanie wasn't happy at all at the two of us and finally asked that we either quit making a racket or leave. Georgia rolled over, farted, and then, even laughing so hard I'm sure I wet my pants, we both had enough of a core to get up and leave. We never went back, and we were never given any more free passes to an exercise class. Melanie hasn't even come in for a biscuit since then.

I'm not sure why I'm thinking about Georgia and exercise, but I'm thankful for it. I know I should be in alarm mode, that the stakes are rather high for me at the moment, but the thought of Melanie's class, the thought of my friend Georgia and the sound of her laughter, gives me momentum. In fact, the memory cheers me enough to pull myself up against the trunk of the loblolly using my legs and my apparent core I didn't know I had. Just as I get to a standing position, I see lights coming in my direction. It startles me so that I slide straight down and fall over, losing whatever gains one exercise class afforded me.

CHAPTER FORTY-EIGHT

"Lorna!"

For some reason, I start kicking—as hard as I can. I do not know what on earth I think this will do except make me sick again or really, really tired, but it's the only defense I have.

"Lorna." Someone is kneeling beside me, somebody else standing near.

"Lorna!" The kneeler says again, and I recognize this voice as friendly. It's Buford.

"What on earth?" he asks, and I start flapping about like a fish on land. I'm just trying to get up or away or out, or just stop feeling like I feel—trapped.

"Bu—" It's all I can say before I vomit again. I don't even know what I have in my stomach to keep bringing up.

He holds me by the arms so I don't fall when I'm leaning over.

He touches me behind my head. "We got to get you to a hospital," he says, and then he turns to the other person standing with him. "Call 911."

"No, no, no …" I say, shaking my head and then wincing with every movement. "No 911."

"You need medical attention, Lorna. That's a hell of a wound you got."

"I know. I know," I tell him, trying to move. But I don't really know how bad of a wound I got. I just know I need to show Buford what I found, show him before whoever did this to me comes back. We can phone the police on our way out.

"Miss Lorna, let me call the ambulance." It's Leo from the front gate. And I sense a return of my reasoning powers, since I deduce that he must've called Buford.

"No," I repeat to Leo. "I need to take you to what I found. I need you to see what's out there." I want to show them the safe, see if they can find any papers that may still be at the outcrop.

I try to get up, and my legs buckle. Buford reaches for me again, and I think he's going to let me show him the safe, but instead I hear him call to Leo, "Pull your car around here."

My left side starts to sag. It's dark now, and I can't make out much of anything except the outline of the house.

"Let's stop for a minute," Buford tells me, standing me in place, his arms still wrapped around me.

I try to steady myself, but I'm dizzy and my legs feel all wobbly. I feel like I'm underwater. I can't see or hear clearly, and it reminds me of when I was a girl before I got the glasses—how it was when Cathedral hid them from me, all that time before I got the surgery, all that time I couldn't see.

"You gonna be sick again?" he asks, since I'm swaying and probably making vomit noises, not the retching ones, but more like those sounds you make before it happens, usually for me it's a growl and a "Help me, Jesus" prayer. I don't know what noises I'm making.

"No," I say but know it's not a real reassuring answer since I do feel myself make a slight pre-vomit growl.

"Do you need to sit down?"

I try to shake my head, but it hurts, so I whisper "no." It'll be too hard to get up. I also feel like we're going in the opposite direction of where the safe is, but then again, it's dark, and I'm a jumble of thoughts and ideas and pain. Maybe we're heading to the outcrop.

Not too much time passes before I see the headlights coming around the corner and pulling up on the lawn where we've stopped. It looks like a police car, some kind of lights on top, and I start to move out of Buford's arms.

"No sheriff," I say with as much energy as I can muster since I do remember Lucy telling me that law enforcement might be involved.

"It's not," he answers. I see Leo get out and run toward us. He must be driving a car from the security office.

He takes his position on my left side, and they walk me to the rear of the car. Leo opens the door, and Buford helps me inside. I immediately fall onto the seat. I feel my legs being hoisted inward and hear the two of them saying something. Then the door closes, and both front doors open. I feel us move, and I want to tell them to drive farther back to the rear of the property to find the safe. I want to tell them about the car in the driveway, ask Leo about the Mercedes, explain how I saw someone standing in Marvin's house, about Lucy's call. But all I can do is close my eyes and drift.

When I wake up, there are bright lights everywhere and voices of people talking over me. I feel pushed and yanked and probed, and my eyes pulled open and somebody giving me instructions that I am not able to obey. I try to ask where I am and what is being done to me, but everything inside and out is heavy and thick, like Helen Johnston's molasses, and it would take too much effort to formulate a question or demand an answer. I just let myself be drawn into the drama of whatever is happening, and I try as best I am able to comply to the demands I am able to follow. Then I fall long and hard into a sleep.

"Lorna."

I hear my name being called but I don't want to answer. I think I swat away the sound.

"Lorna," they call again.

And then there is silence, and I sleep.

"Ms. Pitchford, can you hear me?" It's a different voice, one I don't recognize. I decide I won't talk to them either.

My shoulders are being shaken, not hard, but enough to make my head buzz and enough to make it clear they won't stop unless I answer.

"Ms. Pitchford, Lorna, I need you to look at me. Just open your eyes."

I try, I really do, but it's like my eyelids are shut tight, taped, or maybe even superglued, which makes me recall Buford gluing together Willis's wound. *When was that?* I find myself asking.

The shaking continues. "Ms. Pitchford, open your eyes."

And, finally, I do. A petite young woman in a white lab coat is standing over me, and there are people close, all gathered around. I try to make out who they are. Buford, I know. He smiles and nods. Georgia is there with something in her hand she keeps jiggling. I think it's Leo Landry standing next to her. He's wearing a kind of uniform. And then there's … and I move past them to see another person in a lab coat, but then I do a double take of the person standing behind everyone else, near the door. I jerk up from the bed, knocking the person standing over me into the IV pole, and I feel something come loose. I am suddenly very wet, and I go out again.

CHAPTER FORTY-NINE

When I wake up, I feel surprised. I'm not sure what else to call it, and for some reason I think of Mrs. Lemmons and wonder if this is what she first felt when she came out of her coma, or Willis when he woke up at Marvin's fountain. I try to sit up and see where I am because it dawns on me that it's possible I've been asleep for a year or maybe even ten.

"Whoa there, Missy." It's a woman's voice, like she's talking to a horse. I hear her come closer. "Last time you did that you took down the doctor and two nurses. Made a mess like you was spring cleaning in the kitchen."

Georgia.

I am confused. I have a faint memory of somebody else sitting near her, but it's just a sliver of a suggestion.

"Where am I?" I glance around. It looks like a hospital room but maybe it's Evergreens. And maybe I've been here a decade. I stare hard at my colleague. She doesn't seem any older than I last recall. She seems exactly the same age she was before I got whacked from behind.

"St. Joseph's," she answers, and I recognize the name of the county hospital.

"How long?" I ask.

"Hard to say," she replies.

This confuses me. It can't be that difficult to know how long I've been in the hospital.

"Depends on how long you can stay awake."

Then I understand why she might be confused. She thinks I'm asking how long I'll be staying.

I shake my head and immediately know this is not a movement I will be trying again anytime soon.

"Oh, you mean how long you been in here?" Clearly, she gets it, makes a kind of laugh because of the misunderstanding.

I start to nod and then think better of that action too.

"Three days," she tells me. "You and the Lord," she adds. "Speaking of, when you got hit, did you see him?"

"Who?"

"You know," she says, like I should.

"The murderer?" I ask, trying to remember if I got a clear picture of anybody when I was assaulted.

"No," she sounds frustrated. "Jesus. Did you see Jesus when you got hit?"

I decide not to answer. "I found a safe," I say softly, remembering the outcrop of rocks, the one that loosened, the dark box with a combination code on the top. *A gun safe*, I think, like the one Buford keeps at his house in his bedroom closet. He doesn't like owning a firearm, but Odelia convinced him to keep one.

"What was somebody keeping in there?"

I start to shake my head and stop myself. "I don't know."

"You go in Marvin's house? You find the secret room? Wayne said he told Ferguson about the secret room but that nobody was supposed to go in it until the FBI gave a clearance."

"Wayne?" And then I remember. Georgia's secret life. "No, it was outside," I tell her. "On the old spot where Willis used to stay in the camper." And then I wonder why I'm telling her this stuff. "Where's Buford?" I ask.

"At the jailhouse." She has been standing at the end of the bed, and she returns to her seat in a plastic chair near the window.

"What? I thought he got out." And I wonder if my memories of him helping me to Leo's car are just some sort of concussion-caused hallucination. "I saw him."

"Yes, you did," she replies. And then she just pauses like she's not going to tell me anything else.

"Georgia!" I know my voice is raised, but it suddenly seems like she might be spying on me. She is being very obtuse.

"What?" she asks, sounding alarmed.

"Is Buford in jail?" I feel around the bed and find a control panel on the side rail. I push one button and feel my feet rising. I stop and push the one under it and my head raises so that I can now see her.

"Buford?"

"Georgia," I say with more than a hint of resignation. We are eye to eye now.

"Buford's not in jail anymore. I thought you knew that. He's been here practically the entire time you've been brain frozen. You're the one who called Junior to come get him out." She stretches her legs out in front of her. "He went to see Willis."

"Wait. Willis is in jail?"

"Well, him showing up and Junior yelling about a lawsuit against the county is the reason Ferguson let Buford go. Willis turned himself in."

"For what?"

She leans up, seems to study me closely. "You talking head-crazy again?"

"What?"

"Head-crazy. You've been saying some mighty odd things, acting a little nutty. We're going to need to have a conversation about that later."

"What did Willis say?" I ask, not responding to the crazy-head question.

"That he killed Marvin."

And I can't help myself. I shake my head even though it smarts like a karate chop to the base of my skull. "He didn't kill his brother."

She glances from side to side like there may be somebody else in the room and then whispers, "Well, that's what Wayne thinks, too, and I 'spect he'll have to recuse himself from the case." She leans back in the chair. "I heard him talking to a judge friend from Greensboro. Although it's not one of the usual reasons for a mistrial—those being a hung jury or some prejudicial misconduct by the prosecutor—a judge with advocacy on the behalf of a defendant is a clear and present threat to justice."

I don't reply because I can't decide which is more puzzling, Willis confessing to a murder I'm convinced he didn't commit or Georgia talking all lawyerly.

"Willis didn't do it," I tell her.

"Well, hopefully you got some evidence for Ferguson to abrogate his confession."

"Abro-gate?" I repeat.

Georgia just smiles like she's all proud of herself calling out a new word. She nods and obviously the movement doesn't hurt her at all.

I'm about to ask her for the definition of *abrogate*, when the door to my room swings open and in walks the sheriff.

CHAPTER FIFTY

He turns to Georgia first and nods like he was expecting her. Then he steps fully inside and closes the door behind him.

She smiles. "Ferguson," she says.

He smiles at her, but not real friendly, and then he looks at me. "Lorna." He steps closer to the bed. "Heard you took quite a knock on the noggin."

"I was hit on the back of the head, yes," I answer. I am not giving too much away.

"At the scene of a crime," he says, grinning. He removes his hat, smooths down his hair, and holds the hat in his hands—looking exactly like he has been every time I've seen him recently: smug, in control.

"At Lakeview," I reply.

"At the home of Marvin Lemmons."

We lock eyes. Georgia clears her throat: to try and break the staring contest, I suppose. "You get breakfast, Sheriff?"

He glances over at her. "Actually, I had a doughnut at the station," he replies, and pops a toothpick in his mouth. I am not sure where he had it before now. "Since you've closed the shop and Eugene quit making the cinnamon rolls."

"You closed the shop?" I check the clock on the wall. It's only 10:30 a.m.

"Buford needed a break, and you can't be in here by yourself," she explains. "Everybody knows you need somebody sitting in the hospital with a patient. They might wheel you into an operating room and amputate a leg if there's not a person asking them the right questions, checking on them all the time. Well, that and they need to make an X on the leg they're taking."

Neither Ferguson nor I know how to respond to that.

Then I remember what she's talking about, and I try to think what episode she's recalling of the reality show she loves, something about botched surgeries or operations gone wrong. She tells me lots of the storylines, but I don't recall her talking about a show with an improper patient identification that led to an amputation.

She waves off the questions. "It's just for today," she says. "I did some baking before I got here. We'll open up tomorrow per usual."

Ferguson nods like he approves of the decision and the explanation. He turns his attention to me once again. "You want to tell me what happened?"

"You want to tell me why you locked up Willis?" I raise the head of my bed a little higher and feel queasy, so I drop it down again.

"Lorna Gayle, you have been too involved in this case from the very beginning. I told you to step aside, and you clearly didn't. A murder case is not a situation that is to be discussed with the public."

I close my eyes to stop the wobble.

"He confessed," Ferguson adds.

I wonder if keeping my eyes shut will get him to talk more, but then there's only silence.

I open one eye and see Georgia sitting on the edge of the chair, listening intently.

I open the other eye. "Because he wanted you to let Buford go," I reply.

"Well, Buford should've known you'd have taken care to call his lawyer and would eventually get this sorted out."

"I called his family. Besides, making a man stay in jail to try and lure somebody else in is low, even for you."

I hear a "*Pffft*" from the end of the bed. I guess I sound a bit harsh, or it's Georgia's way to cheer me on.

"Well, sometimes the ways of lawmen aren't always understandable to the general public."

"Why are you still working the case anyway?" I ask. "You told me the FBI made you turn it over. Why is it so important that you solve the case instead of letting them do their work?" And I turn his same question back on him. "Why are you so involved in this murder?"

Then I hear an "Mmm-hmm," and what sounds like a call to "Preach."

"You been talking to my deputy?" he asks.

"Darrell?"

He doesn't answer, but it's clear this is who he means.

"No, I haven't been talking to Darrell about your actions."

He quickly turns to Georgia. "You hear something from Judge Farley you shouldn't have heard?"

And just like that, she reddens. Georgia is busted.

"I don't even know what you're talking about," she answers, sounding believable to me but apparently not to Ferguson. He seems to be studying her expression.

I step in for the save. "The FBI is involved because Marvin was into something illegal. There's supposed to be a file he has that implicates people in some kind of crime, and it seems to me one of those people killed him for that file."

It's clear I have his attention.

"Go on," he says.

"So I went to Marvin's to find this file. Somebody else was there, in the house, probably searching for the evidence Marvin had on them. They saw me out back …" I stop here, take a breath, because I'm not sure I want to tell Ferguson about the safe in the rocks. "And hit me from behind."

"You get a description?"

I don't want to give him any more information, like the make of the car in the driveway when I got to the house or that Leo Landry probably saw the person driving, that this is the real suspect we should be trying to find, because even though I've told him more than I planned, I'm not that sure I trust the sheriff of Owensboro.

"No," Georgia answers for me. "And Lorna is overtired right now, so you'll need to come again at another time for her report."

He glances over at Georgia and spins his hat in his hands. He does a sort of bow, like he's excusing himself. "Thank you, Miss Georgia, for your care of your friend." He faces me. "Perhaps you will give me a call when you're up to an interview."

"I will gladly contact you, Sheriff," I say, yawning, doing my part to lend credence to Georgia's observation on my recovery status.

"It would be greatly appreciated," he responds. He starts to open the door behind him and turns back. "And just so you know, Willis posted bail. He's out of jail." He smiles when he says this. "For now."

This makes me happy, but I try not to let on that it lifts my spirits as much as it does.

"Well, I'll be expecting a call," he says and reaches for the door.

"I'll make sure she remembers," Georgia responds for me.

He opens the door and exits, leaving the door standing agape behind him.

"Well, Lucy, I guess you got some 'splaining to do." Georgia is imitating Ricky Ricardo from the *I Love Lucy* show from the sixties, and I think about the girl from Tennessee, the girl who calls herself Lucy.

I try to shrug but find that hurts as much as a nod or a shake, so I just lie back on the pillow and close my eyes.

When I awake again, Georgia is gone and the sunlight has faded. I blink a few times, trying to get a better view of the clock.

"It's well past dinner," someone says from a place in the room where I cannot see. I raise myself up from the bed but then have to drop down quickly. The nausea returns, and I reach for the remote.

"It's okay, Lorna. You rest. They just put some more medicine in your IV. Seems like you were hit pretty hard. I'll come again when you can answer a few questions."

I sense that I know the person talking, the voice, but I can't identify who it is.

"I'll be back," he says.

And then I know something is terribly off about this visitor. But before I can scream or press the button to call the nurse, I'm pretty sure the person who hit me from behind at Marvin's has left the room, and I feel myself falling into another deep sleep.

CHAPTER FIFTY-ONE

"But you don't know who it was? You didn't recognize the voice?" Buford has pulled a chair beside the bed.

I glance around and see that we're alone. It's dark outside, and I can't see the clock.

"What time is it?" I ask.

"Nine," he answers. "I've been staying the evenings. The nurse gave me a cot to sleep on."

I turn to see the narrow bed pushed against the wall next to the window. I hadn't noticed it before. Now I see there are blankets all ruffled on top, his pillow from home, and there's a suitcase at the end of it.

"You been here every night?" I face him for the answer.

He smiles. "You'd do the same for me."

He's right. He's my person.

"So can you think again of the man in here earlier?"

I close my eyes. I only recall the voice, and I remember that it was the same voice as the one who was talking to somebody while I was being restrained and dragged from the outcrop to the tree line. I didn't remember his voice until I heard it again, at my ear, while I was in this hospital bed.

"I just know he was there at Marvin's," I tell him.

Buford is thinking.

I am thirsty, and I reach for the plastic cup on the bedside table. Buford picks it up for me, holds it while I drink from the straw. When I pull away, he sets it on the table.

"But you didn't recognize the voice?"

"Not exactly," I say, remembering not to shake my head. "It's a little familiar, but I can't place it."

"Did you get a look at him?"

I think about the image in the window, the person standing with their back to me. Wavy hair, narrow hips, a suit. It feels familiar. Such a slippery thing, this confusion.

"You think of something?"

"I don't … I don't know, maybe."

"What were you doing out there?" he wants to know, and I thought we had talked about this, but then I can't keep the details in order of my time in the hospital. I can't remember who I've talked to, who asked the questions I have already answered. It's like a mishmash of memories, flashes of people in and out of the room.

"How did Willis find out about you in jail? Where was he before he came to confess?"

Buford shakes his head. "I don't know exactly. I imagine Ferguson tried to make sure everybody knew he had me arrested. He was quite intentional that Clara got a good show, bringing all the bells and whistles to the house with the search warrant. She probably broadcast it, and that's how Willis got the news."

"Yeah, but his stuff was all cleared out from the creek. He had already moved out. I thought he must've left town."

"Darrell did that."

"What? Why?"

"Ferguson made him. I heard him give the order of a 'deputy dump.' Made him clear away everything of Willis's." He blows out a breath. "Darrell told me after he had done it that he hadn't thrown it away and that if I saw Willis to tell him he had it all in the back of his pickup."

"And then Willis just showed up?"

"I don't know," Buford says, sliding his hand across his forehead, something he does when he's tired or just trying to solve a puzzle.

"Junior had already gotten Ferguson to let me out."

I close my eyes and feel myself relax.

He reaches in and squeezes my hand. I open my eyes, and his face is very close to mine.

"I was really worried," he says. I know he's not talking about Willis.

I close my eyes again and then open them. I am trying not to cry or nod or shake my head, but I don't have the words I want to say, the way I want to thank him for being there, for saving me, for staying the nights here. A tear trickles down my cheek, and he kisses it away.

"How did you find me?" I ask.

He leans away slightly, still holding my hand. "Leo called when you didn't come through the gate and leave. He was worried after a couple of hours, went looking for you, found your truck but not you."

"I was surprised he let me through in the first place." I am able to remember that entry, how I got in the Estates.

"He said you seemed to have worked very hard on your excuse to get in. He knew you never served biscuits on a tray." Buford smiles.

"I just needed a reason to get to Marvin's."

"Well, he said he didn't know what you wanted in the Estates but he knew you are good people and he didn't need to ask you too many questions. He also said it was mostly boring before you drove in and that he was actually glad to see a friendly face driving through the gate. Seems like all the residents treat the workers like they're servants or merely ornamental. He said most of them don't even acknowledge him when he lets them in or waves them through when they use their remotes. He likes it better than walking around a locked warehouse, but not much more."

When Buford finishes what he's saying, the car in the driveway comes to mind. The Mercedes pulling up close behind me so I can't get a good view from my rearview mirror, the same car parked at Marvin's, probably the same person who found me at the outcrop and knocked me out.

I'm just about to explain this, just about to tell Buford to ask Mr. Landry about the Mercedes, when the door opens and the overhead light comes on. I immediately close my eyes, the glare causing my head to ache.

CHAPTER FIFTY-TWO

"Well hello, Sunshine!"

It's the young female doctor that I think I remember punching the first night I was here. Then another thread of a memory floats across my mind. *That man was here when this first happened. Somebody sitting with Georgia ... somebody ... but if he was here, wouldn't Buford have noticed him?*

Buford pulls his hand from mine and stands up. "Doctor," he greets her, and now I know it's her.

I feel slightly embarrassed about the knockout.

"Mr. Painter, good to see you again."

She doesn't look like she's more than twenty-five years old, tiny slip of a thing. It's a wonder I didn't break her in half when I decided I needed to escape. She can't weigh more than a bucket of lard.

Buford nods and puts out his hand. She takes it with what appears to be a strong shake.

"And how you feeling tonight, Ms. Pitchford?" She walks to the other side of the bed, checks the monitors, looks at my IV.

Buford takes his seat. He seems comfortable here, as if he belongs beside me.

"I'm feeling much clearer," I tell her, watching as she continues to check things, taps a few keys on her laptop, documenting what she sees, I'm assuming. I want her to leave so I can tell Buford about the car in the driveway.

She puts down the laptop on my bedside table, takes a breath, and comes closer to me, choosing to take the risk of me lashing out. She takes out a little flashlight from her lab coat pocket, flashes it in my eyes, seems pleased with what she sees. "Follow my finger," she tells me and moves her index finger from side to side right in front of my face. "That's good," she says, and I feel overly proud, like I scored highest on a math quiz.

"How's the nausea?"

I smile. "Under control as long as I don't gesture with my head."

She smiles with me.

"Have you eaten anything?"

"No."

"Well, that's our benchmark. When you can hold down a meal, that's your ticket out of here." She pauses. "How about any chest pains, shortness of breath? Have you been out of bed yet? What's it been now, three days?" She glances over at Buford with the last question. She's asked so many, I don't know which one to answer.

I wait.

Buford nods. Three days.

"So no getting out of bed yet?"

"Not that I recall," I respond.

"Hmm," she says, typing. "Well, we might want to try that in the morning."

I like the idea. I'm getting sore staying in the bed.

"I'll tell the nurse to add an extra dosage of pain medicine with your breakfast and then maybe we can get PT to swing by and try getting you up. It's probably going to be a bit of a bob to start."

"Bit of a Bob?" I ask, wondering if that's the name of a physical therapy apparatus or some exercise for concussions.

"Oh, a wobble, you know, feel a wee bit off-center. You sustained a major concussion. CT scan shows some swelling. That's why you've been so nauseated, confused, and emotional."

"Emotional?" This is news to me.

She glances over to Buford. "She doesn't remember?"

I slowly turn to him and then back to her. "Remember what?"

Buford pats my hand. "It was nothing."

Baby Doctor looks amused. "It was a little more than nothing."

And then I remember.

"Did I beg you to stay?" I ask Buford, feeling mortified at another glimpse of a memory, a sliver of data that just flickered across my brain. "Did I cry and beg you to stay?"

"You had a head injury," he answers.

"It happens," Baby Doctor adds.

"Oh geez," I say, recalling the tears, the over-the-top weeping, everybody exiting the room except Buford. No wonder there's a cot in the room. He didn't stay because he wanted to be with me. He stayed because apparently I had a meltdown.

"It's fine," he replies, and Baby Doctor gives a laugh, a sort of sarcastic little teeny laugh.

I have decided I do not like this tiny slip of a thing anymore. Frankly, I wish I had swung a bit harder when I got upset the first time she was standing near me.

"I'm going to order you a liquid diet tonight. You like broth?"

I think about a dinner of thin soup. It does feel like about the only thing I could swallow, but I want to ask her if anybody really likes broth. I think better of it.

I start to nod. I quickly stop myself and answer with words. "Broth is fine."

"Okey dokey," she says and is out the door.

CHAPTER FIFTY-THREE

I am released from the hospital on the fifth day, when I was finally able to walk the halls without needing an arm or a walker to lean on, eat something solid, manage without the IV pain meds, and answer some questions to demonstrate I'm not chronically impaired—even though I imagine that might have always been questionable to a few people.

I take a pill by mouth to help with the headaches, but I notice a bit more clarity now that I'm off the morphine. Things are starting to come back to me, like the walk to Marvin's from the boathouse, flashes of color from flowers, the smell of pine trees, and the phone call from Lucy when I was down at the creek trying to find Willis, the phone call that led me to Marvin's in the first place. Mostly everything has started to make sense, and I don't feel nearly so confused or lost, but it's not all there, not yet. The memories are still blurry and sporadic.

There are several hours that are completely lost, and one part of the hospital stay that still doesn't quite make sense or seem altogether real. I don't know what is factual and what I have dreamed. And it's frustrating when I ask people who else might have been in the hospital room or who drives a Mercedes or what Marvin could have been up to. They all pretend I'm daffy or dazed or just soft in the head. So I quit asking and am planning to get to the bottom of things as soon as I can take three steps without leaning against a wall.

I did ask Buford and Georgia who was there with them, and neither made mention of the mystery man. They said it was just them and Leo and that Junior stopped by before heading to Raleigh, that there were a lot of doctors and nurses in and out of the room when I first got there and that the preacher was there, said a sorry prayer, according to Georgia, and later Georgia's daughter when she came to pick her up and take her home. There were also a few lawmen, she said, but didn't explain exactly. I know Ferguson and Darrell visited.

I had a few X-rays and scans and neurological tests. It's no wonder, Buford said, that I might think there was a stranger in the room. I get the feeling he doubts the man who hit me ever showed up even though I'm sure I said the man was standing near the door when I first woke up. *Or did I even say that? And is it even right?*

I'm not sure what I know to be true anymore. I have more clarity five days later, remember more and more each day, but everything still feels faraway, just beyond the grasp of my mind.

Buford's staying at my house for a while. He said he'd stay until I was strong and steady, and I told him he's likely to need more than just one suitcase then.

Willis is still charged with the murder, just out of jail. He has to wear an ankle monitor and gave Buford's address as his temporary residence. Ferguson wouldn't let him go without that, saying he was a flight risk. Georgia said Judge Farley agreed and signed the papers making him wear the monitor and check in every morning with Mavis at the sheriff's office.

I feel crazy that I don't have answers. The FBI left town. Nobody seems to know if they're still on the case, or if they just gave up and are letting Willis take the rap and Ferguson take the credit for solving the crime. They did come and talk to me about the attack at Marvin's but never seemed fully interested. I told them about files that may have important information in them, incriminating information. And I let them know about the outcrop and the safe, but they didn't seem concerned. The young one, the one who stopped by the bakery acting all high and mighty even though he was responsible for biscuits and coffee for everyone else, kept his face in his phone during the entire interview, and the female agent looked like she was going to fall asleep. She must have yawned a hundred times.

I don't think they believe my violent event had anything to do with Marvin's murder since they kept asking me if I had possibly slipped and fallen, if I maybe tripped out there and just knocked myself unconscious.

When I asked about restraints on my ankles and wrists, marks where the ropes were tied, one of them said there hadn't been any medical report of rope marks, rather there was a note in my record of a serious reaction to ant bites on my legs and arms. I tried to make them take me to the outcrop and find the safe. They refused but promised they would search exactly where I told them I had been assaulted. When they called to tell me they were leaving town and wouldn't be following up with another interview, the agent also reported that they had done a thorough search where I told them and didn't see anything like I claimed to see. There was an outcrop of stones behind Marvin's house, behind the line of trees, but there was no secret rock to turn over and no safe hidden under any stones.

I admit I feel a little crazy, and if I could figure out how to get out of the house and into my car, I would drive to Lakeview myself and find out what happened to the safe. I would drive through those gates and straight to Marvin's, walk all the way past the loblolly pines and find the answers, but I can't even make it down the hall without taking a rest and I'm pretty sure Georgia hid my car keys. As much as I'd like to understand what has happened and what is going on, I am forced to lay low and rest.

So, for now, I am propped up on the sofa, eating a Popsicle—an orange one with vanilla inside—when I hear a light tapping on my front door. I don't really feel like getting up so I just yell from the living room, "It's open," which I know to be true because I told Buford not to lock it so that Georgia could get in when she was stopping by with dinner.

The tapping continues.

"Come on in," I yell a little louder. The knocking stops, and the door opens. I know it's not Georgia because she'd already be talking if it was.

"Who's there?" I ask, trying to swing around to face the hallway and see who is in the house.

No answer. I feel a little nervous.

"I got my phone," I say. "I'm punching in 911," I add.

There's a shadow first and then I hear, "Miss Lorna."

I put my phone aside since I know who it is.

"Willis," I call out.

He turns the corner to come into the room. He's thinner than the last time I saw him—the night we had dinner over at Buford's. His hair needs a cut, and I wonder why Buford hasn't insisted Willis sit long enough for him to give him proper care. As he steps closer, I can see he also is growing a beard. Maybe he's just letting himself go since he thinks he's going to prison anyway. Surely, Junior will make him clean up before the trial.

"How you doing, Willis?" I motion with my chin over to the recliner next to the sofa. "Come on in and sit down." I realize I still need to try and keep my head still.

"I'm ... I'm okay," he says, sounding rather tentative. He walks over to the chair and then stands in front of it like he's waiting for permission.

I will not nod. "Have a seat. I was hoping I would get to talk to you."

He does, and he fidgets and glances around all nervous—like he does when he stays too long in the bakery or the barbershop. I imagine this will be a short visit, so I will try to make the most of it, see what Willis knows about things at Marvin's.

"How about you?" he asks. "How are you?"

"I'm much better," I tell him.

There's silence, and I hear a car pass in front of the house but I don't look for it out the window. It does make me wonder, though how he got here, but then I see the sweat rolling down his neck, the stains under his arms, and I know he's walked.

"This happen to you at my brother's house?"

I don't know how much Buford has told him. "It did," I answer, and then decide to explain. "I was over at your place at the creek, and somebody called to tell me Marvin had some files, that he hid them out where your camper used to be."

He studies me.

"You know anything about that?" I ask.

He shakes his head. He rubs the palm of his left hand with the thumb on his right. It's a nervous habit.

"You know, Willis, I never asked you, but what happened in the fire? The one that burned your camper and caused Marvin to ask for a restraining order?"

He bites his lower lip, turns away, and I don't know if it's something hard to talk about or if he doesn't remember, but I hope he will have a few answers.

"It just started out of nowhere," he tells me. "Marvin accused me of starting it with a cigarette, but I quit smoking months before then."

"So, what, you just noticed the flames and ran out?"

"I did, because I saw somebody around outside in the dark. I tried to tell Marvin that somebody was nosing around the place, but he wouldn't listen. And you know, he wouldn't really come out of the house." He turns to me.

"Allergies," I say, and he nods.

"You tell Ferguson and the fire chief that?"

"I did," he answers. "But they just took Marvin's side, didn't believe me. Far as I know, they never even checked it out."

"I know how that feels," I reply, thinking about my history with law enforcement, both when I tried to get them to keep searching for Cathedral and more recently, when the FBI acted like I'm crazy.

"You think it might be the same person?"

I'm not sure I follow him.

He explains. "The same person who burned the camper was the same person that knocked you out?"

"Well, it could be, I guess, but there's been a lot of time between the two incidences," I answer.

He nods, like he hadn't thought about that.

There's another bit of silence.

"How's your mama?" I ask, not having heard any updates about Mrs. Lemmons.

"She's real good," Willis responds. "She's moving out of Evergreens," he adds, and this comes as a surprise. "She's moving over to Marvin's."

And this is even a bigger surprise. Before I can ask about this decision, he says something that is a real startle.

"Marvin's lawyer, the one from Charlotte, he came by a few days ago—maybe right after you got knocked out—and visited her at Evergreens. I saw him there, and when I asked what he was doing in town, he said he came to tell her that she would be the main beneficiary of the estate."

There is something in hearing about this visit that starts to make me feel very queasy.

CHAPTER FIFTY-FOUR

"He was there!" I have paced so much waiting for Buford to come home, I'm pretty sure I've worn a rut across the living room carpet.

I look down at where I've been walking, and it dawns on me that I should probably get some new floor coverings anyway. I'm thinking this used to be shag, all brown and messy, but now it just looks like regular office carpet, it's so old. I realize I should pay more attention to my living quarters.

"Who was there?" he asks, not even all the way in yet. His arms are filled with paper bags from the Piggly Wiggly. Buford doesn't care for plastic.

He sets them on the dining room table.

"The lawyer!" I say, walking over, pulling out a chair, and taking a seat. "It was the lawyer!" I add, for a real dramatic effect. I've actually been rehearsing this conversation.

"Junior?" He leans down and gives me a little peck on the top of my head, careful not to touch the goose egg on the back.

"No," I say. "Not Junior."

He waits.

"Marvin's lawyer!"

He takes off his hat and sits in the chair beside me at the table. "The one we saw in the courthouse with Willis when he got fined and had the restraining order placed on him? The one who stopped by the shop the day Marvin was murdered?"

"The very one," I say, and I know I sound all breathy. I have been waiting over an hour for him to finish work and get home, waiting over an hour to tell him the news. I'm leaning toward him now.

"Where was he? Where is the 'there' you're talking about?" He slides the bags toward the end of the table so we can see each other more easily.

"Well …" and I realize this might be harder to explain. "Willis said he was at Evergreens, but I now believe that he was the one that came to my hospital bed—the one who said he was coming back, the one who hit me on the head." I thump my fist on the table before finishing. "The one who murdered Marvin." I relax in my chair, trying not to bounce into an exclamation point.

Buford just nods. "Willis tell you anything else?"

I'm a little surprised he isn't as excited as me, that he doesn't jump up and make a call to Ferguson, but I answer his question, thinking maybe he wants to hear more of the conversation I had earlier.

"He just said he told Mrs. Lemmons that she was the beneficiary of Marvin's estate, and that she's decided to move over there."

"And she's going to do that? She's well enough to leave the nursing home?"

I don't know this part. "He said she was."

"Hmm," is what he says next.

"Hmm?" I ask.

He reaches over for my arm, and I do not like how this is turning out. It is not at all as I imagined. I thought he would be proud of me for solving the crime.

"Lorna, why would Marvin's lawyer kill his best client?"

I pull my arm away. I get a terrible taste in my mouth, and it is not the orange Popsicle. "Because whatever Marvin had on him became a threat."

"And whatever Marvin had on him was what the FBI was searching for?"

"Yes, that's right," and I feel a wee bit better that he's finally coming to the same conclusions as me. And then he shrugs.

"What's that?" I ask.

"What?"

"That shrug? What is that?"

He holds out his hands in front of him like he's giving up and then shakes his head. "I just don't know, Lorna," he explains. "The FBI dropped their case. They didn't find anything. They're letting Ferguson prosecute Willis." He reaches over and takes both my hands in his. "There wasn't anything behind Marvin's house, just a gathering of quarry rocks, no hidden safe, no files. They didn't find anything in his secret room pointing to a crime either."

I pull away again. I want no part of his sympathy or empathy or whatever you call this.

"So, what? You think I made up what I saw? You think I fell and knocked myself out? You think it was ants marching around my ankles and wrists and I wasn't tied up?"

He doesn't respond, so I ask one more question. "You think Willis killed his brother out of revenge or after a fight—"

He starts shaking his head before I finish. "No, I know you were hit from behind. You didn't fall, you were hit. And you did have some pretty bad ant bites, but that doesn't mean you weren't tied up. I can see that ..." He looks me in the eye. "But I don't actually know what I think about Willis anymore."

"What?" I lean up from my chair, and the quick movement causes the sharp pain I've been trying to avoid all day. "You were the one convinced he didn't do this. You've been his biggest ally!"

He nods. "I know, I know, but ..."

"But what?"

"But some things came to light while you were in the hospital."

"What kind of things?"

"Ferguson's evidence."

"What's he got on Willis beside the circumstantial stuff?"

"Preacher Goodlaw," he answers, and I don't know what he means.

"What about Preacher Goodlaw?"

"He was the one who sent you the photos. He was walking early that morning Marvin was killed, up there at the Estates. He was staying with somebody, a parishioner, I think. Her husband had died and she asked him to stay until her family arrived, so he did. He was walking that morning, showed up at the murder scene after it happened."

I don't respond, but I remember Maynard saying the preacher was there at that time.

"Anyway, when he got to Marvin's, he saw the door was open and went in. Then he saw Willis running away. He called 911. He made the report."

"But the photos?" I ask.

"He saw the video on the table, played it while he waited for Ferge."

"Who left the video on the table?"

Buford doesn't answer.

"And so, he just kept it?"

Buford nods.

"And he made photographs from the video? And sent them to me? That doesn't make any sense."

"He claims that after he saw Willis running away and found the tape, he didn't want to show it to the sheriff, that he figured it would incriminate Willis and he didn't want to get him in trouble. He said he took photographs of the tape so that you would know the predicament Willis is in."

I start to feel all wobbly again, and I recall the weird encounter at the nursing home. Preacher Goodlaw was trying to tell me what he had done. He hid the tape because he believed it was the right thing to do.

"He gave them to you because he thought you would know how to help Willis get out of town."

"The preacher thinks Willis killed Marvin?"

"Well, let's face it, the photographs are pretty incriminating. I think the tape is even worse. It shows the murder weapon."

I think about what that would be and remember what Buford found in the guest room where Willis was staying.

"The knife? The one you got rid of?"

He nods.

"But how did Ferguson ever find out any of this?"

"Preacher started feeling guilty. Eventually took the sheriff the tape, confessed to what he had done."

I stop him. "I don't care what evidence there is. It's not Willis," I say. "That lawyer was the one who was at Marvin's house when I was over there. He could have left the video on the table because he wants to frame Willis. Don't you see what he's done? And then, he went back to the scene of the crime. That's classic *Law & Order* stuff." I cannot believe Buford doesn't recognize what is going on.

"He has a key, Lorna. He has permission to be over there. You're right about that. He was probably there that night."

"And he was at my hospital bed. He threatened me."

"Even if that were so …"

And those words sting.

He continues although it is obvious he knows what he's saying is hurtful. "Even if he came to the hospital room, what you said he told you, that he'd be back when you could answer his questions, that's not really a threat. Maybe he just wanted some clarity about what you were doing at Marvin's house, what you told everyone you found. Maybe he wanted to find out who might have done this to you to help you."

Even though it's terribly painful to do so, I shake my head violently. "How can you not trust me?" I ask. "Why don't you believe me?"

Buford is silenced.

"I know what I'm talking about. I know it's the lawyer. I know Willis is innocent. And I thought you knew that about Willis too. I can't believe you'd give up this easily."

He turns away. "Junior is going to do everything he can to help him."

"You need to leave," I tell him. Before he can respond, the back door swings open.

"Dinner!"

And Georgia has arrived.

CHAPTER FIFTY-FIVE

I make Buford go home. I tell him I am fine and don't need a babysitter. I get a call from Draymond, and he says he can come over after work if I need him and, besides, I am seeing only red—and worried about what else I might say—so I tell Buford to leave.

Georgia sees right away the rift between us and pulls out the dice from her front pants pockets. I tell her I don't need no future reading at the moment. We need to stay right where we are for now, right in the present in which Buford so much as admitted that he has doubts about what I remember, doubts about what I know to be true. And then, after he leaves, when she wants to talk to me about it, get the skinny about what happened between us, I make her leave too. I thank her for the chicken-and-biscuit casserole, but I make her go. I even call Draymond and tell him not to come.

I don't want to see anyone. I want to figure this out. I want to catch that lawyer myself. I want to show everyone what he's done, what he's doing.

But right now, after all that drama, I can't make my legs take me anywhere. Even if they could get up and move me back to Marvin's, I don't know where my keys are, and I'm pretty sure Mr. Landry wouldn't let me through the gate without calling Buford. So, as much as I don't want to, as much as I want to solve this crime right now, I've decided I'll get a little rest and clear my head a bit and then decide on my next move.

I make it to my bed and lie down, but I can't make myself sleep because I am a bundle of hard nerves. I'm angry at the FBI for not following up on what I know are solid leads. I'm fed up with the sheriff for just deciding Willis is guilty before even launching an investigation. I'm mad at the preacher for turning over the tape, Willis for confessing to the murder, and I can't even believe Buford's betrayal. I'm also thoroughly disgusted with myself that I can't remember what happened the night of the attack—a bundle of hard nerves, for sure.

And then, as I sit up a bit, lean against the stack of pillows I have pushed behind my head, something else dawns on me, something even harder than anger and confusion and feeling betrayed and disbelieved. I suddenly realize I am alone. Utterly and completely alone. And as long as I have tried to push that fear away, store it out of sight, squash it way down deep so it wouldn't suddenly jump out and smother me, I see now that things have turned out exactly as I have imagined they would be my whole life. I am alone.

First, Mama left. Then Grandma died. Cathedral ran off. Buford joined the military. Authorities just sent me home like I was a child when I came to them for help. And, finally, after years of hearing nothing, Draymond and I just sold the trailer and went our separate ways, trying to find our own paths out of the sadness.

It's what I have always anticipated for my life and maybe even what I made happen by keeping myself all bottled up and closed down. It's clear that I've lived as careful with my emotions as Marvin lived protected from bugs and blooms. I have wrapped my heart in as many layers as he wrapped up his arms and legs, all just trying to keep out the sting of being left alone.

I see it now. I see exactly what has happened. Nobody believing me and Draymond when Cathedral was missing, the dismissive way the FBI treated me, Buford refusing to let me in when he found out he had cancer, his disbelief that I know what I'm talking about even now, that look of pity on his face. It's clear to me that that I am forever on the outside trying to see in. I have always been and will always be on my own. Alone. And I swear coming to this revelation is a bigger blow than a rock to my head.

I close my eyes and try to breathe.

My phone dings. It's a text message.

You okay?

It's Buford.

I wait before I reply, punishing him, I suppose, sorting through what words I could say to conceal this ache, this deep, deep pain.

I am, I type.

Ready for bed?

Yup.

I watch the three dots in the bubble as he types.

Draymond there?

I ponder the answer. I think that if I say no, that I told my brother not to come, that Buford will insist on driving over. He was in the room, after all, when Baby Doctor said I shouldn't stay alone my first night out of the hospital. He'd come over before I can tell him not to.

???

I'm fine, I write.

Three dots more and then they disappear. I'm about to put the phone on the table when I hear the ding.

I'm sorry.

I don't respond.

I silence it so I won't have to hear any more dinging or have to talk to Georgia, since I know she'll call later. I tell myself I'll make sure to turn the ringer on again before I go to sleep. And I'll reassure them both that I am fine in the morning.

I slowly slide my legs over the edge of the bed, take a minute, and stand. I feel a heaviness in my legs and a throbbing in my head, but in spite of the way things are, at least the nausea seems to be gone. I walk to the bathroom, splash my face with water, brush my teeth, and then take a pain pill to help with the headache and maybe let me sleep.

It's hard and slow going, but I change into my nightgown and robe, drop my dirty clothes beside the bed, and move real slow into the living room and then the kitchen to turn off the lights. I draw the curtains together on the front window, taking one last peek outside. I see the streetlight burning, notice the full moon that is high in the night sky, and turn back for the bedroom.

When I walk in and look up, someone is standing by the dresser, facing the bed. He's dressed all in black. At first, I can't see who it is, think he's just a figment of my imagination— but now I recognize him. I am not imagining him. He's in my room, and I know who it is. That wavy hair, those narrow hips.

"Sorry to break in like this," he says.

Maybe it's the pill or maybe it's the newfound knowledge of my isolation, but I'm strangely calm. "You said you'd be back," I reply, slowly sitting on the bed. I glance over at the bedside table and eye my phone, but it's too far to reach for it before he could stop me.

"I did. I most certainly did." He tilts his head like he's thinking about this. "I wasn't sure you'd recall that little interaction." He grins. "You were pretty out of it."

"Thanks to you," I say.

He nods, raises his hands in front of him, like he's surrendering, even though I'm pretty sure that's not what he's doing here.

"I am sorry about that," he replies. "You did surprise me, being out there like you were. I think I'd have a pretty good case of trespassing if it ever came to that. Turns out, I saw you when I was looking out the kitchen window, trying to figure out where Marvin hid the papers. So I must thank you for that, because I had no idea he'd keep anything out there."

"The safe in the outcrop," I reply, wishing now I hadn't told Draymond to stay away.

"Silly Marvin. He has a secret vault in the house. And we all know how he hates to be outside—what on earth persuaded him to put a safe in a pile of rocks?" He's shaking his head, and he sees me turning to my phone again.

He walks over and places it in his pocket. "No need for calls," he says and walks to the end of the bed.

I feel the pain pill starting to take effect, and I try to stay alert as best I am able.

"What is it he had on you?" I ask, thinking I might as well get all the answers I can, him being so chatty and all.

"It's not nearly as exciting as the FBI first thought." He clicks his tongue against the top of his mouth. He sounds like a cicada. I'll have to ask Buford which one makes the clicking noise. If I ever get to ask Buford anything again. If I ever get out of this.

"Marvin got himself in a few money problems, and so, a number of years ago, we dabbled in a few things. Nothing too reckless, just a few offshore accounts that the IRS doesn't know about, a little side hustle that really is no big deal, a few trades that probably wouldn't even be investigated, but all of this together could be damaging to a fine, upstanding attorney, if you know what I mean."

I think I do, but I don't say so.

"And then recently, it seems like he was having a change of heart for some reason, moving money around, keeping some things from me. Seems like Marvin had a bit more going on than he even let on to me."

"The Lemmons cartel?" I say, feeling proud of myself that I was right about Marvin and the family business.

"What?" He appears confounded. "No, don't be ridiculous. This is Owensboro, North Carolina. He was just not being careful."

"And you killed him for that?"

He throws out his hands. "I am his lawyer and his business partner. I do have a stake in Marvin's businesses and in his silence."

I feel so sleepy now.

"Drugs?" I ask.

"Drugs? What kind of man do you think I am? No, wrong again. Well, no to a business but yes to giving you a little more than what was prescribed by your doctor."

No wonder I feel so sleepy. I glance away and think I might make it to the window before he stops me, but I don't know what good that would do. It's locked, and there's a screen. And feeling as wobbly as I am, I'm not even sure I could get there without falling.

He laughs. "How many did you take?"

I smile and don't answer.

"So what do you want from me?" I ask, wondering if anyone will believe me now.

"Well, it seems someone has been telling you things, a few of our little secrets, even a few I didn't know … Marvin apparently confided in an old girlfriend. So that when I found you out there snooping, when I found the safe, I realized somebody's been chatty. I need to know where she is."

Lucy.

I just want to lie down, close my eyes, sleep, but I also know this is becoming quite serious.

"You drugged me and then expect me to tell you how to find Lucy?"

"Don't be silly." He walks toward me. "I drugged you so I can bring you along with me until she calls you again. And then, when you get her on the phone, I will find out where she is. After that, well, I haven't gotten that far. But it shouldn't be too hard to dispose of you. At first, I thought you and that barber lived together, which would've been a little trickier. But …" He glances around. "Seems like you're on your own."

I don't know why, but I start to laugh, and it hurts. I reach up to hold my head in my hands. "Do what you got to do," I say and drop my head on my pillow.

I feel him lift me from the bed, and I'm surprised he's as strong as he is, being so wiry and thin. I feel myself bouncing against him. Just before I fall asleep, I hear myself say, "Night, night, lawyer man."

CHAPTER FIFTY-SIX

When I wake up, I'm in the dark, but I'm moving. I can feel the road beneath me, every bump causing a jarring and intense pain at the back of my head. I slide my hands out from behind me, happy I'm not tied up. I'm still in my gown and robe. I reach up and touch the sides and the top, all soft, like new carpet. Even in the blur of darkness and some superpowered drug, I realize I'm in the trunk of a car.

"Mercedes," I say softly to myself and think about how I always wanted to ride in one—but not like this.

I can even stretch out some more, which surprises me because I thought the lawyer drove a sports car. I also thought there wouldn't be that much trunk space.

"This is nice," I say, and I laugh because I'm still flying a little high.

We hit a big bump and my head falls against something hard. It hurts like the devil, and I almost black out.

"Keep it together, Lorna Gayle," I tell myself. I try to practice some of that deep breathing Melanie talked about before she kicked us out of class, try to remember how to meditate.

Inhale, hold the breath, exhale.

I do this a few times but it just makes me feel like I'm going to hyperventilate, so I stop. I try to clear my mind of the cobwebs without shaking my aching head. I roll over to smell the sides just to see if there's the new car smell in here. And then, just like that, I remember how to get out, what I need to do.

Buford and I were watching some real crime show, some *20/20* or Lifetime movie, and the victim was in exactly the same pickle I'm in. I remember thinking how strange it was that she didn't get out, that she stayed in the trunk until the killer opened the trunk and murdered her.

"There has to be some switch in the newer cars, right?" I had asked, but Buford was reading the sports section in the Raleigh paper. He wasn't even watching the show any longer. "There was a law written," I add.

"Hmm?" He wasn't even listening.

"I remember," I had told him. "The U.S. National Highway Traffic Safety Administration mandated emergency trunk releases in new cars starting with the 2002 model year in the fall of 2001. She was in the trunk of a 2010 Honda Civic." I turned off the television. "She should have pulled the trunk release," I said, and I made Buford give me a high five even though he didn't even really know why.

I realize that I am smarter than I think. If I can just keep my eyes open long enough to stick to the plan. I take in a breath and start feeling around the sides of the trunk. We hit another bump, and that's when I see it. A glow-in-the-dark button right next to a latch. I reach for it before I even know how I will manage jumping out of a moving car, but it's too late. I lift the latch, the top of the trunk pops open, and the next thing I know the wind is whooshing in my face.

CHAPTER FIFTY-SEVEN

I am out and running down the highway before the lawyer can stop the car and catch me. I don't know how I got out except that the Mercedes is low to the ground and as soon as the trunk lid raised up, I just jumped and rolled, like we learned in elementary school about what to do in a fire. Except this wasn't a fire. This was me falling out of a moving car.

I keep running. It hurts but not as bad as I thought it would. Not that I had a lot of time to prepare for what I'm doing.

I turn around and see that the Mercedes is on the side of the road. I notice the brake lights glowing, and I have a hope that maybe he's going to drive away, that maybe he's going to let me go. But I can tell the engine is now in reverse, white lights glaring, and he's driving in my direction.

I do not know where we are, and I don't see headlights on either side of the road to wave someone down. I can't recall how far we've traveled, since I think I must have been unconscious when he put me in the car. I don't even know what time it is, since I took off my watch in the hospital and haven't put it back on. And, of course, I don't have my phone. That's in the front with him.

I know wherever I am, I'm alone in the middle of nowhere with a car moving quickly in my direction. And my head is pounding and I still feel woozy, but I know there's no time to throw up or change directions. So I just run as fast as I can, which I have always known isn't that fast. I'm able to see enough with the full moon that I am coming up on a curve, and then I make out the bridge, and I know exactly where I am.

I run toward the creek and fall to my butt and slide down the bank, landing right where Willis used to have his tent, the very place I had been only days ago. I run toward the rock I had rested on, and I hear splashing near me. I remember the duck that had been close by, the one that startled me that day. I glance beside me, at the edge of the water, and I see a glint of silver shining in the moonlight. I reach for it. It's a knife, and I think it must be the knife Willis hid, the knife Buford found at his house and said he threw into the river! I can't believe my good fortune. I pick it up and keep moving along the path and farther into the woods. Then I stop and listen.

I can hear a car idling somewhere close by, know it's him. I hear all kinds of sticks cracking, and I can tell he's running in my direction. I hear another splash and then a bit of rough language and realize that he's fallen into the water. I keep tearing through the woods until I also fall, only I'm a ways up and it means I got a ways down to go. I just feel myself roll and slam into something—a tree, I think—and roll some more, like a ball in a game at the arcade, first against one obstacle, then another.

When I finally land, it is not a tree that stops me but a set of legs. I start to crawl away as fast as I can, find the knife that had fallen out of my grasp, and try to jump up and start running again, but a hand reaches down and touches me on the shoulder. I try to resist.

"Lorna," comes the whisper, the familiar voice, the one I just heard earlier in the evening. "What are you doing out here?"

Willis.

Before I can answer, the lawyer has made his way to us, and he is holding a flashlight and a gun. The moon shines through the trees, and I take a long look at the man with the wavy brown hair and the narrow hips.

"Well, well, well," he says with a sinister laugh, shining the light on me and then Willis. "If it's not the troubled brother."

Willis helps me to my feet, steps in front of me like a shield. I spot the knife and pick it up, holding it behind my back.

"I should have whacked both of you harder when I had the chance."

"Mr. Donovan?"

"Willis, I thought you were in jail," he responds. "Well, no matter. I've handled you once or twice before, I'm sure I can manage you again. And please, no need for formalities at this late date. It's Byron."

And then he speaks to me. "Hello again, Biscuit Chef," he says with a sneer. "Seems you're slightly more formidable than I first thought."

"Byron Donovan," I reply, finally taking note of his name.

"Esquire, attorney-at-law," he says.

"You should probably leave now, Mr. Donovan," Willis says, and I glance up at the back of his head, thinking how brave he sounds.

"What? You kicking me out of your fine residence?" He laughs. "You sleep out here with the other skunks?"

Willis doesn't reply.

"You get a new trailer?"

Willis is silent as a stone.

"Marvin felt bad, you know, when we took out the restraining order. He even defended you. He never really believed you started that camper fire. It took a bit of convincing that you were smoking again."

"It was you," Willis says.

"It was," Byron Donovan, Esquire, attorney-at-law, responds. "I am paid for my art of persuasion."

I make a hissing noise.

"I really needed you out of there, so I did what needed to be done. And I gave the sheriff even more evidence of crimes to keep you away. Although I don't think they ever used that against you. But you had to go. You were sort of cramping our style, *glamping* in the backyard, if you know what I mean."

I wonder if Willis does; I sure don't. But I do understand now Buford's worry of precedence. This lawyer had made it very bad for Willis.

"And I have to say, I always thought it was weird how he liked having you there. And now I know why."

"The safe," I whisper and feel Willis move slightly.

"Thanks for that, by the way," Byron Donovan, Esquire, attorney-at-law, says. "Took a lot of digging, but I managed to dislodge it."

Willis is angry. I feel his muscles tighten, since I'm leaning into him.

"Plans have changed. Originally, I thought I needed you to answer when the girlfriend from Tennessee calls you again. Then it dawned on me: I don't actually need you for that. I take the call, and I find her. Just like I found you."

I peek around Willis, and the lawyer throws out his hands like he's inviting us into his arms. He points the gun at us.

"So, as crazy as I first thought it sounded, I might actually be able to use that birdbrain cartel theory of yours—make your deaths look like a mob hit, even deliver the books Marvin was so desperately hiding," he says, coming closer. And there's that laugh again. "You know, I think one shot straight through you, Willis, to her, would be very satisfying. Kind of like a two-for-one special ..." And for whatever reason, I think about Mae's marketing plans of a Double Day Promotion at the bakery: Two biscuits for the price of one. Coffee half off.

"I don't even think anybody will notice that she's missing."

I quit thinking about biscuits.

"Everybody'll notice she's missing."

And in spite of the dire circumstances we are in, Willis's words make me feel all warm inside.

Willis takes one step in the lawyer's direction, and I am right on his heels. I even bump into him when he stops.

Suddenly, I feel Willis lunge toward Donovan and fall, causing me to stumble forward. I suddenly remember I'm still clutching the knife, and I hold it up.

"You going to slice me in half and add some butter?" He steps toward us.

"I will do what I got to do," I say, raising my hand higher, the weapon in my fist.

"Then have at it, sweetheart," Donovan says, pulling on the hammer of his pistol. "But you know what they say about having a knife in a gunfight, right?"

"That it better be a big knife?" comes a voice from behind him. And we all turn in that direction.

"Byron Donovan, you are under arrest for the murder of Marvin Lemmons as well as the assault of Willis Lemmons and Lorna Gayle Pitchford. As well as a few other charges once we sort through all this mess. Drop your weapon and put your hands on top of your head. Get down on your knees."

And I suddenly think that I have never seen anything better than a sheriff standing in front of me with a loaded gun.

The lawyer turns to run, but Willis is quick and tackles him to the ground. Ferguson and I watch as the two fall from the path and land near the water. I hear a loud rustling and realize that the duck has made its exit from the river yet again.

"Willis!" I yell.

Ferguson slides down the embankment toward them. There's a tussle, and I can't make out what's happening. Before long, I recognize the sound of Miranda rights being recited, and then Ferguson is standing in front of me with Donovan, handcuffed, next to him.

"You can put that down now," Ferguson says, and I feel frozen.

The sheriff cautiously takes the knife from my hands and I remember to breathe, and then I hear my name being called. From the light of the full moon, I become very clear that there is something much better than seeing a sheriff with a loaded gun.

"Buford!" I call out.

And there's a man running in my direction wearing a neatly ironed smock and the truest and oldest look of love I have ever known.

CHAPTER FIFTY-EIGHT

"Okey dokey."

I recognize that voice. Baby Doctor is back.

I open my eyes, slowly, carefully.

"There she is."

I am instantly blinded by a bright light. I shut my eyes hard. It hurts.

"Seems like you can't stay away from here."

I feel her face close to mine, her breath like cherry bubblegum.

"Must be the broth."

I am then jostled around, and the beeps near my head sound way too loud. I cringe.

"Oh, sorry about that. I'm almost done," she says. She reaches over me and seems to be working on something over my head.

"There, I turned off the alarm. Auditory sensitivity can be a booger pill."

She pulls away, and I start to relax even though I'm still imagining exactly what a booger pill is.

"Started you on a morphine drip."

And just like that, I'm drifting.

"You got a visitor. I made the others leave," she adds. "Okay, you two, take it easy for a night." And I hear her leave the room.

I try to open my eyes, but only one is cooperating this time. I feel a hand on mine.

"Buford," I whisper.

"Lorna," he says, and I feel everything around me soften. "I'm so sorry I didn't believe you."

But it doesn't matter anymore. It was Buford who called Ferguson and told him about the lawyer, made him drive over to my house to hear my story. And then, I wasn't there and since my truck wasn't gone and it seemed strange that I would be missing after having just gotten home from the hospital, he called Draymond and Georgia. Neither of them knew where I was, and he ultimately concluded I had been abducted. It was Buford who thought to search at the creek, although the reason for that hasn't become clear. Luckily, Ferguson heard us at the bank and got to us just before the lawyer got off a shot.

"I'm so glad you're okay," Buford tells me.

"How long have I been in here this time?" I ask, trying to remember when everything broke loose.

"There was more swelling in your brain," he responds. "Three days."

"Like the Lord," I whisper.

"What's that?"

"Nothing." And I smile. "How's Willis?"

"He was here until Tiny Doc made him leave. He's staying over at my house."

"The charges?"

"All dropped. Seems like Mr. Donovan tied up all the loose ends for Ferguson. The safe was at his house, complete with files that showed money transactions and accounting records, stuff that the FBI hauled away like on one of those raids you see on television. There was even some video equipment that could be used to doctor the security video that he had placed at the scene. Turns out, after Donovan killed Marvin, he edited the footage to indict Willis."

"But how did he get Willis to go to Marvin's house that night?"

"Willis still doesn't remember, but we think Donovan was promising reconciliation for the brothers. We don't know how he got inside the gate, but there was a lot going on that night with Mr. Friddle's death, so he probably just snuck in." He sighs. "I don't think it would have been that hard for the lawyer to talk Willis into going there; he would have done anything to try and make it right with his brother."

And just like that I think about Cathedral, and how I still miss her, how guilty I feel for giving up on her, how even after we quit looking, I know I would have gone anywhere to find her and bring her home.

Buford leans his elbows on the side rail of the bed, and I can smell the gentle scent of sandalwood cologne. "Ferguson had it all confirmed. The FBI was on to Marvin because one of his employees was an informant, had been reporting details of business deals that weren't exactly aboveboard."

"Then why did they drop the case?"

"They didn't really, but they didn't have the evidence to prove a murder or even show there was anything illegal going on. They didn't really know about Donovan's participation and apparently were just hoping something more would come out during the trial with Willis."

"There were just going to let him hang for something they didn't think he did instead of building a case for his innocence?"

Buford looks away. "I guess they think some people are expendable."

I nod only slightly. This was what Buford expected would happen, that the homeless veteran would not be believed.

"Willis was telling the truth all along."

"And I'm so sorry for doubting him, for doubting you."

I try to shake my head but can't. I want to tell him to let go of the guilt; we've all made mistakes in this chaos. But what I say is that I should've never told him to leave when I got home from the hospital.

He bows his head.

"Byron Donovan, Esquire, attorney-at-law," I say in a whisper.

"Did he really say all that?"

"Well, only once. I just keep repeating it."

Buford laughs. "So, the lawyer—"

"Byron Donovan, Esquire, attorney-at-law," I say before he does.

He smiles. "Yes, him. He sets Willis up to take the fall, knocks him in the head." He puts his hand on my brow. "Like you." I melt into his touch. "And he tried to find the files. I think he had a suspicion Marvin was stopping the shady businesses, since Marvin called him to Owensboro. Donovan's secretary in Charlotte said he had made an appointment to come down here because Marvin told him he was making some changes, including writing a new will. Seems like he got some news that made him want to take the straight and narrow, take care of his family."

"His mother?" I ask, but then remember that she didn't wake up until after he was murdered.

"Maybe he knew she was getting better," he says and shrugs. "Anyway, it looks like Willis is a wealthy man now—him and Mrs. Lemmons. Without any other living relatives and without a will that anybody can actually find, they get everything of Marvin's. It's all got to be worked out with the lawyers and such, but she's already planning to move over to Marvin's, and he's buying one of them fancy motor homes to park out back."

This makes me happy. Willis living in style, outside.

"So all's well that ends well."

"I'd say so," he replies.

And I yawn. My eyes are so heavy.

"Lorna ..."

"Uh-huh."

"Would you have really stabbed the lawyer?"

"You always said it best," I reply, and I see the smile spread across his face.

"You do what you got to do," we say together.

I stifle another yawn and start to drift again. And there's now a gentle buzz from somewhere in the room, or maybe it's just in my head.

"Horsefly," Buford says and swats at something above my head.

"Whore-spy," I say. "Georgia."

"What's that?" he asks, but before I can answer, I have faded away into the gentle night, or something warm and familiar, like words from an old poem.

When I wake up, the sun is full, shining through the window, and I feel rested. I start to stretch and then realize that is not something I should do, since my head feels like it's in a vise. I reposition myself ever so slightly.

His hand is still on mine, and Buford has fallen asleep, sitting in the chair at my side. I turn my head just enough to see him still sleeping, his lips pursed like he's blowing bubbles, a few new wrinkles across his brow.

His face rests on his arm and, my God, he is the most beautiful thing I've ever woken up to. I don't know if it's the morphine or the near-death experience or finding out he was the one who made the sheriff go searching for me—that he did believe me after all—but I am undeniably, completely, in love with this man. And I do not want to waste one more minute being angry or petty or guarded or unsure of myself.

"Buford," I whisper, and he starts to rouse.

He bats his eyelids, waking slowly. He raises his face from the side rail, yawns, and then smiles softly at me.

"I have been wrong to think that what we have is enough, because it isn't."

His brow crinkles in that way I love so much, and I realize I'm not saying things exactly right, so I try to pull myself together.

"What I mean to say is, I don't want what's just enough. I don't want what's just comfortable and routine and boring. I mean, I like comfortable and routine and boring, I do."

I'm rambling. This is not going as I had hoped. I start again.

"I was wrong to push you away, and I don't want to be wrong anymore. Not about that. Not about us. I want you to be able to talk to me when you're sick, let me be the one who takes you to the doctor for a test, me to be the one who waits with you for the results. I want to make a life with you. A comfortable, routine, boring life, but one in which I get to be your wife, for you to be my family."

He leans away from me and reaches into his front pocket, pulling out a small jewelry box. And now I'm the one with the crinkled brow.

"Lorna Gayle Pitchford, are you proposing to me?" He opens the box and there's a diamond ring, and I have no idea how long he's had it. "Because if you are, then maybe I should get this resized for my finger."

He drops to a knee.

"Buford, I can't see you down there," I tell him. And he tries to slip the ring on my finger, only it doesn't quite fit because my hands are both swollen and my fingers have turned into tiny fat sausages. He starts to push a little, and before I can tell him just to hold on to it until I'm back to myself, the hospital door swings open and bangs against the wall, startling us both and sending the ring flying in that direction.

"I only got the butters left. That dang peanut of a doctor took the fruity ones."

Georgia.

She holds out her hand and catches the piece of jewelry like some professional ballplayer.

"Where's somebody that tiny going to put three biscuits? She's ain't more than a minute. Ain't no bigger than Flora."

She puts the plate on the bedside table. "And Lord Almighty, speaking of my granddaughter, now she's up and decided she don't want to wrestle no more, which is a blessing for sure. But now she says she wants to take up pole dancing, claims it's a sport. Where does that girl come up with her notions?"

She stops and then looks from Buford to me and then back to Buford, then at me and once again at Buford, and then finally at the ring she just caught in midair. Then the biggest grin is plastered across her face. She hands the ring to Buford, pulls the dice from her pocket, and gives them a kiss.

"Praise the Lord," is what she says, and she throws them on the table, turning up a six and a one, gives a whoop, and then just claps her hands.

EPILOGUE

The wedding is to take place at Marvin's in six months, as soon as the estate is settled. In the meantime, Willis is clearing out the back lot so nobody has an allergy attack, and we plan to rent a tent from Harper's Funeral Home to put up, as long as there's not a death in the community. We'll add little white lights to wrap around the inside.

Preacher Goodlaw agreed to officiate, and Mrs. Lemmons—now fit as a fiddle though still a little forgetful—is helping with the planning. Besides marrying a thieving, abusive man and being in a coma for more years than she can count, not having a daughter-in-law or a wedding to plan has been her greatest source of disappointment.

Georgia has agreed to be my maid of honor, bought herself a fancy dress, a purple frock from Winston-Salem that her daughter Mae helped her pick out, and Junior will serve as the best man. Even Odelia and her wife plan to come from California and stand with us next to Draymond—who's giving me away—and Lucille, Buford's sister who will stand up next to Junior.

Mavis volunteered to play a portable organ, and Darrell has offered to sing. He gave us a preview, and I swear it was the prettiest ballad I've ever heard. He's going to sing the solo while we light a candle of unity, blending our families, honoring our commitments.

The deputy's talent of singing was quite a surprise for us all. He shared it at the bakery one Saturday morning when he sang his song about love and the ocean, an Irish fisherman's song. I swear Georgia bawled like a newborn.

I told Darrell later that maybe he could find something a little more uplifting, since I thought we were already tempting fate by holding the service in a funeral home tent. I certainly didn't want the service to be mournful.

Robbie is on the lookout for pots of geraniums to mark the path to the tent, the big ones like I told him I saw at the house in Lakeview Estates, and there'll be bouquets of wildflowers for each table. Georgia and I decided to have biscuits and gravy as a side dish to the meal we're going to ask Eugene to cater and punchbowls full of something pink and bubbly Clara intends to make. I already know folks are planning to spice it up, since I see the men in the shop handing over dollar bills to Buford's nephew Leon, who I know runs liquor up from Florida.

Donna plans to bring Miss Abigail as her plus-one, and she still leaves her at the bakery when she's trying to sell a house. But I get the feeling Miss Abigail has been playacting all the time, since she always winks at me before she drops her head onto the table or starts playing in the grape jelly.

R.J. will be the photographer, and Thelma says she'll fix my makeup and hair at a discount. We've been talking about colors for the wedding party, and Donna has offered to give ideas. I think she's leaning toward lavender.

Buddy, the mayor, accepted our invitation for the fall date and even gave us a discount on a mattress. Judge Farley plans to attend alone, his wife now staying permanently with her sister in Little Rock. I watched Georgia when he made the announcement, and in classic spy form, she didn't flinch. She just smiled like she already knew that marital bliss was coming to an end while she fingered the dice in her pocket.

We even invited Baby Doctor and a few of the nurses from the hospital before I was discharged. Buford asked the FBI agent, the young one, the smug one, to join us, since it became apparent that he is sweet on Evelyn, the CNA he met when he went to pick up Willis from Evergreens.

It will be everything I could have imagined for my wedding. Hopeful, joyful, tender. And when Buford looks me square in the eye and promises his love to me, in front of the preacher and the gathering of our beloveds, in front of God and all our witnesses, I worry I may just fall out again. And I'm pretty sure it won't be because of the concussion. It will be a simple reaction to love. But the truth is, I actually invited Baby Doctor in case there is some medical emergency; can't be too safe these days.

Georgia has gone for the day, and I'm closing up the bakery when I notice a young woman sitting in the front table in the dining room. I don't remember her coming in.

"Hello," I say as I walk around the serving line to start wiping off the tables and sweeping the floor. "Can I get you anything?"

She holds up a cup, and I assume Georgia must have taken her order while I was cleaning in the kitchen. I don't know how long she's been there.

"You want a refill?"

She shakes her head. I don't recognize her.

I start moving the tables on the other side of the dining room when I hear her chair move, letting me know she's getting ready to leave.

"Lorna," she says and smiles, and I faintly recognize the voice.

"Yes," I answer, an automatic response. "Wait ..."

She smiles wider as I figure it out.

"Lucy," I say and drop the broom. I don't know why, but I walk right over to her like we're old friends and take her hands in mine. "Here you are. I'm so glad you're safe."

"Thanks to you," she says, and I shake my head.

"Not me," I tell her, and she seems confused.

"It was the efforts of a lot of people," I tell her. "And you were so smart and brave. You knew to get those fancy burner phones, to leave Memphis when you did—"

"To call you," she adds.

I sit down beside her.

"Thank you," she says, "but I know you were the one who figured out who the murderer was. And why. And I know you never gave me up."

I start to contradict her but decide there's no use to try and change her mind about what happened. I nod and smile.

She sees the fingers on my left hand and immediately notices the engagement ring. She holds it up. "Well, now, this looks new."

"It is," I say, stretching my hand in front of her.

"When's the happy day?" Lucy asks.

"In the fall," I answer. "We're waiting for Marvin's estate to be settled, for Mrs. Lemmons and Willis to be affirmed as the next of kin and to become the rightful owners of his property at the lake. That's our venue," I tell her. "You should come."

Lucy doesn't answer but turns toward the window facing the street, and I see her watch a young woman coming in our direction. There is something familiar about the gait, something that takes me back to what feels like a hundred years. She's got long blond hair, practically white. She's lanky, skinny, pale. And she's wearing a long-sleeve shirt and long pants, a floppy hat when I know the temperature has reached the eighties today.

"Marvin," I mouth. She's dressed just like Marvin used to dress.

I turn to Lucy, my face a question mark. "You had a child with Marvin Lemmons?" I ask.

The young woman walks in, stands at the front door—and it's more than just Marvin whose appearance she bears. There's something else old and familiar.

"She's not mine," Lucy answers, smiling at the young woman. "But she might throw a wrench in the estate settlement."

And the girl comes toward us.

"Lorna, I'd like you to meet somebody."

I know my mouth is gaped wide open. I can't believe my eyes.

"This is Cathedral and Marvin's daughter. This is your niece, Aurora Pitchford."

And I feel myself fall backward, right into the arms of Buford, who has come from the parking lot and slipped in behind me.

"Aurora Gayle Pitchford," the young woman adds. "She named me after you, said you were a good big sister."

And I am at a loss for words.

"Marvin only found out a few weeks ago," Lucy says. "Not too long before he was murdered. I think he was searching for her before he died."

I still can't find one word but now it makes all the sense in the world that he was going to change his will. He had a child.

"Well, what do you know? This wedding is even better than we could have dreamed," Buford whispers to me, and I'm dizzy with the surprise.

I reach out to the girl—the one who looks just like Cathedral, looks just like family, and with all the love in my heart, grab her arms and pull her into myself.

LORNA GAYLE'S TOP TEN TIPS FOR THE BEST BISCUITS

1. Use cold butter only. This way, when the butter melts, steam is released and creates small pockets of air. Then you have airy and flaky biscuits.

2. Try to use only fresh baking powder. This is the leavening agent in biscuits and is known to be a double-acting release agent. To test to see if your box is fresh, mix a spoonful of baking powder with ¼ cup of hot water. If it doesn't bubble vigorously, it's time to get a new box.

3. Try not to guess in measuring. It's best to keep measurements as accurate as possible.

4. Use cold buttermilk or make your own with 1 tablespoon of lemon juice and enough milk to equal 1 cup. Let stand 5 minutes.

5. Use a rolling pin. It's fun to use and helps create a more even surface.

6. Handle the dough as little as possible. Don't overwork it or you'll develop too much gluten, which makes the biscuit tough.

7. Press straight down when using a sharp metal biscuit cutter. If you twist the cutter, the biscuits will likely bake unevenly on top.

8. Use a metal baking sheet without sides for more balanced baking.

9. No need to grease the baking pan; there's plenty of grease in the batter.

10. Place the dough ½ inch apart for biscuits that rise higher.

O, BISCUIT'S FAVORITE FLAKY BISCUIT RECIPE
Makes 14–16 biscuits

Ingredients
- 4 cups all-purpose flour
- 10 teaspoons baking powder
- ½ teaspoon baking soda
- 2 tablespoons sugar
- 2 teaspoons fine sea salt
- 12 tablespoons cold butter
- 1 ½ cups + 4 tablespoons whole milk

Directions
1. Preheat oven to 425°F. Lightly grease and flour a baking sheet.

2. In a large bowl or food processor, mix together the flour, baking powder, baking soda, sugar, and salt.

3. Cut the cold butter into cubes, and place the cubes into the mixture. Mix together until the butter is in small chunks and mixed well.

4. Make a hole in the middle of the batter and pour in the milk.

5. Stir until a dough forms.

6. Place the dough onto a lightly floured surface. Sprinkle a little flour on top and then work the dough together with your hands. Add flour as needed if batter becomes too sticky.

7. Press the dough into a rectangle about ¾-inch thick and then fold the dough into thirds. Spin the rectangle about 90 degrees, and then repeat this process two more times.

8. Form the dough into a rectangle between ½-inch and ¾-inch thick, then use a biscuit cutter to cut biscuits.

9. Place the biscuits close together on the baking sheet.

10. For scraps, you can make more biscuits, but do not overwork the dough.

11. Bake the biscuits 12 to 15 minutes until the tops are golden brown and have risen.

ACKNOWLEDGMENTS

O, *Biscuit* began as a silly idea that led to a joyful experience in its writing. I am grateful to the early listeners who created space for me to share my joy.

A huge thank you to Warren Publishing: Amy Ashby, Mindy Kuhn, and Lacey Cope are all professional, kind, and always available. From the very beginning until publication date, I have known that I was in very capable hands, which made the publishing process collaborative and enjoyable. I have been cared-for and supported. I am thankful to editors Rikki Jarrett and especially Erika Nein, as well as Lacey and the marketing team.

I am so grateful that I am able to live a creative life, to have support from friends and family and readers who encourage me daily. My life is a gift, and I continue to wonder at the marvel of all that never fails to delight.

www.ingramcontent.com/pod-product-compliance
Lightning Source LLC
Chambersburg PA
CBHW030642020726
47493CB00006B/1829